Hurricane Megan

Hampton Thoroughbreds
Book Two

Diane Culver

JUL 2 5 2016

Copyright © 2013 By Laurie Bumpus

E-book and cover formatted by Jessica Lewis
http://www.AuthorsLifeSaver.com

This book is a work of fiction. The characters and events are solely the products of the author's imagination and are not real. Any resemblance to actual people is totally unintended. In a few instances where the place names are real, the related characters, incidents or dialogues are entirely fictional. The places may still exist, and if so, the author hopes you will frequent them to get the true feel of the Hamptons.

ISBN: 1483993493
ISBN-13: 978-1483993492

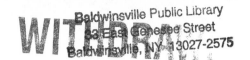
DEDICATION

This book is dedicated to my husband, sons and daughters-in-law. Without your support I would not have been able to cross another item off my bucket list.

And to my parents:
Mom – who taught me to stand up for what I believe. You made me who I am today.

Dad, "The Professor" – who taught me that an education can lead you to things you could never have imagined you could achieve. And being a teacher was the greatest profession by far.

I love you all very much.

PROLOGUE

Gabreski Airport
Hampton Beach, Long Island

The sun gave off a soft orangey hue in the early hour of the morning. "Red at night, sailors delight. Red in the morning, sailors take warning." The ancient mariner's forecast meant nothing to the three men standing in the hangar, which housed two private planes. Instead the trio warily eyed a Cessna, wing lights flashing, taxiing towards them. Not one of them cared about the beauty of the Hampton morning, only about the plane's passenger.

The jet's nose-light focused on the airport employee signaling the pilot to steer the craft to its final destination. Shadows cast by the buildings eerily crept over the runway as daylight dawned. The men took great pains to remain out of sight.

"What do you plan on doing?" the tallest man asked. He was lean and solidly built. His hair was a military brush-cut with a touch of grey at the temples. Dressed in khaki pants, navy blue shirt opened at the collar, and a dark blazer, he stood, hands at his sides, clenching and unclenching his fists.

"I don't think we should be here," the man next to him says. He, too, looked as if he had lived a military lifestyle, standing erect in a brown business suit with a yellow dress shirt and tie. "I don't like being summarily summoned without an explanation. Are you sure this isn't some sort of set up? We've no idea who's on that plane with him."

The third man, dressed in chinos and a blue polo shirt, complete with company logo, turned to his two companions and replied, "*You* don't. But I do. Stay out of sight. I've no intention of letting our uninvited guest make it off that plane. If I'm not back in ten minutes, you make your way on board...no matter who you take out in the process. Understood?" The duo nodded.

As the private plane came to a halt, the first two men backed into the recesses of the hanger as the man in the polo shirt jogged out onto the tarmac. When the jet dropped its staircase to the pavement, he immediately took the steps two at a time, only to be met by two bodyguards, their hands reaching for their holstered weapons. He quickly flashed them his credentials and disappeared into the interior of the plane.

Seeing his person of interest, an imposing man with a groomed black beard, lounging in a tan leather seat, he made his way to him. He had met his visitor on several recent occasions. Having felt the need to vet him after their encounters, he had discovered his unwelcome visitor was from a wealthy family in Saudi Arabia with ties to several unsavory terror organizations in the Middle East. He slid into the leather seat opposite the man, carefully positioning his body to make sure his guest could not easily signal the staff onboard.

"I'd ask you to make yourself comfortable but you already have." The Arab's voice was laced with anger.

Apparently, the man in the black and white turban wasn't used to being one-upped. But the Arab wasn't calling the shots today. He was.

"I told you, Kalil, I'd meet you in New York *tomorrow*. You've taken a great risk filing a flight plan. This may be a small airport, but the FAA now has documentation you came to Hampton Beach." Kalil's reply was a simple shrug of his shoulders. "I came onboard to be sure you weren't recognized. For me, being at Gabreski is no big deal. I fly out of here on the company's private plane on a regular basis. *You*, however, would make international news tonight if you walked off this jet."

Kalil's face reddened at being admonished by an American. The man watched as his visitor tried to control his infamous temper. White knuckles gripping the seat's armrests were a dead give away.

"I am here because you did not return the call to Amid. He tells me he has called you three times. So I came to hear for myself. Your plan...it is in place?" Kalil asked in a clipped tone.

This time is was the outsider's turn to shrug his shoulders. "You must trust my expertise and that of my men. Show some patience. If not, your operation will be doomed from the start." The man paused. "Do you have the money?"

Kalil drew a long, thick envelope from his jacket pocket. "Here is the first installment. It cannot be traced?" The Arab's impatience would be the undoing of everything they'd put into place. His investigation had led him to the fact that the Saudi had gone over and above whom he worked for. But what his team and Kalil were about to do together would affect millions if they were successful.

He rolled up the envelope and stuffed it into his pant's pocket. "Absolutely.

No one is the wiser. I must go. You've been here too long." Getting up from his seat he made his way off the plane without incident. Without looking over his shoulder, the man walked briskly to the hangar. He heard the roar of the Cessna's engines power up as he stepped inside, seeking the men he left behind.

"Well?" Two voices asked in unison.

"Head on out. I'll give you an update at Wednesday night's meeting." Without giving out any other information, he turned and walked into the daylight, donning a pair of Oakley sunglasses. He climbed into a red Audi convertible parked nearby and sped off. If all went well, the money in his pocket would be invested in the beach club's account by sunset. No one would be the wiser.

CHAPTER ONE

Arlington, Virginia
Two weeks later

When not out on assignment, Megan Spears was used to wearing her official black pantsuit with her white camisole top on a daily basis. But that was to the Agency office in Langley, Virginia. When Megan had received the official summons to appear before the Director of the CIA at her private compound, Megan made certain she looked sharp and well polished. She even replaced her practical black pumps with high heels, which, at the moment, tapped nervously on the white marble floor.

As Megan sat ramrod straight in a black Windsor chair outside the door of Elizabeth Hallock's inner sanctum, she clicked open her makeup mirror. She checked once more to see if she'd covered up the remnants of her black eye, a small souvenir for closing out her latest assignment. Her left cheek was still slightly puffy and swollen, but she had hidden the bruising under a fair amount of foundation and blush. From what she saw of her reflection, she would pass inspection and no one would know. She hoped.

Hearing the doors open, Megan slid her makeup case inside her purse. She looked up to see Sam Tanner, the Director's second-in-command, staring down at her. Was that a quirky smile on what was normally a somber looking face? He'd always been all business whenever she encountered him at the Agency.

"Ah, Agent Spears. Prompt as usual. Come in." With a sweeping gesture, Sam ushered her into the massive, wood paneled library. "The Director is on the phone as you can see, but she's just about finished."

As Megan followed Sam into the office she stifled a gasp. The splendor of her surroundings, especially the three large arched windows that let in the morning light, was unlike anything she'd ever seen. The room reminded her of an article she recently read in *Home Interiors* magazine. Sitting behind a large desk with papers and folders piled high on each side of her was the formidable woman Megan had come to see. Somehow the Director didn't seem as intimidating here as she did at the office, but Megan was wary nonetheless.

Sam motioned for Megan to take a seat in the white leather wing chair in front of the Director's desk. Megan did so, turning to survey the office that also looked like a library as she waited. Megan surmised her entire studio apartment on F Street would fit in the room ten times over. Elizabeth Hallock was the head of one of the country's most influential institutions. Why wouldn't the Director's home base of operations be in keeping with her position and status, especially within the hierarchy of the intelligence community? But who did she entertain in such a glorious setting? Megan's mind was intrigued by the thought.

"Coffee or tea?" Agent Tanner interrupted her musings.

Anxious and slightly afraid she would spill the offered cup, Megan shook her head. "Nothing. But thank you."

"I'll have a pot of tea, Sam." Elizabeth Hallock hung up the phone. The Director locked eyes on Megan immediately. "Agent Spears is a tea drinker. A girl after my own heart. Loves Earl Grey." Megan arched her eyebrows, surprised that one of the most powerful women in the President's administration knew what she drank at breakfast. Elizabeth winked, the corners of her mouth turning up into a grin. "It's amazing what one finds in a background check, isn't it?" Directing her next comment to Agent Tanner, the Director instructed, "Have Juanita brew up a pot for us, if you will."

Sam mumbled and headed out the door, closing it behind him.

"He'll be back." Elizabeth stated with a smile on her face. She pointed to Megan. "So, tell me, Agent Spears. Who got the worse end in your encounter at the Lincoln Memorial? That's a heck of a makeup job, if I do say so."

The dark foundation Megan had used that morning now not only covered the bruise, but the blush that formed from the embarrassment of having been caught off guard.

Trying to inject a light tone into an already nervous voice, Megan replied, "I'm glad to say I did. But believe me, Madam Director, I am not happy the money in the briefcase you entrusted to us is gone."

The trademark tortoise shell reading glasses, normally perched on the top of the Director's head, now sat on the tip of her nose. "What's a couple hundred thousand dollars?"

Megan tried her best to keep her jaw from sagging at such a nonchalant comment from the head of the CIA. But Elizabeth Hallock seemed unmoved by it. "This is eating you up inside, isn't it? Never failed at anything before, have you?" The Director shuffled through a stack of papers and pulled a sheet from the pile. She read out loud, "Top of your class at Harvard. Number one in your training here at the Farm. You've been assigned to seven missions - all with successful outcomes. For the record, I was impressed with your recent work in Paris."

Megan sat up straight not quite knowing how to respond to the comments about her resume and the compliment. It was the kind of thing she knew Elizabeth Hallock rarely bestowed. "I take great pride in my work. But yesterday was supposed to be a simple surveillance op. I - don't – fail. My record speaks for itself."

Elizabeth's eyes widened. Megan's first thought was she was in trouble, but it appeared as if the opposite was true. The Director seemed downright pleased about how Megan felt about her personal failure to complete an assigned task.

Both heads turned as the door suddenly opened. Sam entered. In his hands, he balanced a tray, which included the requested pot of tea, along with a steaming mug of coffee.

"Where would you like this, *Madam*?" Sam asked. As in any office, the rumor mill ran rampant that Sam and Elizabeth had been lovers at one point in their careers. But no one had any hard facts of an affair other than it was true they had partnered in England and Europe more than thirty years ago.

Elizabeth stretched and stood up, pointing to the opposite end of the room. "Place it on the table by the fireplace if you would. The couch is much more comfortable than this chair I've been sitting in all morning. I need a break." She rose and walked past Megan, who remained seated, waiting for an invitation to join them. "You were right, Sam. Megan's upset about the botched assignment. I think we better tell her why we brought her here today… and not her partner. Don't you?"

Megan snapped to attention. Finally! An explanation of why she seemed to be the only invited "guest" to the tea party. She wondered where her partner, Derek Taylor, had disappeared to after their surveillance op. She had expected to see him sitting out in the hallway when she arrived, but he had been MIA since the mission went sour.

"Come." Elizabeth waved to her. Megan rose and walked to the club chair on the other side of the coffee table. "Make yourself comfortable, Agent Spears. May I call you Megan? It's much less formal, given that we're not at the office." Megan nodded as the Director continued, "Take a big deep breath, dear. Sam and I aren't here to take your gun and badge. Quite the opposite in fact."

Inwardly breathing a sigh of relief, Megan reached for the tea hoping the cup and saucer wouldn't shake in her hands. She did all she could to contain her nerves as she looked at the two people who had summoned her.

"Love a duck, dearie," the Director's soft southern drawl came out on occasion. "Drink that tea. We're not here to bite your head off over that briefcase. As a matter of fact, the scenario played out just as we wanted it to.

Didn't it, Sam?"

Sam sat beside Elizabeth, nodded and drank from his mug.

Megan was totally perplexed. It was the second time the Director alluded to the fact that all had gone as planned. Bringing the cup to her lips, Meg blew on the hot liquid and took a long sip. The minute the warmth hit her stomach the tension she'd felt from being summoned eased significantly. A good cup of tea always did the trick. Putting the cup and saucer down on the coffee table in front of her, she folded her hands in her lap and stared at the two people who seemed to be assessing every move she'd made since she walked in the door.

"May I be blunt, Madam Director?" Megan asked.

"You may. As a matter of fact, I hoped you would. If I were in your shoes, I'd be asking some pretty direct questions."

"As I'm sure you are well aware, Derek and I were on surveillance to be sure the drop off to Petroff was made without incident. We followed protocol and secured the interior of the monument pronouncing it ready. We watched our agent set the briefcase down inside the Lincoln Memorial by the left pillar's railing and walk away as planned. But just as Petroff walked up the stairs to the spot where the case was to be exchanged, a masked individual came from out of nowhere and knocked Petroff to the ground. That individual grabbed the case, bolted over the railing and made his way to a Moped stashed behind the souvenir stand located at the foot of the staircase. The suspect sped off toward the Tidal Basin. Derek gave chase in the Agency-issued SUV. The last I saw of my partner, he was following the suspect headed for the Key Bridge.

"I spied another man, dressed identical to the man on the motorcycle, trying to make his way down the gravel path toward the Washington Monument. When he realized I had made him, he took off running. I gave chase. As he hopped over a copse of bushes by the World War II Memorial, I tackled him to the ground. That man, to my knowledge, is now in custody. Pardon my directness, but what was my role supposed to have been? You're now telling me it happened exactly the way you planned and yet I failed in my mission. Quite frankly, I'm beginning to wonder what the mission was in the first place." Megan's voice rose. Realizing she sounded as if she was berating her boss, Megan quickly apologized. "Forgive me. I didn't mean to take that tone. And I certainly didn't mean to question the mission or its objective. Everything is very unclear."

The Director placed her glasses back up on top of her coiffed, grey hair. Sitting back into the cushions of the white sofa, Elizabeth Hallock took several sips of tea. There was no doubt in Megan's mind she was contemplating her choice of words very carefully. The hair on the back of Megan's neck stood up. Perhaps, she had gone too far. She had crossed the line. Something was going to happen. To her or her job.

"Sam, would you care to enlighten Megan?"

Sam swallowed the last remnants of his coffee and placed his mug on the table. "As *you* are aware, Megan, our agents never proceed on an assignment without being well briefed. But this one…we had to hold this one close to the vest. Your superior informed us if he were to choose anyone for what we have in mind, it would be you."

"Excuse me, Agent Tanner. I don't mean to interrupt, but you're telling me you want someone who can screw up an assignment?"

Sam and Elizabeth glanced at each other. As far as Megan was concerned, she felt as if she was going around in circles.

Sam continued. "No. It's because of what you bring to the table. This next mission is extremely sensitive and you have what we need to get the job done."

Elizabeth leaned forward. "Megan, we've watched you very carefully over the last three years. We recruited you because of your overall background. You speak three languages, including Russian and Arabic, a plus for any organization here in DC. Add to that, your background in microbiology. We knew at some point we would move you from being a general field agent and promote you to a higher level operative—one who could assume the lead. It took awhile, but I knew there was a mission to give you, and only you, based on your credentials. That time has come. Paris was just a trial on the international scene. You've proved yourself in more ways than one."

There had been very few times in Megan's life when she was speechless. This was one of them. The Director of the CIA had been watching *her*, Megan Spears, formerly from a little known town in upstate New York, who happened to land a full scholarship in microbiology to George Washington University. Her love of languages had been an added bonus. Maybe the tumble she'd taken and the nasty slap across her left cheek before she gotten the upper hand over her accomplice had been worth it after all.

"Megan? Megan!" The Director's voice broke into her thoughts.

"I'm sorry." Megan sat on the edge of the couch, almost at attention and crossed her legs. She was filled with nervous anticipation.

"No, dear. Don't be sorry. I'd be wondering what the Agency had planned for me if I were in your shoes."

"And what is that?" Meg glanced from Sam to the Director.

Sam sat forward, his forearms on his legs, his eyes looking directly into hers. "Megan, we needed to be sure *that* particular briefcase was taken by the very man who stole it. It was a set up on our side from the start. Only we couldn't divulge that to you or to Derek.

"You see Petroff got himself into some legal trouble working with an arms supplier from Russia and was arrested several years ago. We worked out a deal to use him as a credible participant when we need him. The other day was one of those times. We leaked information to the parties under investigation and, sure enough, the money was picked off. The bills are marked. If what we believe is true, the money will show up in Hampton Beach within the next few weeks. *You* are going to be our eyes and ears there, Agent Spears."

As Sam talked, Megan began to relax, sinking back into the comfortable cushions of the blue-flowered club chair. She finally felt at ease enough to ask, "Why hasn't the FBI stepped in? Why is the CIA working this?"

"It's rather complicated," Elizabeth stated. "Not only do we have a problem with finding out who's laundering the money, which, you're right, the Feds normally handle, but a Russian family on the Agency's radar has resurfaced. We have information that they've been doing business with operatives from Saudi Arabia."

"And I fit in because…?" Megan's heart started to hammer in her chest just as it did at the start of every new mission. The challenge of having the opportunity to do what she did best had adrenaline rushing through her body.

"Because you have the perfect resume to be dropped into our covert operation. Your cover will be perfect. No one will be the wiser."

Elizabeth reached for a large manila envelope. She leaned across the coffee table and handed it to Megan. "I don't need to tell you what's in here." Megan was fully aware it contained everything she would need to know about her new assignment. "You are to stay here at the compound for the next few days. You will be briefed and learn everything you can about the situation. This isn't a typical assignment, Megan. It's complex and needs someone who can multi-task and play different roles. That's why I need *you*. Ask whatever questions you need to before you leave. Once you're there, you'll be the lead agent on the ground. You know the drill."

Megan nodded. "One last question."

"What is it?" Elizabeth asked as she rose from the sofa, stretching her arms out in front of her, her eyes pinned on Megan's.

"What happened to Derek and the accomplice that tangled with me? Where did he fit in? Am I to look for him in Hampton Beach? You said you identified the man who took the cash."

Sam cleared his throat before he spoke up, "The man who took the cash may have made Derek. Right now, we're not sure. But we are positive he cannot identify you. We made sure of that. The 'accomplice' really was an extra to throw you off. That man you wrestled to the ground was Agent Tompkins, who, by the way, says you have one hell of a mean right hook. You owe him a drink when you get back to DC."

Thank God, Megan thought, she wasn't going back into the office anytime soon. She'd never live it down. She knew Tomkins, and he'd be out to get her. He didn't like women working in the field.

Megan rose from her chair, the envelope clasped in her hand.

"You'll be staying in the east wing," Elizabeth directed. "My niece, Katherine, used to stay there when she visited. Juanita will see you have everything you need. Why don't we plan to discuss things over dinner at six?"

"I didn't bring any clothes."

"That's all right. There should be a few pairs of jeans and some shirts in the dresser. You're about Katherine's size. Help yourself. After that, we'll outfit you for Hampton Beach." Elizabeth walked back to her desk and picked up the phone.

The meeting was over. And Megan, who thought she'd never lead an assignment at this early stage in her career, was headed to the Hamptons. From the little she knew of the area, it was a series of small towns where the rich and famous loved to live, play, and party. And apparently, with all the wealth and power people who lived there, it was the perfect cover to sell arms and do all sorts of dirty deeds and get away with it. That wasn't going to happen on her watch.

* * *

Elizabeth sat in the shade of the patio umbrella by the side of the pool. Even the lemonade she drank didn't quench her thirst. She wanted to be in the comfort of her air-conditioned office, but Sam insisted they talk outside the four walls of the house. God, the man was stubborn. She had learned when he got into one of his moods there was no reasoning with him. It was late afternoon and she still had a lot of "I"s to dot and "T"s to cross before she could release Megan into the field. For the time being though Megan had followed orders and disappeared into the study to look over the dossier she'd been given.

Elizabeth knew that Sam had something to say and he'd tell her in his own good time. But it was hot and she was tired. Besides, she hated to sweat.

"Lizzie!" Elizabeth ignored his deep warning growl as she bit into a slice of apple danish. She redirected her line of sight toward the pool, taking in the lush gardens that had come into bloom with the unusually warm spring weather. Anything not to look into the eyes of the man who could read her like a book. "You're not planning what I think you are?" Sam asked. "Are you?"

Elizabeth twirled the straw in her glass, making the ice cubes clink. If she turned to look at him now he'd know. Well, the two of them had butted heads over many an issue before and she'd come out on top. She twisted her body in the cushioned patio chair and leveled a look at him devoid of any emotion. "What ever are you referring to? You know perfectly well I'm sending a well trained agent on assignment to Hampton Beach."

"You better not be playing matchmaker again." Elizabeth didn't utter a word. She sat stoically silent. "I knew it!" Sam slammed his hand on the glass patio table. Elizabeth jumped in her seat. "You're sending Megan there *and* using Matthew's beach club as her cover. Don't you dare deny it." Sam wagged his index finger at her as she turned away to gaze at the gardens. "I know what that mind of yours is up to, *Madam Director*. You've had this planned long before you decided to bring me in to strategize logistics."

"Samuel Tanner, how could you possibly accuse me of such a thing?" Elizabeth tried her best to look shocked but failed miserably. "Megan Spears is perfect for this sting. We both agreed her qualifications warranted her being tapped for the operation."

"Oh, no." Sam shook his head vigorously. "Don't go twisting my words around. I know you far too well. We've been together too long, my friend. Your mind's already wrapped around the fact Megan is just what *Matthew* needs. What exactly are your plans for her? I hope no one will question a new face showing up within the Hallock inner circle."

"I have it covered."

"Oh? You have? Just like last time, I suppose?" Sam stretched out his legs, crossed his arms, snorted and he scowled at her, "Could've fooled me."

"That was different. Katherine came running *to* me *from* Hallock Farm."

"And the minute she told you what *she* needed, you immediately knew that John Clinton was the perfect agent for Operation Hide and Seek…and for her."

Elizabeth placed her glass on the table and crossed her arms defiantly. "I don't see either of them complaining now, do you? John finally retired from the Agency. He and Katherine are happily running Clinton Stables and doing amazingly well financially. And little Lizzie is the apple of their eye. Besides, didn't we catch one of the world's most wanted operatives in the process?"

Sam grumbled, making Elizabeth smile inwardly. "Your little scheme worked because Kate was a trained agent *before* she left to work as a vet at Hallock Farm. Have you forgotten, even with their backgrounds, Kate and John were almost killed? Listen, I give Matthew a lot credit for what he's accomplished considering family dynamics and the cards that have been stacked against him. But he knows squat about being involved in anything of this magnitude. Have you run this by the DHS?"

Elizabeth looked her faithful partner in the eye. "I have faith Megan has what it takes to do the job and not endanger Matthew. And do you honestly think I'd proceed unless the Department of Homeland Security hadn't given their stamp of approval? Especially knowing who and what we're dealing with?"

Elizabeth took in Sam's reaction. He was shaking his head in disbelief. But she knew that meant he was surrendering. Elizabeth hadn't told him every pertinent detail, but Sam always had her back and she had his. Operation Hurricane was about to commence.

CHAPTER TWO

Hampton Beach, Long Island
Two weeks later

The ocean had always been in Matthew Hallock's blood. Many times his love of the sea had made him the black sheep of the family. Looking out the large picture window of his office at the Sunfish Beach Club, Matt watched as the waves crested, broke, and rolled onto shore. Mesmerized by the ebb and flow of the water, he yearned for the good old days. The time when nothing mattered but waking at the break of dawn, eating a light breakfast, and racing to the beach in his Jeep to ride the waves all day long.

He arrived early at the office, dressed in beige cargo shorts and a paint-splattered, white tee-shirt bearing the logo of the club. Not his typical dress, but today was a workday for everyone. The windows overlooking the dunes were open and the air smelled of sand, surf, and seaweed. Being part owner in a beach club had been his dream since high school. When the Sunfish had gone into bankruptcy at the end of last season, Matt and three friends pooled their money and snapped up the prestigious club. Their offer was accepted on the spot. To this day, he pinched himself from time to time to be sure the life he was living was real. He, Matt Hallock, whose father had said he would never amount to "a hill of beans" because Matt chose to go on the national surfing circuit rather than head to an Ivy League school after high school, was part owner of one of the most sought after waterfront properties in Hampton Beach. Now he was entrusted by his silent partners to make the money flow in and not out. Matt prayed his knowledge acquired working his way around the world at various surf camps and businesses would pay off big time.

Wrapping his hands around the cup of coffee he'd picked up at Eckart's on his way to work, Matt raised it to his lips and took a swallow of the dark liquid. The door to his office creaked open. Turning toward the sound, Matt found Sarah Adams, his new manager, standing patiently inside. As he sat down, taking another swallow of the needed caffeine boost, he beckoned her to sit in one of the captain's chairs that faced his desk. "Hey! Good morning. Got the work schedule set for the day?"

Sitting down, Sarah took a pencil from behind her ear and placed her ever-present clipboard on her lap. "Yes, Mr. Hallock. It's rather long. For what we need to have done, we'll need to hire a few more temporary workers to get this place ship-shape."

Matt shook his head and smiled. "Sarah, how many times are we going to go over the fact that my name's Matt. I've known you since you were ten years old." He winked at her.

Sarah grinned back and laughed. "Yeah, you're right, Matt. But this is my first real job and I wanted to sound professional." Sarah tapped her pencil nervously on her clipboard. Obviously, she was ready to start.

Matt took a long look at his new manager. Sarah's life hadn't been easy. She hadn't grown up having everything given to her like he had. She didn't live in a mansion on Moriches Bay. Her parents had died when she was young. Her grandparents raised her in a small house in the village. "Sarah, you're the best thing to come knocking at my door. I hadn't planned on being this far ahead with renovations and hiring personnel."

"About that, boss." Sarah scribbled something on her paper and looked up at him.

"What's wrong?" Matt asked.

"We've got a major problem in hiring professionally certified lifeguards since the county changed the rules. Add to that the fact that when the crew's final paychecks bounced last year, we're having some trouble getting people to answer the ads we've put in the papers. The word around town is to beware of possible start-up money problems."

Matt leaned back and ran his fingers through his windswept brown hair. He contemplated what she told him and took another long swallow of coffee, then placed the cup on his desk. "How many do we need?"

"With three stations on the beach, we need four rotating crews of four people per crew. Plus we need a two-man crew at the pool. One guard at each end, plus break replacements. So…" Sarah stopped, looked down and checked off something on her clipboard. "From my count, a minimum of twenty and a few to sub if one of the crew is injured or calls in sick. I'd hire twenty-five to be safe."

"When are tryouts?"

"Two weeks from Saturday. Doesn't give you a whole lot of time."

Matt scratched at the stubble on his chin. "Why don't I make a few calls tonight to some of the kids I met at a camp last summer. Maybe some of them might be interested in coming to the Hamptons. What do you think?"

"I think that would be great. Tyler can run the tryouts. He knows what you need, Matt. That will free you up. The workload around here is picking up big-time. You're going to be busy signing checks. The painters are scheduled to start tomorrow and the pool men are coming to find the leak."

A hard knock rattled the screen door. Matt looked over Sarah's shoulder. He grinned when he saw who stood there. "Hey, good buddy." He looked at his watch. "You're early. Give me a minute." Matt was surprised to see Sarah cringe when she turned to see who stood waiting to see him. "Sarah and I were just finishing up some work details for today." Looking across his desk, Matt asked, "Anything else we need to go over?"

"Not at the moment. Here's your copy of the work orders. Why don't I touch base with you at lunchtime?" Sarah rose from the chair, making every effort to give a wide berth to his visitor as she passed by. Matt couldn't help but notice how Sarah's eyes never met Draper's on her way out. "See you later, Matt. I'll get another ad placed in the paper." The door creaked behind her as she left.

"That girl does not like me." Jeff Draper said as he helped himself to the chair Sarah had just vacated.

Matt gave his old friend a quizzical look. "Any particular reason why?"

Jeff shrugged his shoulders. "Haven't the slightest. But every time I'm anywhere nearby, she heads in the opposite direction. So… How's the lay of the club, partner?" Jeff stretched out his long legs, put his hands behind his head and yawned. "Sorry . But damn, Hallock. This is way too early to have a meeting."

Matt eyed his partner, taking in Jeff's appearance. "Ah, no offense, but you look like hell. Where did you run off to last night? You're in the same clothes you wore when I left you and the others at the bar at the country club."

"That's normally your line, Matt, not mine. But since you asked, I had some business to attend to." Jeff yawned again.

Matt eyed his friend warily. "Everything okay? You can talk about it if you need to. Won't go farther than these four walls."

"Hell, Hallock, you're my partner, not my shrink." Matt was taken aback by Jeff's sharp retort. "Listen, I'm out of sorts this morning. Where are the others?"

Matt squirmed in his chair. He had known this was going to be an uncomfortable conversation. The other two partners had given him the task of talking to Jeff about a situation that had occurred recently. Matt downed the last of his coffee, which was now cold. "I feel awkward having to talk to you about this." Matt cleared his throat and barged ahead. "I needto be sure your quarterly deposit went in the bank yesterday. Last time you missed the deadline and the three of us had to pony up the deposit. It put the three of us in a bit of a financial bind, Jeff. Unfortunately, I drew the short straw and got to be the one to talk to you about holding up your end of the partnership. Sorry for putting you on the spot."

Jeff's right hand started to tremble as it gripped the arm of the chair. Matt knew from years of being one of Jeff's best friends that the man had a serious issue with anger management. By the look on Jeff's face, he was pissed for being called on the carpet. Matt tried his best to speak to his friend in a calm voice. "Listen, Jeff. I know what's it's like to go it alone. You know the crap I've dealt with over the years with my father. And I know your family is struggling with their finances. Your mother was in tears talking to Mother at the house the other day."

Jeff's hand shot up. "Enough already, Hallock. I met the damn deadline. Call the bank. The deposit went in *on time*. It won't happen again. My cash flow is improving. So call off the others and tell them all is well." Jeff rose, almost knocking over the chair in the process. "I've got to run. I need to shower, change my clothes, and see a few investors about a new prospectus before noon."

Matt came around to the other side of the desk, his hand outstretched. The two men shook hands. "Sorry about the inquisition. Just doing my job. See you at the club's board meeting on Monday night?"

"I'll be there. The Coast Guard meeting got moved to Wednesday night." Jeff turned and walked out the door. It seemed to Matt that Jeff couldn't get out of the club's office fast enough.

Matt walked out onto the small landing where staircases led to all parts of the Sunfish complex. His eyes zeroed in, found, and followed Jeff as his partner made his way through the myriad of employees busy at work as he made his way to the club's front entrance. For some reason, he didn't buy Jeff's story about changing his clothes. Not one bit. From Jeff's years in the Coast Guard, he was a stickler for being meticulously dressed and pressed in public. Matt watched Jeff jump into his red Audi. The Audi's engine roared to life and as the car took off the backend fishtailed in the parking lot. No. Jeff Draper had something on his mind, and Matt was determined to find out what that was.

At the moment though, Matt had other things on his mind. His first priority was to get the beach club up and running ASAP. Memorial Day was just a few weeks away. Sarah's list on his desk was long, which told him it would be another long day and night. As he walked back into the office, the door screeched.

Note to Sarah. Buy a new screen door.

CHAPTER THREE

North Fork
Long Island

Almost to shore, Meg reached up and pulled the hood of her black wetsuit off her head and made sure her gun was securely holstered in the belt around her waist. Her eyes scanned the beach for any unwanted company, relieved to see only the glow of the far away campfires on the grounds of Orient Point State Park. Jumping out into ankle deep water, Meg beached and pulled the kayak from the water. She stored its paddle inside the craft and sat beside it. The calm waves created by the small cove lapped onto shore. The fog had rolled in faster than she'd anticipated and she was lucky to have made it back to the exact point where she launched the kayak several hours earlier. It was taking some time to become familiar with the North Fork, but she had put in a good night's work. Her objective was to stake out several key positions from the water in which she could get a good view of the southwest side of Plum Island.

Meg's thoughts drifted to the ferry ride she had taken several days earlier from Orient Point to New London, playing the role of tourist so she could see the island from the high vantage point of the ferry's upper deck. The weather had cooperated, sunny and clear, the waters calm, not choppy. As the ferry passed by Plum Island on its way to Connecticut, she felt as if she could reach out and touch the outcropping of the rocky cliffs. The high-powered zoom lens on her Agency-issued camera was perfect for rapidly taking pictures of the beaches and terrain as the boat passed. She'd managed to photograph rare footage of the testing lab hidden by the scrub pines on the top of the sheer cliff. With her photos coupled with the NASA satellite images, Meg would be able to piece together topographical information with her team, which would enable them to move forward in the planning process.

Needing to vacate the park's beach before being detected, Meg hoisted the blue kayak effortlessly above her head, jogged up through the soggy sand, and snuck into a copse of pine trees. Finding the black Land Rover lent to her by Reginald Litchfield, the Director's contact on the North Fork, she tied the kayak to the SUV's roof rack, checking to be sure the straps around the watercraft were securely fastened.

Meg had discovered on her arrival that Reginald, aka Reggie, and his wife, Victoria, were old friends of Elizabeth Hallock. They owned the Sound View Marina as well as the Fox Hollow Bed and Breakfast, where she'd taken up temporary residence. The ten-room inn was the perfect location for the team to get their bearings of the North and South Forks of Long Island. It was at Fox Hollow where she was able to pretend to be a tourist and question the locals about the beaches and tides. More importantly, over the last few days, Meg had been able to get a feel of the routines of the comings and goings of the townsfolk.

The ride back to Fox Hollow took longer than Meg anticipated with the fog nipping at her heels. The single lane roads that sharply twisted and turned through the small villages on the North Fork were trying to drive even on a normally clear day. Visibility that night became poorer as time passed. The fog came at her from both bodies of water—the Long Island Sound to her north and Peconic Bay to her south, a nasty combination according to Reggie.

Arriving back at the inn, Meg headed for the garage at the back of the property. Meg drove the black car into the open bay and parked. Keys in hand, she tugged her black duffle bag, packed with her gear, from its place on the passenger seat. As she stepped from the car, she bumped into the chest of a tall, burly man whose arms came out to steady her. Meg's instantaneous reaction was to reach for the gun at her side.

"Easy lass, 'tis only me." Meg released her hand from her weapon, hearing the familiar voice with the Scottish accent. Reggie. "I was beginning to think we were going to have to come and find you. You're running a wee bit later than usual."

"Time got away when I discovered a small cove I wanted to explore. The fog didn't help either." Retrieving the bag she'd dropped, Meg walked to the open garage door. "I'll fill you in after I've given my report. There are some things that need to change or this set-up isn't going to work. The Director isn't going to like what I found tonight."

Meg didn't mean to be abrupt with Reggie but she was on a time schedule. One glance at the glowing face of the watch on her wrist made her remember she had a report to file by midnight. Slinging the black bag over her left shoulder, she headed for the back door. Reggie followed close behind. Meg breathed in the scent of the flowers of the English garden as she passed by. In her brief time at Fox Hollow, she'd come to learn quite a few interesting details about her host and hostess, especially that they had served as CIA's operatives.

Opening the door to the large country kitchen, bedecked in a Nantucket theme, Meg took in the smell of shepherd's pie that wafted through the air. Her mouth watered. She was tired and hungry. It had been a long day and she hadn't taken the time to eat since breakfast. It would be even longer if she didn't get her work done. Her report was bound to shake up the Agency plans, which had been in the works since she'd arrived in Hampton Beach. And if it's there was one thing Meg learned in her tenure at the Agency it was that Elizabeth Hallock did *not* like change once she'd set a plan into action.

"Reggie, be a dear and set a plate for Meggie. You're hungry, aren't you, luv?" Victoria stood at the six-burner gas stove, a flowered apron tied about her thin waist. Meg met the woman's welcoming smile with a broad grin. Victoria blew a wisp of errant red hair from her face. It was evident from day one that she ran the house and Reggie ran the marina and the lines didn't cross.

"Yes, your highness," Reggie responded with a small bow. He came around the counter and wrapped his arm around his wife's waist only to be pushed away. "Keep the food warm, Vic. Meggie has to check in with Elizabeth. Then, I believe we'll need to talk, lass. Am I right?"

Meg opened the kitchen door slightly to see if any of the inn's other guests were nearby. Looking back over her shoulder, she said, "Yes. We need to talk logistics. I don't know how the Director will take to me wanting to change her plans."

"Don't you be worrying about Lizzie," Victoria put Megan's supper dish back to warm in the oven. "Do what needs to be done. You're the one here on site. Make the call as to what's needed. We'll back you up. Elizabeth's not here to see for herself. She's got to trust your team's instincts and observations. You're a good agent, Meggie." Megan saw both parties exchange knowing glances. "Now go." Victoria shooed her out the door. "Use the secure line in the master suite's office. Then, hurry back for your dinner."

Meg nodded, peeking out the kitchen door into the hall to see if anyone was about before she made for the bedroom. Elizabeth Hallock wouldn't like what Meg had to tell her. What had been laid out for her in her original mission statement wasn't going to cut it. Whoever had done the reconnaissance for the job left several huge holes in the logistics of being able to carry out a successful mission. Meg drew in a deep breath as she picked up the phone to place the call. The outcome to the world at large would be catastrophic if the previous intelligence briefings were on target. Change was needed. And time was not on their side.

* * *

" "I understand completely, Megan."

Meg sat in the white wicker chair in the suite's office, amazed that everything she relayed to the Director wasn't being met with a definitive "No."

"You understand where and why I think I need more backup based on the layout of the operation?" Meg cautiously weighed her words. "The location of my cover *and* the need for me to be on the North Fork at night is going to pose a problem in regards to the efficient use of the team's time and mine. Getting from Hampton Beach and back to the Inn everyday is posing a major problem."

"I agree," came the reply. During the past twenty minutes, Meg laid out a scenario for the Director to change the placement of personnel for Operation Hurricane. Not once had the head of the CIA challenged her on any of the items on her list. In fact, it had seemed to Megan as if she had carried on a one-way conversation. "Have you had a chance to talk to Reggie and Vickie yet, Megan?"

"For just a few minutes, ma'am. I wanted to wait until I confirmed I had your approval, then I'd lay out the new assignments."

There was a moment of silence at the other end of the line. "I've taken copious notes. I'll be in touch with you tomorrow morning. Agent Tanner and I will rework the part we've discussed. A few things definitely need to be readdressed. You've done good work, Megan. I had a feeling there would be a need for more presence within the area. But I hadn't planned on Matthew giving you the *chief* lifeguard position. That's thrown a wrench in the works, but let's work it to our advantage, shall we?"

"In what way?" Megan asked. Where was the Director heading with that thought?

"I need Agent Tanner's take on this, Megan. I've an idea, but I need to run it by him. Now, go get yourself some dinner. You've earned it. Just be sure to talk with Reggie and Vickie. Is that all?"

Is that all? Judas! Megan had given the woman a list that practically changed everything from the original manila folder placed in her hands that day at the compound. Most of the agents Meg worked with in the past relayed that Elizabeth Hallock *never* wanted or solicited mission advice from any agent. Her word was law and heaven help you if you didn't follow protocol. This case was proving to be the opposite of what Meg expected.

"I'll check in at 0800 hours tomorrow for the final round of instructions, Director. Have a good evening."

"Sleep well, Megan. I hope Victoria has made you some of her infamous shepherd's pie. My mouth can water whenever I think about her cooking it."

A click came over the line. Their conversation was over.

Meg dropped the phone into its cradle. She lounged back against the comfortable blue and white striped cushions, yawned and stretched. Meg needed a day that had forty-eight hours in it, not twenty-four. She'd been at the Sunfish Beach Club well before dawn to check out the surrounding area. That was followed by a trip into the small hamlet of Hampton Beach that lay to the north of Jessup's Bridge. Meg needed to find the quickest routes between the beach club and the inn. It certainly wasn't going to be easy. The Hamptons were not like DC, where there was a highway in every direction or a Metro to take you from point A to point B underground in a matter of minutes.

Meg's stomached growled, a signal that it was time to eat and sleep. Tomorrow would be another day. What awaited her from that point on had her mind drifting in a thousand different directions. Her late grandmother had once told her patience was a virtue. Obviously, Gram hadn't worked for the CIA.

CHAPTER FOUR

Hallock Farm
Hampton Beach

"Make a legal u-turn. Recalculating route."

Lost, Meg stared at "Genie," her GPS, and glanced down at the crude map Reggie had drawn for her on a piece of paper that sat on the car's console. She'd left Fox Hollow a little over an hour ago. Her travels to the South Fork should have taken thirty minutes. This was definitely a sign it was not going to be a good day. As a matter of fact, since talking to Reggie and Victoria three days ago, and now in possession of the new logistical plan that the Director and Agent Tanner had reworked, given her input and needs, things were *so* not what she'd expected. But one followed the orders given, no questions asked.

"Recalculating route." Genie shrieked again from the top of the Beetle Bug's dashboard. With her mind filled with a new set of assignments and objectives, Meg hit Genie's mute button and pulled off to the side of the road. The tires of the Beetle Bug crunched on the asphalt strewn with broken sea shells, and came to a halt.

Inhale. Meg's heart hammered in her chest. She never liked being behind schedule and she was at least three hours off her mark. Being late had set off an inner panic. This feeling was not like anything she'd experienced before. *But you've never taken on the role of lead agent. Take a deep breath. Regroup. As soon as you get to where you need to be you'll reassess.*

She couldn't be that lost, could she? As she looked out of the right side of the windshield, Meg became mesmerized and was unprepared for the spectacular view of the large body of water that had been hidden by large, meticulously trimmed hedges of the houses she had just passed. The big "pond" was Moriches Bay. The scene before her had her drinking in its beauty, as if she were standing in a museum looking at a watercolor seascape. The sky was a robin's egg blue dotted with white puffy clouds. Seeing the sun making its way into the western sky was one more reminder she was behind schedule.

Numerous yachts and watercraft zipped across the wide expanse of water. Some boats were anchored, bobbing up and down in the wakes of boats that motored by. Her eyes tracked a lone water-skier trailing behind in the wake of a large cruiser. Even at a distance, Meg could tell the skier was having the time of his life.

It was unusual for Meg to feel envious, but she was. Oh, to have the luxury of living a life with such freedom. When was the last time she took a day off to kick back and relax? To do something solely for Megan Spears, the person, with not a thought or care about the Agency. Taking one last look at the peaceful, calm scene that stretched for miles, she thought about her personal life. And lack thereof.

Since graduating from George Washington and attending the Farm's boot camp, Meg had given her all to the Agency and her various assignments 24/7. No men. No complications. No family. She liked it like that. It was a lonely world, but she had made her choice. Besides, seeing the world had been a dream of hers since she was young. Guns, art thieves, and speeding through the canals of Venice hadn't exactly been in those travel plans, but she lived for the rush an assignment gave her.

Meg reminded herself to focus on her present predicament. How did an accomplished CIA agent get lost in a tiny hamlet with a car programmed with the latest gadgetry?

Deciding to give the GPS one more try, Meg unmuted "Genie" and pulled the Bug onto the carless single lane road.

"Make a legal u-turn."

Okay. I'm game. Let's try this one more time. Following "orders," Meg swung about, steering her little car in the opposite direction and traveled on for a few more minutes.

"You have arrived at your destination."

Looking at the large orange arrow on the view screen, Meg glanced up and to the right where the GPS indicated she was to turn off the single lane road. No way! Pushing her sunglasses onto the top of her head, she peered incredulously through the windshield. This wasn't right. But apparently it was according to the map. Meg was about to enter a massive tree-lined drive leading her in the direction of a house, the size of which she'd never seen before. She had been intimidated by being called to the Director's home and was in awe of her surroundings there, but this? This house was over the top. At the edge of the road was a sign set into two brick columns announcing the entrance to the property. After admiring the red, white, and pink azalea bushes that were in full bloom, she read the sign printed in large black cursive writing: "HALLOCK FARM." OMG! Meg sat back in the driver's seat shell-shocked. No, this could not be happening. Hallock? As in Elizabeth and Matthew?

The tinkling of several pieces of the puzzle clicked into place. Needing to get to the bottom of something that was beginning to take shape in her mind, Meg reached above the rear-view mirror and pressed the Onstar button.

"Digit dial," her voice was terse.

"The number, please." A robotic voice replied.

Megan read off the number and waited. On the third ring, the phone was answered. "Hello, Sunfish Beach Club." Sarah Adam's sunny, pleasant voice came through loud and clear.

"Sarah, it's Megan Spears."

"Meg!" Sarah exclaimed. "You made it down okay." Meg was temporarily caught off guard. Not her typical assignment, she had to remember Sarah and everyone who worked at the club thought she had come to take a summer job, a break from her teaching career in Syracuse.

Before Meg could explain why she was calling, Sarah continued, "Well, how do you like your summer digs? Pretty nice, don't you think?"

Well, well, well. Apparently she wasn't lost. But this was *not* what she and the Director discussed as an alternative living arrangement when Meg explained her need to be closer to the beach club. "Uh, Sarah. I think there's been a bit of a mix up. I'm not looking at an apartment to rent. Am I suppose to meet someone here to take me into town?"

Sarah laughed. "No, Meg. You're going to being staying at the estate! Mrs. Hallock was thrilled to have you and a few of the other guards stay in the house for the summer. It took us all at the club by surprise when she offered the other day. We were scrambling to find places that were relatively cheap, which is almost impossible to do at this time of year. What do you think? Pretty impressive?"

Meg drummed her fingertips on the steering wheel. Sarah didn't want to know what she really thought. Neither would the Director. How the hell was she going to have the latitude to move about undetected living under the noses of all these people? It had been her understanding she'd be living in an apartment above one of the shops on Main Street, thereby having the ease to move as she pleased after her day at the club, no questions asked. At least that's what had been *agreed* upon.

Meg gritted her teeth and tried her best to sound enthusiastic. "Great! Just great. Where do I report?"

"Meg, you really need to lighten up."

"What?" Meg didn't have time to play games.

"You said 'report' like you're being called up to active duty. Listen, my boss is all for you staying there, too. In fact, Matt was pretty elated, now that I think about it. But I'm getting off track. All the bedrooms have been empty since Matt and his three brothers and sister moved out. Plus, the house is only a half a mile from the club. It's convenient to work and to town." Meg took a quick glance at the scope of the property before her eyes, and started to click off her new mental "to-do" list. Sarah kept talking as Meg thought of the dilemma she was in. "Pull in the driveway and head up to the main house. The others are due in shortly. Oh, and to give you a heads up. Mrs. H is very much into the Hampton social scene. So, be prepared for a few parties here and there. If you didn't bring a few fancier things there are plenty of shops in town. Oh, it'll be fun, won't it?" Meg rolled her eyes and glanced at her watch. She felt a migraine coming on just listening to the happy chatter. "Lots of people think she's stuffy at times, but she's a real pussy cat. Go get settled in. And don't forget you have an early start for training in the morning. Take care. Bye."

Silence. Knowing the first thing she'd have to do is a new recon of the area when the timing was right, Meg shifted her car into drive and started down the long brick-lined driveway. If she thought the water view was breath taking, it didn't compare to what she saw ahead of her through the front windshield. Nearing the house, she slowed the Bug to a crawl. The line of trees gave way, leaving her speechless due to the magnificence of the mansion before her. The house spoke of money. Lots and lots of money.

Following the drive that encircled flowerbeds of red roses, Meg parked at the steps leading up to the front entrance and its sweeping veranda. Check that. The house had two verandas, one that circled the first floor and one on the second. Seeing no welcome committee, she stepped out of her car. Taking in the trim shrubs and manicured lawns, she noted how everything in the flowerbeds was symmetrically placed. Off to the right, large, red stables and what looked like some sort of training facility could be seen with a multitude of activities taking place in the pens adjoining the buildings. The farm was a massive piece of real estate and seemed to go on for miles.

Meg was awestruck. No, she definitely hadn't planned on this. As she stood taking it all in, she tapped her foot on the pavement, arms crossed, thinking of a few choice things she'd like to say to a few people back in DC and on the North Fork. Meg was convinced Reggie, Victoria, and the Director knew of her "relocation" venue. What had they been thinking not warning her about the impact the scope of the farm could pose? Was there some rationale for being here and not at the apartment in the village? And, if so, why had they not shared that with her? Her job was not getting any easier.

Meg turned at the sound of the front door opening. Standing on the steps, dressed in khaki chino pants, an oxford shirt open at the neck, and boat shoes on his feet was the man himself, Matthew Hallock. The smile on his face was one of *those* kinds of smiles. As he walked down the front staircase, her radar pinged that her employer would need to be set in his place. And the sooner, the better.

During tryouts Meg turned to find Matt near her whenever she had a minute to acclimate to her surroundings at the club. He seemed to be taking a particular interest in *her* drills, not those of the other female guards. She could have sworn he had an excuse to be near the water whenever she exited in her red training bathing suit, his eyes taking in every move she made.

Most often she felt downright uncomfortable, but then sometimes, she didn't.

As the man made his way toward her, Meg needed to figure out how to keep the man close enough in order to see if the intel on the money stolen and its subsequent trail was true, but far enough away so he wouldn't get the impression she was out for a summer fling. She had heard the locker room rumors. Matt was a ladies man and loved one-night stands. Those were not in her play book. Not now. Not ever.

But today as he lithely trotted down the stairs seemingly eager to welcome her, Meg couldn't tear her eyes away from his handsome, tanned physique. As he came around the corner of the Bug, she put her hand out to great him. Clasping his hand in hers, Meg wasn't prepared for the warm jolt of heat that radiated up her arm and settled in her belly. From her churning stomach and the look Matt sent her way, it felt as if she'd walked unknowingly into the path of a hurricane. It was the calm before the storm.

* * *

"Matthew!" Matt's hand dropped the sheer drape he had pulled to the side in order to get a better view of the long drive. He had paced back and forth on the Oriental rug and checked the driveway at least five times in the last half hour waiting for one particular individual to arrive.

"What ever are you doing?" Helen Hallock, the matriarch of the prestigious Hampton clan, asked, as she peered questioningly at him.

Caught. Now would come a litany of questions. It was a known fact he never visited the main house unless "invited" for a mandatory family dinner. Matt had done everything he could do to steer clear of the main house without hurting his mother's feelings over the past few years. It was his father, Robert, he avoided at all costs. Nicknamed the "black sheep" of the family by his father, Matt was quite content living in the caretaker's old cottage. Over the last year, he had remodeled the run-down bungalow located at the very back edge of the estate. Nestled behind the paddocks and barns, the small house afforded him the privacy he sought from the rest of the world. He could come and go as he pleased with whomever he wanted to.

"Mother." Matt stepped away from the window and out into the room. Matt wasn't ready for the Helen Hallock inquisition. She was a master at retrieving the most amount of information in the least amount of time. It was his personal opinion that his mother would even give Aunt Elizabeth a run for her money. Matt stepped forward. "I thought I'd be here to welcome the lifeguards. Make them feel at ease. From the clock, I think they ought to be arriving very soon."

"Matthew, dear. We *always* make our guests feel at ease." Now it was Matt's turn to raise his eyebrows and stare at his mother.

Matt was tempted to respond differently, but stopped. Several years ago, he wouldn't have agreed with her. But since his youngest sister, Kate, had married former Agent John Clinton and gone to Virginia to establish a new horse farm, his parents' demeanor had changed dramatically from stuffy Hampton upper crusted snobs to almost downright nice people. Of course, his adorable niece, Lizzie, was the primary catalyst for the sudden transformation. Lizzie's birth had been a major turning point in familial relations in the Hallock household.

"Really." Matt paused. "Well, I think to some people this house is a tad intimidating. I just wanted the people who are going to reside here for the summer to feel warmly received." There that should do it, he thought. His mother was always one for proper etiquette.

"Well there's no need for you to be here, Matthew. You should be on your way." Was she tossing him out? What was going on? "You've got more than enough on your plate down at the club getting ready for opening day, according to Sarah. Or is there a different reason for you physically being in this house without being summoned? This is *quite* unusual."

A brief twinkle sparkled fleetingly in his mother's eyes and the touch of a grin appeared at the corners of her mouth. Had she any idea he was waiting for Megan Spears? A car door closed loudly outside just as he was about to reply. For some reason, Matt was unable to move and stood rooted in place. What had come over him?

Helen Hallock, who had sat down on the couch as she questioned him, crossed her legs and folded her hands in her lap. She made no move to the door to welcome whoever had arrived. "Excuse me," she said, "but Hannah's in the kitchen readying everything for the party tomorrow. Aren't *you* going to see who that is? You did just say you were welcoming the guests coming to live here." Sitting ever so prim and proper, the woman before him grinned like the Cheshire cat. For some reason, his mother was taking great relish in his discomfort.

Without responding, Matt walked out the door and onto the mansion's porch that wrapped around the entire first floor of the house. His eyes lighted on the brown-haired beauty who stood next to her car scanning the surrounding scenery, a look of awe upon her face. That was until her eyes landed on *him*. Then the corners of her mouth turned down. He bounded down the steps and came to a halt in front of her, his large calloused hand reaching out to take her more diminutive one.

"Welcome to Hallock Farm, Megan! I hope you found the place okay."

Meg immediately retracted her hand from his, as if she had touched a hot stove. He saw the start of a smile, but it faded as she eyed him warily. "Listen, Mr. Hallock."

"My name's Matt, Megan. Mr. Hallock is my father."

"I'm thinking there's been some mistake." The woman seemed nervous. Matt watched as she rocked back and forth on the soles of her feet. He couldn't take his eyes off her sleek tanned legs. She stared in every direction but at him.

"What would you make you think that?" Matt asked. He crossed his arms and eyed her thoughtfully. Yes. From the tone in her voice, the woman was definitely not happy about something.

"I just spoke to Sarah Adams. She told me I'm residing here." Meg pointed in the direction of the estate house. "Your *parents'* house. For the *entire* summer." Matt locked eyes with her and drummed his fingers on the roof of the Bug. He was starting to like making her feel uncomfortable. "I don't think I can impose on your parents' hospitality. Perhaps there's a smaller place in town where I can rent a room?"

Matt countered her opposition. "Being here works better than what the front office planned, Megan. The house is empty and besides, Mother was so delighted to be of help in boarding some of the guards, I couldn't say no. She and Father are planning a welcoming barbecue for tomorrow evening. A mixer for all the employees at the club for the summer."

Matt's eyes traversed the length of her body, drawn to her legs poking out of a pair of cut-off denim shorts. A form fitting tee-shirt fit her upper torso in all the right places. He watched as she tipped back the rim of a navy blue ball cap.

"Like what you see?" Meg's comment took him by surprise.

Bold with a touch of sass. Just his type, Matt thought. His face reddened though, caught beyond the bounds of what was right between boss and employee. Matt took a few steps back and cleared his throat. "Here, let me help you with your luggage. Mother asked me to help you get settled in." Meg popped open the trunk of her car. He glanced down seeing only a duffle bag and one small suitcase. "This is it? This is all you brought for the summer?"

"I travel light. All I needed was a swimsuit, rain gear, and some changes of tops and pants. Sarah said I could buy a dress in town for any party I might need to attend."

Matt stood rooted in his place, speechless. There wasn't a woman of his acquaintance who didn't travel with at least four or five suitcases brimming with designer clothes of every brand, coupled with shoes and accessories to match. Having secured her meager belongings, he headed in the direction of the front staircase. "I'll introduce you to Mother and Hannah."

Meg fell into step beside him. Trying not to let the sweet smell of lavender walking beside him get the better of his libido, Matt desperately thought a change of conversation was needed. "We've a major management meeting tomorrow followed by defibrillator training. Since you're chief guard, you and I will be working pretty closely together. You've got to be excited."

"Thrilled." Matt detected a tinge of sarcasm in her voice. He couldn't see Meg's face, but the woman didn't sound enthused. Maybe she was simply tired from her trip. "Lead the way…Matt. I'm all yours."

Matt stopped at the door, turned, and gazed down into her chocolate-colored eyes. The woman was actually blushing at the sexual innuendo that slipped out.

She reached for her duffle bag he held in his hand, but he wouldn't give it over to her. Mother would have a fit if he walked in the door not doing right by a guest coming to stay in their home. Matt wiggled his eyebrows at his new chief lifeguard trying to put her at ease. "I guess you are. Aren't you?"

Matt was extremely pleased that Megan Spears would be working in close proximity 24/7. From the first time he'd seen her, he wondered how he would pull off the possibility of spending time with her outside of the beach club. It was as if his mother had read his mind by inviting Meg and some of the crew to live at the estate. He had thought of asking, but with the rocky relationship with his father, he hadn't wanted to broach the subject. No doubt, Sarah had intervened. He smiled. Being a hopeless romantic, that girl was always matchmaking for someone in town. Apparently, he was her next target. And she'd brought Meg into his life. Matt made a mental note to give the girl a raise.

CHAPTER FIVE

Hampton Bays Diner

"He's late. The meeting ended a half an hour ago. Didn't he say he'd be right behind us?" Mike Kranepool was not happy with the turn of events. "Where the hell do you suppose he is?" Mike took a sip of coffee and placed his cup on the table in the booth he had corralled for their meeting. Surprised how busy the diner was on a Wednesday night, he wasn't comfortable with the crowd that had gathered. Anyone could eavesdrop. If he'd known the place was going to be hopping with locals, he would have made Steve pick a place in a more remote setting. Memorial Day was rapidly approaching and people were venturing to the Hamptons in droves to ready their houses for the summer. The diner was on Montauk Highway, which was on the main drag to getting to all the Hamptons.

"Well, where the hell do you think he's taken himself off to?" Steve countered. "Between you and me, I don't like the way he's sneaking around. I don't like being left waiting all the time. Do you?" Steve leaned across the table and whispered, "I thought I was being followed today."

Dumbfounded by Steve's revelation, Mike stared at the man sitting across from him. "What? Now you really sound paranoid. Look. Jeff said he'd be right behind us. Didn't you see he was talking to one of the new men? You know he's in charge of setting up their training for the auxiliary. Plus he's probably had to check the status for taking the boat out tomorrow night."

Steve leaned back, the rickety, knotty-pine bench creaking under his large, muscular frame. "That's another thing. That new guy. Didn't he look a bit too polished? You see his suit? Who the hell wears a suit like that to a Coast Guard meeting?" He pointed down at his worn jeans and checkered shirt and gestured incredulously.

"What *is* your problem tonight, Baker?" Mike asked. Out of the three men, he had the least patience dealing with Baker's eccentricities and constant obsessions. Steve labored over every minute detail of anything they did and it drove Mike nuts. But this time, he had to honestly admit even he had reservations regarding Jeff Draper. There were moments when he wondered if Jeff was out for himself in the grand scheme of things.

Take the other morning at the airport. Both he and Steve were left to cool their heels in the hangar during the money transfer. If Steve was even remotely correct, maybe they better be wary and cautious in the bustling atmosphere of the diner. Several locals had spied them when they walked in and waved. Tomorrow morning at Eckart's, the locals' breakfast haunt, their comings and goings might be fodder for those who loved to talk about everyone's business.

So engrossed in his thoughts, Mike was taken aback by a shadow passing over their table. He jumped and Steve's cup slipped from his hand, spilling its contents. Mike didn't know who was more startled, him, Steve, or the waitress who'd come to refill their coffee.

The teenager, dressed in a white shirt, black pants, and black apron scrambled to use a wet rag to mop up the liquid. Even though the table wasn't completely clean, she asked, "Do you want to order now?"

Mike shook his head. "No, just a refill. We're still waiting for our friend. Sorry to take up space like this. He should be here at any moment."

"It's all right." She refilled Mike's cup and looked at Steve. "I'll get you a new cup and someone to wipe up the mess." She pointed at him. "Don't let your shirt get wet. Decaf, right?

Steve watched as the waitress walked off. As his gaze drifted over Mike's shoulder, Mike saw him stiffen. "Draper's here. It's about time."

Mike swiveled in his seat to watch the man in question weave in and out of the crowd gathered waiting to be seated. Jeff acknowledged them and headed for the back corner booth.

Before Jeff could make his way through the throng of people, Mike swung out of his seat and motioned for Steve to move so they could share the seat. Jeff took his place on the side Mike vacated seconds earlier. The waitress appeared out of nowhere. Jeff tossed aside the menu she handed him. "Just black coffee with the haddock dinner."

The waitress set Steve's new cup in front of him, filling it. "You fellas want anything to eat?"

"Nothing for me." Mike wanted the conversation to be short and brief, but from the looks of things, that wasn't going to happen since Jeff ordered dinner. And, from the look on Steve's face, his friend had something to get off his chest.

"Took you long enough." Steve growled. Mike didn't like the sharp look Jeff shot Steve's way.

"Listen. I didn't have much choice. I don't know why I'm going to explain myself, but," Jeff took a long swallow from his cup, "the new member needed to fill out some paper work and Ben wasn't there to do the honors. On top of that, the dock master gave me problems about getting the boat for tomorrow night's excursion. I had to sign my life away over some rule change. Since when are we filling out boat plans for training outings into the Peconic?"

The waitress arrived back with Jeff's dinner on her tray. She topped off their cups and abruptly turned away.

Mike spoke in a hushed voice. "Obviously you haven't read the recent security addendums in the emails. Since Homeland put Plum Island under their jurisdiction, we've got to file any movement we make with any kind of boat if it's moving from the Peconic or the Sound around that facility. That goes for anything recreational or military. I've been trying to contact you, but you never answer your damn cell phone." Mike paused, seeing a pair of dark eyes staring him down from the other side of the table. "What's your problem now, Draper? I'm getting a bit peeved on being kept out of the loop. We thought we were in this together. Your style of communication sucks." Mike nodded his head in Steve's direction. "Steve feels the same. Like you've taken it upon yourself to run the show. Hasn't it occurred to you we're taking as many risks as you are? Don't you think we should be involved and know all the details?"

Jeff Draper chewed his food, swallowed, and shot a smoldering glare at Mike. "First, I thought it was better the two of you operate on a 'need to know' basis. That's until we have something to work off of. Dealing with the Arab hasn't been easy. It's for your own safety I've kept you away from the man. He seems to think he can do what he wants when he wants—like that day at the airport. I told you the damn man filed a flight plan for his jet." Jeff paused and wiped his mouth with a napkin. "Now, he's not paying the money on the schedule we had agreed upon so I've got Hallock and the other investors on my back. Hallock is monitoring banking deposits, dates, and time. The transfers are becoming more difficult to hide. I wanted to wire it from that offshore account, but felt it would be a bad move on my part.

"Second, I don't think it's a good idea that the three of us be seen together, other than the meetings. Which one of you picked *this* place? We should be meeting down at the Liars Club at the pier. Nobody goes there but Buddy Owens, and he's half wasted most of the time. We can talk and nobody will be the wiser. The fishermen come and go from there. New faces all the time." Jeff stopped. "What's wrong with you, Kranepool? You look like you've got something to tell me."

"I think you better listen to Steve. We may have other problems."

Jeff rested his knife and fork on his plate and leaned back, arms crossed over his broad chest. "And just what might those be?" He looked intently at Baker. "I'm not getting sucked into your paranoia again, my friend. If you can't hack it, you're welcome to back out of this deal at any time. But I don't need to tell you what might happen."

Out of the corner of his eye, Mike saw Steve grip his hand around the knife of his place setting. If they weren't in a public place, there'd probably be some kind of incident. Their feud had been brewing for months. "Funny. I thought you needed us for muscle and brawn and our knowledge of the bays and coastal waterways. But you're at bit in over your head, Jeff, when it comes to dealing with John Steeler."

Jeff's eyebrows shot up. "What do you know about Steeler?"

"Both of you may think I'm paranoid, but the years have taught me to be... cautious. You've been seeing John about cooking up another set of books for the club, haven't you?"

Steve suddenly had Mike's undivided attention. Where had he gotten that piece of information? Mike continued to watch Steve and Jeff, their eyed locked in silent combat.

Steve continued. "I know John's forte ever since we were kids. I kept my nose clean and wound up at the Academy. He wound up with a sealed record after his old man did some money laundering with those friends of old man Hallock. He looks cleaned up and respectable, but most people don't know what happened our senior year of high school. You do."

"Why you..."Jeff's voice rose. Heads turned in the tables and booths surrounding them.

"I'm not finished." Steve whispered, leaning across the table. "I told Mike I was being followed today. I'm pretty damn sure we all might be."

"Enough! Both of you!" Mike spoke in a hushed tone as well. "It's not the time or the place." Mike pointed his finger at Jeff. "Obviously, Jeff, *you* owe us a more detailed explanation. No more of this crap of 'on a need to know basis.' We're in this as thick as you are. And if Steve thinks he's being followed, we need to check it out. Could be we're being watched by the Arab...or for that fact, anyone who might be on to you. And we deserve to know more of the role Steeler's playing in what we're about to do."

"All right," Jeff said, his patience definitely at an end. Standing up, he threw twenty dollars on the table. "Meet me at the Liar's tomorrow night. Ten o'clock. *Don't* come together. And come in by water. *Don't* use the whaler. There's someone I want you both to meet."

Without another word, Jeff turned, making his way through the throng of people, and walked out the front door.

"Do you trust him?" Steve tapped his fingers on the wooden, chipped table.

"To be honest, after tonight, I'm not quite sure anymore. But, I'll tell you I'll be packing tomorrow night. The Liar's Club? When was the last time we went there?"

"When we followed your old man, only to find out he'd gone to pick up his mistress. Jeff's out of touch with who goes there. He's been away from Hampton Beach too long. I'm worried something's going to seem out of place and someone will talk out of turn."

Mike placed his arm around Steve's shoulder. "I think, my friend, for once, you may be on to something. My take is Jeff's playing dumb. I can't believe he didn't know about Homeland's new policy regarding the island. Him? We all got the briefings. And with the DC contacts he's got? His security clearance is far higher than either of us. Brushing aside our concerns clinched it for me. Come on. I've got some thinking to do before tomorrow night."

Trying to locate the teenager who'd waited on them, Mike and Steve finally gave up and added to the money Jeff placed on the table moments earlier to pay their non-existent bill. They made their way to the diner's exit.

As they climbed into their respective vehicles, both men were totally unaware of a young, dark haired man peering through the curtains of the diner, watching them as they left. Waiting on him was the very same teenage waitress who'd serve them their coffee and Jeff his meal. A sly smile curled up at the corners of his mouth as he diligently wrote in a notepad as the waitress talked. Mike and Steve turned onto Montauk Highway, each driving in opposite directions. Steve's paranoia had become a full-fledged reality.

CHAPTER SIX

Hallock Farm

Her body's reaction to the rigorous final day of workouts surprised Meg. She felt all of her twenty-nine years, and then some, when she jumped from the lifeguard tower earlier that afternoon. The hot sun hit her sunburned shoulders as she sprinted to the water for one set of drills. It was an odd sensation given the fact she'd kept up with her training regime for the Agency.

Standing in the shower, the hot water pounding on her aching muscles, was pure relief and heaven rolled into one. But her lingering caused Meg to be late dressing for the barbecue. She needed to hurry.

As Meg donned her outfit for the welcome party, the chatter of people gathered on the patio below drifted up through her open bedroom window. Not sure the curtains hid her from view, she stepped to the side as she toweled off and listened to the conversation from below. A group of three women stood beneath her window immersed in the topic of one special man—Matthew Hallock.

A tall, lithe woman, whom Meg had met briefly in the locker room, said, "I'm telling you, my mother said he's bad news."

A shorter woman dressed in a flowing orange caftan responded. "What ever are you talking about, Teresa? I think the man's rather intriguing. Beside, he fits the bill of being tall, dark, and handsome. Tanned from his days at the beach. Admit it. He's yummy just to look at. From his reputation, I'd say he's just my type. Besides, he's got the Hallock money, girlfriend."

Meg struggled to zip up her dress while keeping an eye on the taller woman who gingerly sipped her cocktail. "You do like Hampton playboys, don't you? But Matt goes through women like you go through shoes, Sally. I thought you were after something more. Didn't you tell Mel and me you were done with summer flings?"

The third woman, more elaborately dressed for a casual barbecue than the other two, spoke up. "That man's way out of our league, ladies. Face it. He's a born player. Always has been. Always will be. Like father, like son. And besides, he's way too old for us anyhow." She took a sip of her own drink. "And have you forgotten? *He's-the-boss.*" She enunciated the last three words.

Meg watched Teresa scan the crowd that grew increasingly larger by the minute. "And how, pray tell, do you know so much about him?" Teresa turned and directed her comment at the third woman—Melanie, one of Megan's rotation crew chiefs and a local from the village.

"I've grown up in the shadow of the Hallock family. I can tell you Matt lives by his own set of rules. If you're looking for a one-night stand, he's your man. Any woman in Hampton Beach who's managed to date him more than once finds herself at the curb if she so much as mentions the word 'commitment' or asks where the relationship is headed. He goes after what he wants. Once he gets it, he's out the door." Meg heard the disgust in Melanie's voice. Personal experience, perhaps?

Not one for idle gossip, but trying to learn more about the man, Meg walked away from the window disappointed. She didn't have any patience with men who saw women as apparently Matthew Hallock did. Actually, she was quite dismayed Elizabeth Hallock hadn't included a more personal profile of her nephew. Perhaps the Director was embarrassed by his behavior with the opposite sex. Meg had to set aside her personal bias and carry on. Idle gossip had nothing to do with her assignment. Nor could she let it interfere with her team's objective.

Meg slid her feet into the espadrilles that accessorized the sundress she'd purchased with Sarah Adams in town the day before. When she explained to Sarah she hadn't anything appropriate for the function, Sarah cleared her schedule and made herself available to take Meg shopping at a quaint dress shop in the village. Obviously, Meg couldn't publicly announce she'd only come to work the beach club and be dressed for nocturnal visits to the north shore when Sarah and Mrs. Hallock had questioned her lack of a dress. Dabbing on a touch of makeup, Meg looked in the mirror of the antique dresser and pronounced herself good to go. She headed for the patio and the multitude of guests who had arrived while she dressed. Grabbing her wrap from her bed, in the event the evening turned cool, she silently closed the bedroom door behind her.

* * *

The luscious green lawn off the brick patio was filled with circular tables with white linen table clothes and matching white chairs. The nautical decorations lent a beach theme to the party. Seashell centerpieces dotted the candle lit tables. White lights were strewn across the tops of the hedges that bordered the property from the rest of the farm offering a soft illumination. Diners were already enjoying their meals. Spotlights of red, white, and blue were focused on the dance floor that had been built for the occasion. Oldie-goldies played softly in the background.

Good Lord, Meg thought, as she took in the crowd. All these people work for the Sunfish Beach Club? Her time had been mainly spent with the guards. But where had the rest of these people been hiding? She made a mental note to ask Sarah for the party's guest list without arousing any suspicion. Meg vetted the employees using the CIA database, but upon seeing the size of the crowd it was time to double check those on the party's invitation list.

Meg's stomach growled, her cue to get in line at the buffet table and find a place to sit. She scanned the crowd looking for two particular individuals. Two people she hadn't planned on seeing in Hampton Beach, but was relieved their assignments were adjusted, bringing them to the club and the North Fork. The two would be valuable assets in the weeks to come.

"Hungry?" A sultry voice whispered in her right ear.

Startled, Meg jumped, nearly dropping her white plate and its contents on the ground. She looked up to find her boss staring down at her, a rakish grin on his face. She took several steps backward accidentally bumping into the person in line behind her. She apologized and turned back to the buffet. But he was so close it was impossible not to look up at him. Meg had to admit the women on the patio had him pegged—tall, dark, handsome. Even she had to admit she was drawn to his surfer physique and piercing blue eyes. *Stop. Wipe those thoughts from your mind.*

Back in control, Meg replied, "Yes. As a matter of fact I'm famished. After those workouts today I really built up an appetite." Meg nodded to the table lavishly spread with seafood dishes, burgers, and salads. "Your parents really know how to throw a party. I don't think I've ever been to one quite like this. There's enough food here to feed the entire town."

Matt chuckled, "This is nothing. Wait for the gig Mother's planning to hold at the end of the season. She's already booked the country club. My brother, Ethan, is already regretting he said she could have the party there."

Feigning no knowledge of the Hallock family, Meg politely asked, "Your brother works at the country club? It seems your family is spread all over. What does he do?"

"Well, Ethan doesn't own the club, but he'd sure like to given the opportunity. Ethan's been its president for the last several years. We all have our hands in different business arenas since Father retired."

A somber look passed over Matt's face. Meg knew from researching the history between Matt and his father that Robert Hallock had dealt in some unsavory business dealings with the Russian mob several years ago, forcing him to relinquish his title as CEO of Hallock Farm. The Director had given Meg a brief synopsis of the Hallock family relations, but didn't delve deep enough, as far as Meg was concerned. There was more digging to do—including whether or not the stolen DC briefcase had actually arrived in Hampton Beach. The Director had been extremely vague, saying it was only imperative to find if the whereabouts of the Washington money led there. When Meg pushed for more information, especially regarding the elder Hallock, Agent Tanner discreetly shook his head. Meg stopped her inquiry, sensing she'd obviously hit on a delicate subject. She tucked away her questions for a later place and time.

Matt moved closer as they moved through the line and began to put food on both their plates. Meg had only to look up and over the buffet table to see that his actions had caught the attention of several of the younger staff members.

Not wanting to appear rude, Meg stammered, "Thank you, Mr. Hallock. I think I can take it from here." She took the salad tongs from his hand. The last thing she needed was anyone thinking there was more than a working relationship between the two of them.

"We've covered this before." For some reason, he sounded displeased. "Mr. Hallock is my father." Matt pointed at the elderly couple greeting guests coming through an archway by the rose garden.

"Okay…Matt." Meg tried her best to smile. "But I can help myself to my own food. Please don't wait on me." Another look of discontent crossed his face. His blue eyes gazed down into hers and he frowned.

"I'm not waiting on you. My crew chief looked tired and since you arrived a bit late, I thought I'd help you out, introduce you around to some people you haven't met. That's all." Matt slapped a healthy helping of potato salad on his own plate and followed behind her.

Maybe, Meg thought, she was making too much of nothing. "Well, thank you. I'm going to grab a drink and eat all this before it gets cold."

Meg bolted out of the line before he could reply and hoped Matt wouldn't follow. Unfortunately, he wasn't taking the hint to leave her alone. He came up behind her at the bar. It was obvious the man wasn't going to be easily deterred. She'd met his type before. A man with his eye on a prize. Unfortunately, she was his intended target for that night if what she'd heard from the ladies on the patio was true.

"Soda, beer, or a wine?" Matt offered as he signaled the bartender.

Meg chose the first thing that came to mind. "Beer."

As Matt handed her the cold bottle, he was distracted by the bartender. Meg took advantage to make a hasty retreat. As she turned to seek out a spot to sit and eat, she saw two people signaling her—Jake Donahue and Samantha Hewitt, the two people she'd been trying to locate earlier.

Nodding at them, Meg glanced over her shoulder and saw Matt looking for her. When his eyes locked on hers, a strange chill ran down her spine. It was then she knew Matt definitely had set his sights on her and was going to follow her whether she liked it or not. Little did he know that their "closeness" would come to a grinding halt if and when he found out why she'd come to Hampton Beach. She had come to save him and his business, not fall into bed for a summer romp. Sliding into the chair next to Samantha, Meg put her plate and beer on the table swearing under her breath.

"Some party, huh, Meg?" Samantha made light conversation, then lowered her voice. "Jake's eyeballed the crowd. Some people of interest are here."

"This just isn't the crowd from the club." Jake discreetly pointed his index finger in the direction of a group of people huddled together in the back corner of the yard. Meg's eyes grew round. Jake nodded. "Yeah. I'm shocked, too. Makes me feel like we're back in Paris. Sammy and I need to eat and get out of here. Reggie, Victoria, and the Eagle need to know who's here. Those two complicate matters."

Meg took a long swallow to quench her thirst. The beer tasted cool and refreshing. "No kidding. At least you two have got an easier time getting out of the estate than I do." Meg heartily dug into the food on her plate. But the food stuck in her throat and her heart thumped in her chest thinking of the ramifications of who she laid eyes on. She needed to make up a good reason so she could get to the inn as well. "I'm trying to figure out the easiest way to escape without being detected. Mrs. H practically does a bed check. I feel like I'm at summer camp."

Both Jake and Samantha glanced at each other and smirked. Jake, finished with his meal, swallowed the last of his beer, and motioned to where Matt now stood on the outskirts of the dance floor talking to two women. "You got the perfect gig here, Meg. Think about it. You're able to keep an eye on the man in question as well as be near the club. The Eagle put enough people in place on the ground to make things run smoothly."

Meg sat back and took in the cacophony of noise and people, lowering her voice, "I'm the lead agent. How the hell can I keep my people coordinated in this kind of set up? Too many obstacles and too much territory to cover."

Samantha nudged her in the side. "Relax. Take it for what it is. You've got a chance to get closer to Matt, find out about the man and his business. And hell, it's a bonus that he's pretty good on the eyes." She laughed, her eyes twinkling in delight.

Meg glared at Samantha. They'd been close friends since meeting at boot camp. "Easy for you to say. Go ahead and joke. But that sixth sense tells me this isn't all what…"

Jake interrupted Meg, taking her by surprise, by quickly standing up. "Mr.

Hallock! Great party, sir!"

Samantha stood as well, her hand sneaking into Jake's as if they were a couple. "Yes, it's lovely. The food was delicious. But unfortunately, Jake and I are going to make an early night of it, sir. We both need to get ready for the grind of the early morning hours. Get our bodies in sync for the early morning wake up call." She glanced down at Meg, who was finishing her dinner. Meg looked away, peeved that her agents had every intention of leaving her to deal with Matt. *Just great. Alone with the man…again.*

Jake put his arm around Samantha's shoulder. "Your timing's perfect. We didn't want to leave Meg alone. She really hasn't had a chance to introduce herself to anyone but the guards." Meg almost choked on her potato salad. Her agent would pay at some point with an unpleasant duty assignment for that comment.

Matt took possession of the seat on Meg's left as Jake and Samantha strolled off. Meg watched as they stopped to bid good night to the elder Hallocks.

"Well," Matt's voice was as deep and husky as the first time she heard it. "This is cozy."

"Ah, Mr. Hallock." Matt's eyebrow arched at the reference to his father and he locked his blue eyes on hers. From the little she'd experienced so far, Meg knew it was time to set the record straight regarding their employer-employee relationship. She plastered a fake smile onto her face and continued, "Matt, please understand I'm not used to referring my boss on a first name basis. I work *for* you, And for the record, I don't mix business with pleasure." *Contrary to you.*

"Message understood." Matt leaned back in the white chair, his eyes roamed the entire length of her. Did the man not get the message? She thought she was sending out clear signals. But her body betrayed her when she shivered at his perusal. Her mission had her treading cautiously. Jake and Sammy had pointed out the obvious—Agent Megan Spears needed Matt Hallock by her side no matter what. She had to deal with that fact. Hell, what a paradox. To put it mildly, this was one freaking mess.

* * *

Matthew Hallock *never* gave up when it came to the pursuit of the opposite sex. Megan Spears intrigued him. He'd been attracted to her physically from the moment he saw her come out of the surf at tryouts. Taking in her red, one-piece bathing suit that highlighted every curve of her tall, athletic frame when she strode out of the water squeezing the water out of her long brown hair and laying the hair to one side across her breasts hit him in the solar plexus. Knocked the wind right out of him.

During training Meg proved she was attentive to detail more so than any guard he had ever worked with. The beach club's guards were in good hands.

She was smart, clearly organized, and always multi-tasking. Must be her teacher training. But tonight there had been a change in her. She was uncomfortable for some reason, as if she was out of her comfort zone. He likened her mood to one of the fillies at the farm, kicking up her heels and running from his side at the bar, headed to the safe haven of where Jake and Samantha had sat down to eat and enjoy their dinner.

Meg sat rigid, pushing her food around her plate. Matt took a sip of his beer. Break the ice, he thought. "So, Meg…Those teenagers teach you to dance?"

Meg's brow wrinkled, momentarily puzzled and confused. But she disguised the look on her face as quickly as it appeared. "I've done my fair share of chaperoning proms. Why are you asking?"

Knowing Meg wouldn't cause a scene in front of the guests, Matt reached for her hand and pulled her from her seat. "I thought we'd take a spin around the dance floor."

Matt would have given anything to know what was going through her mind right then and there, as he whisked her to an open space in the crowd. Her face was devoid of emotion. Deep down, he really thought she'd put up a fight, but Meg acquiesced and followed. She jerked her hand from his as they left the table, but Matt reached for it again, entwining his fingers with hers. She wasn't getting away from him tonight.

Thanking the gods that a soft, slow ballad was playing, Matt placed his arm around her waist and pulled her close. Meg stiffened from the contact of their bodies. He looked down into a pair of eyes ready to do battle, his clue to release the tight hold he had on her, allowing a small space between them. From the minute, she'd blown a whistle in his face at the Sunfish to get out of her way, he'd known Megan Spears would be a challenge. Normally, women followed him everywhere without question. She would be different. He loved a good chase as long as he got what he wanted in the end. And Megan Spears was going to provide just that.

Everything about her fascinated him. He expected her to bolt from the dance floor, but she hadn't. Gently swaying to the music, he eyed Meg as she closely examined everyone around them.

She asked out of the blue, "About that final lifeguard meeting for the rotating crews?"

Work. The woman had a one track mind. Matt cut her off. "No business tonight. Relax and enjoy the music." Matt once again attempted to pull Meg to him. Didn't she realize how perfectly they fit together? But one glance into her beautiful, tanned, freckled face told him they were on different wavelengths. Meg wasn't pleased.

As everyone danced around them, Matt stopped. He needed to know what was wrong. "What is it? Tell me." He had to know. Not only did they have to work together, but he had plans for the two of them. An entire summer full of plans.

"Wrong?" Meg spoke a bit more forcefully than Matt was comfortable with. Heads turned as people listened in. "With all due respect, I don't think dancing cheek to cheek with a new employee is conducive to an appropriate business relationship. Everyone is staring. I have to work with these…"

"Excuse me. May I cut in?" A deep voice came from over Matt's shoulder.

Matt turned to see who had asked to take his place. A large, intimidating man stood tall and erect. Matt had never laid eyes on him before and clearly the man had every intention of dancing with Meg.

Matt heard Meg gasp. She seemed as surprised as he was at the unwanted intruder. Matt stepped away from Meg, perturbed at being interrupted. "Who the hell are you?"

The sleek man in a dark navy blue suit and starched white shirt moved around Matt to stand next to Meg. Taking Meg's hand in his own, he said, "Meg, would you care to introduce me to your new friend?"

Meg stood silent. She looked as if she'd seen a ghost.

"Well…Meg seems to be at a loss for words." The stranger stuck his hand out in greeting. "I'll introduce myself. I'm Derek Taylor…Meg's boyfriend."

CHAPTER SEVEN

Sound View Marina

"My boyfriend? Really? That's the best you could come up with?" Miffed, Meg sat in the passenger seat of a black Jeep hidden in the scrub pines which were off to the side of the marina's boat ramp. She punched Derek in the arm. "Whatever were *you* thinking? Come to think of it, what are you even doing here?"

The only thing that pleased Meg at that moment was the man by her side had served as an excuse to leave the party at the Hallock estate. The look on Matt's face was forever imprinted in her memory.

"If you'd be quiet for five minutes, I'd tell you." Derek drummed his fingers on the steering wheel. "I'd think you'd be grateful I showed up when I did. But per usual, you've done nothing but bark orders since I brought you to the inn."

Meg interrupted, "I am—"

"Shut up so I can explain." Derek Taylor was looking through his night vision binoculars at the boats moored in the marina. "The Director knows her nephew. She had no doubt he was going to be an issue. Especially when she found out you'd be working very closely together. She became concerned you had too much on your plate, what with trying to keep your eyes on anything amiss at the club and being here on the North Fork. So…the Director decided to send me in as a diversion…and back up."

Derek reached for a bottle of water in the cooler behind her seat. Meg leaned against the passenger door as he went on to explain, "Relax, sunshine. I'm about as happy about this "relationship" as you are. Remember, I'm the one who might have been made on that drop in DC. My sources in the department tell me I'm taking a big risk being sent here. But you know as well as I do, you go where you have to when the Eagle says to."

Meg hadn't like Derek Taylor from the time they were introduced at the Agency. She detested the fact he became her partner after Paris. But she had to admit, having him here playing the role of suitor was her ticket off the estate. If she was to guess, Agent Tanner must have realized the logistics of placing her at the farm might not have been the best decision after all. She bet he had swayed the Director to send Derek as a diversion.

"Give me those binoculars." Meg put her hand out only to have Derek swat it away.

"Where are yours, *Lead* Agent Spears? I know you're packing your weapon tonight. Didn't you come prepared?" The man was obnoxious, especially more so since he had been passed over for promotion. And he knew exactly how to push her buttons. Smugly he smiled, looked her up and down and said, "I've been imagining where you put your gun when you're on the beach."

Sexist pig. "Remember, you answer to me, Agent Taylor. Don't cross the line." Meg glared at him. His arrogant expression suddenly disappeared. *Good. Let him think I might put him on report.* That could get him where she wanted him—back at a desk job in Langley. "*My* binoculars are back at the inn in my duffle bag. Reggie was in such a hurry to get out onto the water I didn't have time to grab my equipment. "Your binoculars," Meg put out her hand once more. "*Agent Taylor.*"

Derek handed over the requested item. Now in possession of the night vision binoculars, Meg watched Derek reach for his holster and pull out his Glock. He leaned across her and opened the glove compartment. He took out a magazine and began to load his weapon.

"And you're talking about me," she said sarcastically. "You've been carrying around an unloaded weapon?"

"Didn't think this outing was going to require one. I only thought we were doing a recon as Reggie made his patrol run. Now I know otherwise."

The cool night air drifted in the open windows. Binoculars in hand, Meg searched the boats docked at their berths, zooming the lens out to the end of the pier.

"Flash the lights!" Meg suddenly ordered. "Three times!" Derek sat motionless. "Do as you're told! Flash the lights!"

"Okay, okay. What the hell is going on?"

Meg held up her hand for silence. Through the night vision binoculars, she watched as the *Scottish Lass* made its way past the flashing warning light at the marina's entrance from Long Island Sound; its destination—the large slip at the end of the dock. A flurry of activity could be seen as the crew on board prepared to moor the boat. Reggie stood clearly at the helm, steering the boat, calling out instructions to secure the lines. Meg had a clear view of the scuba divers used in the night's mission. They were divesting themselves of their gear, stowing their tanks and gear in the main cabin. That didn't please her. The divers should have changed out of their wetsuits in the privacy of the wide-open waters. Anyone could be watching.

Moving up in her seat for a better view, Meg said, "Keep your eyes on the docks. Look for anything suspicious. I've got my eyes on the boat. Those three flashes meant there's been clear sailing so far... but..."

"But what?"

"I've got a strong suspicion we're not alone."

"What? We've been sitting here for more than two hours, Meg. All we've seen were a couple of families coming from what looked like a day's outing on the bay. What makes you think there's somebody out there who shouldn't be?"

A solitary light flashed from the top of the *Scottish Lass*.

"Flash again—once," Meg directed. This time Derek did as she requested. "Why? I can't go into it right now. Jake and Samantha identified several people at the party who weren't employees of the Sunfish. Apparently the Hallocks invited a few society friends." Meg paused, her eyes intently scanning for anything out of the ordinary now that Reggie's boat had docked. "Interesting company the Hallocks know from the Hampton social circle. Jake spotted two Russians, one who's been under Agency surveillance for quite some time."

"Please don't tell me there was anyone we may have come in contact with in DC?" Derek pointed suddenly at the *Scottish Lass*. "A double flash. What's up?"

Not answering either of Derek's questions, Meg thrust the binoculars back in his hands. Stepping out of the Jeep, she undid the lens cap of her night vision camera that hung around her neck. Derek opened his door to follow, but Meg motioned for him to stay put. "Keep your eyes on the water. Everything seems to be in order so far. That wasn't a distress code. I'm just going to take a one-hundred and eighty degree panoramic picture. Perhaps it will show us anything we've missed. I've just got a feeling something's not right."

Derek nodded, raised the binoculars and looked toward the marina through the Jeep's windshield.

Meg walked to the edge of the scrub pines and began to snap photographs. As her lens fell on the western edge of the pier, a ripple in the water caught her eye. She zoomed in and immediately began clicking as if her life depended on it. Wedged between two small jet skis was a two-person kayak. From where she'd positioned herself, and even with the zoom lens of the camera, Meg could barely make out two people—one, a burly, masked individual. Using their paddles, they were making a futile attempt to fight the current of the outgoing tide to keep the kayak wedged between two boats. She had to find Derek and get a message to Reggie.

Back at the Jeep, she found Derek casually leaning up against the car. Would he ever follow a simple directive?

Giving him the signal they were not alone had his attention within seconds. As Meg rounded the front of the SUV, Derek was already manning the encrypted two-way radio to make contact with Reggie.

"Here she is. Over." Derek handed over the headset and turned on the ignition. He backed up ever so slowly over the gravel drive.

"This is Sparrow, Night Owl. Over."

Reggie's voice came on the line. "What's up?"

"Perpendicular to your line of sight. Can you make out the kayak? Over."

"Roger that. Sending the raft to intercept. Tide's too low for them to reach the ladder. Meet me back at base. Night Owl out."

Before Meg finished talking, Derek had them back on Route 25A headed for Fox Hollow. In the interim of Meg's move to the Hallock estate, Reggie and Victoria had posted a "No Vacancy" sign. The ten-room inn had been emptied of its guests and converted into the home base of the operation.

"Meg, what is it? What's happened?" Derek asked.

Meg was leery of showing Derek anything at that point, but she lit up the view screen of the camera, holding it so that Derek could glance at the picture while trying to keep his eyes on the road. Meg witnessed his body tense at the visual. "Are you thinking what I'm thinking?"

"I don't know. You tell me."

"That there's a leak in the chain of command." Derek slowed the Jeep, checking all the angles of the SUV's mirrors, cranning his neck to see if there were any cars behind them. Seeing nothing he turned into the inn's driveway.

"Having things go wrong in Hampton Beach is one thing, Derek. But to have something happen so close to base camp has me nervous. We'll know more when Reggie gets back. Pull up behind the back cottage. I don't want this car visible from the road."

"What's your plan?"

Meg turned to Derek wondering exactly what she should say. She eyed him suspiciously. Was he *really* her partner? She hadn't received any directives from Langley. Elizabeth would have informed her he was on his way. Hell, she didn't like not knowing where Derek Taylor fit in the scheme of things. Could she trust him? He'd literally popped out of nowhere! Within the next few hours, Meg was damn sure she was going to find out.

Meg grabbed the camera that sat on the console. "We wait to see who's shown up without an invitation. Reggie hasn't lost his touch when it comes to interrogation. This isn't an issue that can be turned over to the local police department."

With the Jeep parked, Derek opened the door, climbed out and made for the path leading up to the kitchen. Funny, Meg thought, how he knew his way around this particular piece of property. Halfway up the path, he turned to her and said, "Okay. I've got to change out of these clothes. You let me know what you need me to do."

Meg nodded and followed him, wondering about the man's change in demeanor since their work in DC. Her mind whirled with all that had transpired. Not that she wasn't grateful Derek appeared in Hampton Beach when he did. But she couldn't believe someone at the Agency hadn't noticed the man had been a thorn in her side since day one. Something didn't gel. But right now, there were other more pressing issues to deal with. The team had barely begun to start their investigation into the club's financials, when they now had to deal with intruders in their own backyard.

Derek reached the kitchen door and opened it. "Coming in? Victoria's cooking smells divine."

Meg shook her head. "No… Give me a few minutes to collect my thoughts."

Derek shrugged, threw his duffle bag over his shoulder and entered the house. Totally alone, Meg was left to deal with her jumbled thoughts regarding her assignment. Everything usually lined up perfectly in sync. Plans at the ready to be carried out. That wasn't happening here.

When she'd been given the assignment to proceed, as lead agent, it was *her* job to delegate the agents' duties and activities, wasn't it? The Director and she made a verbal agreement that Meg would handle whatever was necessary to bring Operation Hurricane to a close. Over the last week, she'd done nothing but grow increasingly frustrated at the multitude of obstacles thrown in the way. Meg stuffed her hands in the pockets of her pants and kicked at the pebbles on the path. Operation Hurricane had exponentially jumped from a Category 1 to a Category 2.

* * *

Fox Hollow Inn

Practically overnight a secret room in the basement had been converted into control central for Operation Hurricane. Every technological piece of surveillance equipment was up and functioning and currently being monitored by highly trained Agency IT specialists. But even with the use of the most sophisticated of current spyware, Meg and her team had managed to capture two men with nothing more than a pair of night vision binoculars.

A long rectangular table sat in the middle of the room, maps and tidal charts placed on its surface. A large map of the eastern end of Long Island hung on the wall with color-coded thumbtacks strategically placed along the North and South Fork.

Reggie, Victoria, and the agents who led the night's scouting expedition to Plum Island had arrived back at the inn thirty minutes after Meg and Derek.

Everyone had been sequestered in the basement ever since. The two suspects to be questioned were being monitored by the members of the Special Ops team that had gone out that night on the *Scottish Lass*.

Meg and Derek leaned against the wall in one corner watching Jake and Samantha converse with Reggie and Victoria at the table.

Derek spoke softly, "What's your gut telling you right now? You've always had a pretty good sixth sense."

In front of a crowded room filled with some of Elizabeth's top operatives, Meg wasn't about to share with Derek her displeasure as lead agent in not being allowed immediate access to the two men. When she finally made her way into the kitchen after some serious contemplation, Victoria informed her that Reggie would be in charge of the interrogation. She'd halted and stood shell shocked at the news. That was the proverbial straw that broke the camel's back.

"Derek, I know you and I haven't seen eye to eye. But I think we can concur we both have major concerns about the progression of this case."

Derek said aloud what was on her mind. "Roger that. We've been in this room for what," he looked at his watch, "thirty minutes? And we haven't been allowed to retrieve intel from the suspects? Personally, I don't like the fact that Reggie's called the shots. It should be you, Meg. But who are we to question the Director's plan?"

But it's not my plan. Meg eyed Derek out of the corner of her eye. He actually sounded sincere, as if he was on her side for a change. He seemed different from his normal snarly, sarcastic persona she'd been forced to deal with. Did the man have his own personal agenda? While they talked, he had moved close enough to nudge her and indicated for her to look at the people surrounding the table. Reggie was speaking into his encrypted cell phone.

Derek nodded at Reggie. "*You* should be the one on the phone with the Eagle. Don't get me wrong. Reggie's an operative with a big stake in this. But how can we go setting up a line of defense when we haven't the faintest idea who's who or what's what? Or is it only me thinking that?"

Meg had to agree. "You're right. Jake, Samantha, and I spoke briefly when I got in. They're trying to get a handle on Hampton Beach and what's going on at the estate. Jake's done some research, especially that one visitor at the party. He's trying to go back into one of our cases and see what plays out. But, hell," Meg took off her blue cap, undid the rubber band that held her ponytail and ran her hands through her hair. "You and I both know we've always had a set of linear operational steps to follow. Like I said, we've had 'issues', but we've always known what's going down and followed protocol to the letter."

Suddenly Meg and the entire crows went silent upon hearing Reggie's bellow from across the room. He was standing over the shoulder of one of the men at the communication center looking at a screen. He held the phone to his ear.

The Director was on the other end. From what Meg could hear things were going from bad to worse.

"They're what?" Reggie roared. Meg watched him look from one monitor to the other. "Listen, your agents have a right to know what you're telling me....No, I'm not going to follow that directive... Listen to me, Lizzie!" Meg had never seen Reggie display his temper in any fashion. He usually handled everything calmly and rationally, but something the Eagle said had ticked him off. He walked back to the table and slammed his fist down causing all who stood nearby to flinch. "Hell, you've got agents in different places not sure what they're suppose to be looking for. And now you hand us *this*."

This? Meg made her presence known by moving closer to him hoping Reggie would put her on the phone. Why didn't Reggie just put the damn call through on the speaker? "Lizzie, Meggie needs to be in charge. You've got her over at that damn beach club most of the day—a lifeguard for God's sake! She needs more leverage to do her job. Listen to what she has to say, especially in lieu of tonight. God, what a mess."

Reggie paused. Meg thought she'd finally be put on the secure line, but Reggie continued, "Yes, Derek's here." There was a slight pause, and he continued, "Yes, he created a credible diversion. Matt hasn't given Meggie a moment's peace."

Meg cringed at the tone he used. Reggie was letting off steam at her expense. What would the Director think? It was probably better the criticism came from Elizabeth's former field agent and not herself. He, Victoria, Sam Tanner, and Elizabeth Hallock had had each other's back for well over thirty years. Megan recently learned from Victoria that Reggie was none too pleased to be called back to active duty. He had been quite happy manning his fishing marina and charter boat business. And Victoria, after years in the European theatre, was content running her very lucrative bed and breakfast. Operation Hurricane was a favor—a payback. The Eagle saved Reggie's life in Germany during the Cold War. Once this mission was accomplished, their bill would be paid in full. And as Victoria had put it, the end couldn't come soon enough.

"Well, I'll tell you what *I'm* going to do. I'm turning on the speakerphone and we're all going to join in." Everyone could hear the loud, not particularly pleased voice, with the southern accent as they stood around the table. "You don't have a choice, luv. I'm doing it."

Meg eyed Derek, and then looked at Jake and Samantha. No one wanted to cross the woman on the other end. Everyone valued their careers and their reputations. Meg thought they were caught between a rock and a hard place, but right then, if she and her team didn't get a handle on the situation, the assignment would implode.

Reggie laid the phone down and pressed the red button on the black triangular box on the table. The Director's soft southern drawl became more pronounced. "Tell somebody to go up and retrieve our guests. Be sure they sit on opposite sides of the table and *don't* release their restraints. Treat us this way, will they? Like we're can't do our jobs. I'll show them who's in charge!"

Meg looked at Derek and noticed the rest of the team had the same puzzled expression on their faces as she did.

"Elizabeth." Sam Tanner could be heard whispering softly in the background. "The agents can hear you now."

There was dead silence. Elizabeth cleared her throat. "Forgive my rudeness. In a few minutes you'll see what I'm referring too. Stand your ground. These two interlopers will remain our guests for the duration of this operation, Megan."

At the mention of her name, Meg walked over to stand at the table. Not knowing what she was agreeing to do, but that it was a direct order, she stated, "Yes, ma'am."

The door opened and two men, escorted by armed Special Ops soldiers, entered the room, masks still covering their faces. Hands still in Flex-cuffs, they were pushed into the metal chairs that awaited them.

Meg and her team glanced curiously at the intruders and at each other. Meg read her team well. All had the same question on their minds. Why the masks?

"Are they there?" Elizabeth's asked. "Remove their masks."

Reggie chose the man on his right, reached for the man's chin, and yanked off the mask that hid his face from view. Jake and Samantha gasped while Meg struggled to maintain her composure. Her heart thumped in her chest. Victoria grabbed for the closest chair and sat down, a stunned look on her face. Out of the corner of her eye, Meg noted Derek had no reaction. It was definitely odd he didn't share their surprise that Todd Ranger, a well-known and respected, high level DHS agent, sat before them. What the hell? Exactly what was he doing in her neck of the woods? Just what Meg needed on top of everything else - a bureaucratic, territorial pissing match. Federal agencies never got along for the good of the whole. But, her mind backed up and retraced the facts she'd been told in Arlington. The Director had cleared this op with Homeland. Had someone lied? And if so, whom? Meg positioned herself for a better eye view of the unveiling of the second intruder and any reactions from the people in the room.

A sober expression crossed Derek's face when the identity of the second intruder was revealed to the team. Meg's gut told her he knew the identification of their "guest."

"Who are you?" Meg bent down eye level with the man. He dropped his eyes to the floor and sat in stony silence. "You know I'm going to find out sooner or later when I run your fingerprints through the databases. Make it easy on yourself now. Who sent you here?" No reply was forthcoming.

Meg's attention was drawn away from her interrogation at the sound of Reggie's voice.

"Take that smug expression off your face, Ranger." Reggie admonished the man. "Well, Madam Director. What does Homeland have to say about sending one of their men to spy on us? Don't we work on the same side? Or have things changed that much since I retired."

Meg had had enough. She had to step up and take charge no matter the consequences.

"Director, with your permission, my team will continue with the interrogation. I'll file my report in the morning."

"Be sure to have it on my desk by 0800, Agent Spears."

"Samantha, you come with me," Meg directed. "Agent Ranger is going to sit right here. He's got some explaining to do."

"Jake, you and Derek take our other visitor and go with Reggie."

The three members of her team stood motionless. She knew exactly what had crossed their minds. What possessed her to split up the respective pairing of partners? It wasn't done. It violated protocol.

As the Special Ops guards escorted the unidentified man to an alternative site, Meg motioned Jake to her. She lowered her voice so no one else would hear. "Watch him."

"I'm on it. I'll find out what I can with the intelligence I have, but he's not going to be easy to break."

Meg jerked Jake's arm as he turned to go. She wanted his undivided attention for what she had to say. "I know you'll do your best… But it's Taylor I want you to have your eye on. Got it?"

Jake nodded and walked behind Derek who was led the suspect out the door.

Reggie had disconnected his call placed to the Eagle. Meg looked to him for reassurance. "Don't you go thinking you've done the wrong thing, Meggie. Like you, I've a bit wary since he arrived. I'd had my eyes on him, too."

CHAPTER EIGHT

Sunfish Beach Club

Meg didn't know why she glanced at her watch. She knew instinctively it was 0600 hours. The backs of her calves ached from the intense workout she had put herself through that morning. Sprinting up and down the beach had chipped away at the levels of stress and frustration churning away at her insides. She slowed her pace and came to a stop at the bottom step of the stairs that led over the dunes to her office in the clubhouse.

It was time for a shower and a change of clothes before the mad rush of the day began. Meg mentally made a note that she needed to file her report to the Eagle before 0800. The report would be brief, as the Homeland agent was totally uncooperative. But they had landed a bigger fish from the fingerprints taken from the other suspect when run through Interpol's database. Jake's research had paid off in more ways than one. Meg was awaiting her instructions as to how to proceedWalking up and over the boardwalk's gray planks, Meg breathed in the freshness of the salty sea air. She'd come to love the stillness of the mornings, so much so that Sarah had given her a key to let herself into the club to exercise and put to rights anything that needed to be done before the multitude of employees arrived. It was during that time she'd been able to document the events of her time in Hampton Beach out of the prying eyes of others. It was from here she'd sent in her daily reports.

Hearing the screen door creak on the landing on the landing above her, Meg halted, senses alert. She had the distinct feeling wasn't alone. Reaching under her lightweight jacket, she drew her pistol from its holster.

Crouching low to the ground, Meg's eyes darted from the pavilion to the pool, landing on the staircase in front of her that led to the club's central offices. She saw no one. But the slap of a door above her had her focus more intently on the possibility that someone was upstairs.

Glancing down at the steps, she spied two sets of wet, sandy footprints. Due to the previous night's rainstorm, the sand had matted and become wedged in the soles of the intruders' shoes. Taking great care, with her back to the wall, Meg cautiously lifted each foot not wanting to destroy the evidence as she made her way up the stairs. The white door to Matt's office was ajar and Meg heard hushed voices coming from within. She hid herself from view and listened.

"I told you I don't know where the thumb drive is."

A deeper male voice retorted, "I need it, you fool. Without it, I can't access the spreadsheets. I need to change the books."

"Maybe there's a ledger somewhere in the drawer."

Meg heard the locked drawer of Matt's desk being rifled as the perpetrator tried to get access to its contents.

"Stop. Don't waste precious time," a deep voice commanded. "Sarah is way into technology. There's no way she'd keep any paper copies lying around. Everything is digitized. When I came to visit Matt the other day, Sarah left the office clutching a wad of papers to her chest. She may have had the drive on her."

"Then we're screwed…"

Agency procedures dictated Meg call for backup; there was no time. Stupidly she left her radio behind in her locker when she'd gone for her run. Meg needed to corral whoever was in the office. It would be two against one, but she'd been in that position before. Making her way past the open office door undetected, Meg zeroed in on the two men inside. They were lean and muscular. Looked as if they'd been put through a thorough training regiment of some sort. Her first thought was they reminded of some men from the military she'd come in contact with. From the clothes they wore, she doubted they carried any kind of firearm. Meg opened the door wider hoping it wouldn't make a sound. But squeak and creak it did.

As she propped the door open with her hip, she raised her gun, aimed it at the two men and yelled, "Stop right there."

Meg was unprepared for what came next. An overly large, rough hand snaked out from behind the door, grabbing onto then wrenching her wrist. The two men she'd been able to get a good look stopped dead in their tracks at the sound of her voice and the ensuing commotion. Trying to twist away from her captor's strong grip, Meg's wrist accidentally slammed into the doorknob. The blow was painful, so much so she dropped her weapon, which spun across the wide plank floor, coming to rest beneath the wicker couch on the opposite side of the room.

"Well, who have we here?" asked the man whose tone spoke of seriously doing her bodily harm. Out of the corner of her eye, the other two men stood motionless. The odds were against Meg but she had to strike out. Twisting out of the hold of the third man, Meg landed a strong blow to his midsection. She was confident she'd knocked the wind out of him temporarily as he reached for his stomach. She swung her leg up and around, kicking him in the ribs. The man lost his balance. His head smacked the paneling with enough force to send him sinking to the floor unconscious.

Rounding on the men at the desk, Meg felt at a disadvantage without her weapon. Her eyes darted around the room for another to use in her defense. Suddenly, seeing the butt of her pistol peeking out from under the wicker sofa, Meg lunged for it.

"Let's get the hell out of here," one of man screamed. "This isn't worth it."

Time was of the essence as Meg saw the third man slowly sitting up as she bent over to retrieve the gun. Thinking he was disoriented and she had a few minutes to grab the gun, she was taken aback when a foot came crashed down on he shoulder pinning her to the floor. She grimaced as a sharp pain shot down her back and arm.

The man holding her had regained his senses and reacted quickly, " Get out!" He shouted to the other two. "Now! She may have backup. That's the last thing we need."

The two men who'd been trying to break into the desk didn't need to be told twice. They beat a hasty exit. Meg braced herself for what might come when the man would take possession of her gun. But she was wrong.

His leg suddenly lifted, the door opened and then slammed shut. The room was eerily quiet. Shaking off the numbness in her arm, Meg retrieved her weapon, rose and listened. Sure enough, she heard the pounding of footsteps coming from the landing near the front of the club.

Meg rushed through the open door, trailing behind the three men, her gun at the ready. Heading for the front stairs, she looked down and saw tracks left behind. The three had taken a detour. They weren't heading to the main entrance but to the side stairs that led to the private drive where Matt parked his car. Peering carefully around the corner, Meg was just in time to see a black Escalade pull out onto Dune Road. The driver, hidden from view by the tinted windows, spun the steering wheel and gunned the car into overdrive, making for Jessup's Bridge. The Caillac's tires squealed, leaving tread marks on the road. Meg inwardly gasped as the car shot through the red light. She was right. They were headed for the mainland. They'd be long gone from Hampton Beach's small village in no time. With her car parked in the lot across from the Sunfish, there was little Meg could do. Without her radio to put out an APB and contact Jake and Samantha, Meg knew she'd lost them. For now.

"Shit!" she screamed, the sound echoing in the confines of the club. "Shit! Shit! Double Shit!"

Holstering her gun, Meg made her way back to Matt's office. It was going to be extremely difficult for her to determine what might have been taken. Once inside, she looked around. The office looked as if no one had really been looking through Matt's records. Everything on the desk seemed in order except for a couple of scratches where the two men had tried to pry the drawer open with an embellished envelope opener. Meg smiled, reaching for the tissue box sitting atop the filing cabinet. She picked up the opener, her grin now almost ear to ear. Fingerprints and DNA. Just what she needed to pass off to Jake.

But there was serious issue Meg couldn't lay to rest as she tucked away her find. How was she going to ask Sarah about the thumb drive or records without raising suspicion? Seeing the clock on the wall, Meg had to have Jake and Samantha at the club ASAP. Time was of the essence.

Meg couldn't stop thinking about the comment one man made about being in the office with Sarah. Meg subtly needed to find out exactly who had the club's manager been in the office with…and when. Putting that clue together with what she'd manage to retrieve from her scuffle, she could find in forty-five minutes might give her the best viable lead as to where the money might be hidden. Possibly, with luck on their side, the team would be able to access the financials of the individuals who had "dropped in" for the visit. It might be the first major lead as to who was laundering money through the club accounts and how it was actually being accomplished.

Heading to the locker room to grab her encrypted radio, Meg looked across the dunes to the Atlantic Ocean. The sun had broken the horizon on a calm and tranquil sea. No doubt there were rough waters ahead.

* * *

Memorial Day broke all previous attendance records at the Sunfish Beach Club. The weather lured the crowds to its cabana suites, salt-water pool, and beach in unheard of numbers. Memberships to the prestigious beach community had sky rocketed this year thanks to Sarah Adams's aggressive marketing campaign. Before Matt walked into the shaded pavilion, his eyes captured the white flag flying from the flagpole rising high into the air. It signaled to all who could see, from the beach, Dune Road, and beyond, that there were no waves. He spotted the tranquil sea as his gaze traveled up and down the beach. He let out a sigh of satisfaction. Business would be booming again today.

The thought of the cash register jingling with money filled him with pride. Matt and his partners had defied the odds. If Sarah's projections were correct, the club was headed for its first profitable year in a long while. There was a lot to prove—not only to his partners and all the naysayers in the village, but to his family, especially his father, who'd told him he'd never amount to anything when he passed on the chance to go to college.

Scanning the boardwalk for Meg, as he did every morning upon arriving at the club, he spied his chief lifeguard sitting on a bench at the end of the boardwalk. But this time, unlike other mornings, she wasn't alone. Jake and Samantha, his other head rotation guards, were circled around her. All three were deep in conversation and seemed totally oblivious to anything around them. Matt eyed them from a distance. Their body language spoke volumes. Something had gone awry by the way Jake kept gesturing to the clubhouse. Matt frowned, as the trio's talk seemed to grow more heated. Curious as to why three of his guards were at the club before the allotted time to report, much less the obvious debate taking place, he decided to venture toward them.

"Well, this is unusual. What are you three doing here at this time of the morning? Normally, Meg's the only one here." Matt gazed at Jake and Samantha. "Had I known the two of you were going to be here, I'd have brought two more cups of coffee."

Jake and Samantha immediately looked to Meg. It was clearly evident now Matt had interrupted a very private conversation.

Jake spoke up. "Now don't go getting alarmed, boss. Meg called us because when she came back from her run she found your office door open."

Matt locked eyes with Meg.

"I know this place gets locked up tighter than a drum when you and Sarah leave at night," Meg responded, her eyes never leaving his. "So…I thought the best thing to do was to call Jake, who brought Samantha. We were just about to text you. See if you wanted us to report this to the police."

"Have you been in the office? Does it look like anything was taken?" Matt asked.

Meg replied, "To be honest, I don't really know. Everything seems normal to me, but maybe you and Sarah should take a look. I don't know what you have in there. My gut tells me it's that door you've been telling Sarah to get fixed. It may have come ajar in the wind storm last night."

Again, a look passed among his three employees. One that made him feel as if they were not telling him the whole story.

Jake nodded at the complex. "Listen, boss, if it's okay, Sam and I will get the place swept up and be sure everything is all set for the incoming crowd. We still have some rotation planning to do. But you need to know there's a storm brewing. Suppose to come in from the north. That'll set the waves pounding for sure. We need to set up some alerts in the guardhouse regarding the riptides and undertow. Mind if we bow out? You and Meg can sort out the office."

"No. Go right ahead," Matt said. "I'll check out the office and decide what to do. Would you mind getting the coffee brewing? And, text or call Sarah. Tell her I said to get here ASAP. I need her to go through my files, make sure nothing is amiss. She always leaves with the thumb drive of the club's data at the end of the day. Go on. Get your day started."

As Jake and Samantha made their way up the staircase to the guardhouse office, Matt tried to offered Meg the tea he'd brought, but she was deep in thought, back typing on that damn computer she always seem to have with her in the mornings. This time, she seemed to be typing furiously. Whatever was so important? He held the Styrofoam cup in his hand and studied her intently. Her long, sleek hair was pulled up away from her face and tucked into her club-issued cap. She'd zoned out and was deep in concentration on whatever she was doing.

As he silently stood by, his thoughts moved away from the night's event to the knowledge that Meg having a boyfriend put a temporary damper on his summer spirits. Talk about being blindsided. But when had he ever let a boyfriend stand in his way? Maybe the size of the guy had briefly intimidated him, but he was only down for the count... temporarily. Matthew Hallock had *never* been knocked out of the ring before.

Taking a sip of his coffee, he once again eyed Meg pensively. Maybe he should rethink her having a key. Sarah was the one who suggested the idea since Meg had been showing up at sunrise for her morning runs and exercise. Matt had done so grudgingly worried since he'd had another go round with Jeff Draper, unbeknownst to Sarah, over deposits for the club's cash flow. But Sarah berated him about trusting his employees. If Sarah was so confident that Meg should access, so be it.

Matt witnessed her workouts on several occasions. He was in awe of the discipline, dedication and types of drills she put herself through in those early morning hours when she thought no one was watching.

However, after this morning, he was skeptical that the door had been "just ajar" as Jake had stated or was there really something else in play. Every time he'd talked to Jeff lately, there was always another excuse. He and Draper went back to high school, but Matt was beginning to question where Jeff could get the amount of cash he was investing on a consistent basis. Matt's brother, Thomas, had briefly mentioned Jeff in a conversation a few weeks ago when they both had to appear at a Hallock Farm board meeting. The primary topic of conversation was Jeff's family's financial downfall on Wall Street last summer. The Drapers were selling their small stake in the equine facility's rehab clinic which Matt's sister, Kate, had started when she'd graduated from college ten years ago. Life had been good in the Hamptons back then. People had ready cash to burn and invest and the society events were a dime a dozen. Not so now with the market chaos and the collapse on Wall Street. Even though Matt's father considered him the black sheep, Thomas had taken it upon himself to help Matt invest the salary he'd drawn from the board and his winnings on the surfing circuit. Without his eldest brother's guidance, there probably would be no Sunfish Beach Club today.

Shaking off his rambling thoughts and needing to get to work, Matt readied himself to make another go at offering Meg her morning cup of tea.

"So, what do you think? Another good day for my coffers?"

His voice must have taken her by surprise. Meg jumped, papers and clipboard flying everywhere. She clutched her computer tightly to her chest to keep it from dropping and slamming onto the boardwalk.

After gathering her papers and stacking everything on the bench beside her, Meg accepted the Styrofoam cup, took off the lid, and sipped the liquid. "Sorry about that. I guess I was too deep in thought about everything going on."

You're keeping something from me, Matt thought. *And I don't like it one bit.* "You seemed to be in another world. I know you have everything well in hand, Meg. Just keep an extra keen eye on the crews today with the weather report. When the winds turn from the north after lunch, all this," he gestured out to the ocean," will be churning up faster than ever. Last year one of the crews took their eyes off the surf for one minute and someone's raft crashed into the jetty rock."

Matt moved closer to point out to Meg where the jetty jutted out from the sandy beach. "See how close the rocks are to the flag?"

Meg's eyes followed. Getting up for a better look, she inadvertently backed into him. Funny, she didn't pull away as she always did.

Softening his voice, Matt said, "Pretty great down here in the morning, don't you think?" Matt didn't move afraid he would frighten her away.

"Especially when the sun peaks over the horizon," Meg whispered. "The sunrises are…well, there's just no words to describe how beautiful the beach can be."

And you're equally as beautiful. "Rumor has it you've been running every morning."

Suddenly Meg broke their closeness. She took a step away, her gaze directed at the ocean. At least she hadn't put a big space between them.

"I love to exercise on the sand. It's better than the gym. Good for the gluts. Running on the beach is about the hardest workout you can get." Meg patted her butt and winked. Matt didn't know how to respond as he was caught off guard by her hint of flirtation. What changed? Normally, he'd be the recipient of a lecture on professionalism in the workplace.

Take it slow, good buddy. You don't want her to know you've seen her in action. "Good thing I gave you your own key, huh? Sarah told me you keep to a pretty strict routine. If the beach does it for you, I'm only too happy to oblige."

"Thanks. The early workout gives me some peace and quiet to get the day planned out. Once the crowds hit, everyone's coming at me from all directions. I don't need to tell you what a balancing act it is."

Placing his deck shoe upon the bench, he studied Meg. He spent most of his waking hours thinking about her. Doing so was totally out of character and he was having trouble questioning the reasons behind why this woman in particular filled his thoughts constantly. Lying awake in the early morning hours, Matt thought of little else but how to get closer to his chief guard. Ethan and Thomas had commented on the change in him at lunch after the Hallock Farm board meeting last week. Ethan was subtle, pointing out Matt was missed by many at the country club bar on Saturday night. Thomas, his older brother and not a frequenter of the Hampton social scene, informed him Sarah had mentioned Matt wasn't making the rounds at the Marakesh, a club in the village where the singles crowd gravitated.

Oh, hell, go for it. You know you want to know. Ask.

"So where's the boyfriend?"

The smile on Meg's face abruptly disappeared. Her piercing glare told him he'd treaded into unwanted territory. "Back at work…where he belongs."

Matt chuckled lightly. "Well they say absence makes the heart grow fonder. What's the man do for a living?"

A quizzical look passed across Meg's face. "Derek's in investment banking. Works in New York City. What's it to you?" Now the old Meg had surfaced front and center, defensive, putting him in his place.

Matt raised his hands above his head in a gesture of surrender. "I don't mean to pry into your personal life. Just wondered how a teacher from Syracuse hooked up with a banker from the big city. Must make it hard for a long distance…"

By the look on her face, he'd crossed over the line… again. There was not going to be any talk about her personal life. *Back track. Think. Get yourself out of the hole you've dug.* "Well…I noticed the duty roster." He paused and chose his next words carefully. He didn't want to blow it. "I see you have a day off next week. Thought you might like a Hamptons' tour. Interested?" He put both hands out in front him to ward off her reaction. "Unless you have plans with Derek."

Matt heard the hesitation in her voice. "No, as a matter of fact. I don't have plans. He's got a…a… family commitment. Quite honestly, I was planning on taking a map and go touring the North Fork. People say the old potato fields have been turned into vineyards. And supposedly 25A is dotted with antique shops. I'm curious. I've seen your family's home. I want to explore some more. People say it's a bit different away from the beach." Meg bent to gather up her computer and papers.

"You'll never get to see what you want by doing it that way," Matt countered.

"What do you mean?"

"The best way to tour is by water. My family has a boat over on the north shore at the Bay View Yacht Club. Well, it's really Thomas's boat. But he's so busy running Hallock Farm he barely has the time to use it. So it sits with its crew waiting for an outing. I bet he'd be happy if we took it out for the day."

Meg eyed him skeptically. "But the boss doesn't get a day off during the summer."

"Who told you that?"

"Sarah."

Matt smiled. "That's the luxury of being the boss. I can take a day or two from time to time." Matt looked down into a tanned, freckled face warring with conflicting emotions. He was certain he had piqued her interest. There was no doubt Meg wanted to say yes and accompany him. "We can spend the afternoon visiting the vineyards along the Peconic or just cruise and enjoy the scenery. There's some great places to stop and dock the boat. One place in particular has a spectacular restaurant where we can grab a casual dinner. Then, if you're up for it, I'll take you out for some good old fashioned crabbing under Jessup's Bridge. Nothing like netting a bucket of crabs and having a few beers at midnight. Mother and Father would be thrilled. We used to do a lot of that when we were kids."

Meg's eyebrow arched. "You drank beer when you were a kid?"

Matt laughed at shocked expression on Meg's face. "No! Hannah made sure we always had a frothy root beer waiting in a chilled beer mug. Made us feel like grownups...So? What do you say?"

Meg's answer threw him for a loop. Matt thought he had the cat in the bag. "Thanks, but I'll just fend for myself."

Matt wasn't one to give up easily. He was used to getting his way with the women who crossed his path. But for Meg, H=he'd grovel and play the card he had in his pocket if it came down to it. "Come on, Meg. I promise to be a good host. Your boyfriend can trust me. Let me show you around. Mother would expect it of me. She'd hate for you to be out and about when one of the family could take you on your tour."

There. He had played the "Mother" trump card. That particular trick didn't normally work with any of the society girls he dated, but Meg was different, and she seemed to have developed a unique friendship with his mother since her arrival at the estate. From the little he'd been able to glean from Hannah, the admiration was mutual.

Meg eyed him cautiously then warily replied, "Well...If your mother thinks it would be okay, I'll take you up on your offer."

If Sarah Adams had been standing next him, Matt would have hugged her. Matt had taken those baby steps to start building a trusting relationship just as Sarah suggested. And it had worked! He had his first date with Megan Spears. Sarah warned him to be wary of the boyfriend, but Meg had his head spinning like no other woman. He would follow Sarah's matchmaking advice for now. Slow and steady.

Matt was startled by the sound of Meg's cup dropping on the wooden deck of the boardwalk. One minute she was standing beside him, the next she was off running, making a beeline for the ocean. Making sure her computer and papers were secure, he threw off his boat shoes and followed. Where the hell was she going? Alarmed, he set out to find out.

* * *

Meg had too much on her mind, especially after the surprise arrival on the scene of the agent from Homeland Security and another, who, though identified by Interpol, had been deemed classified, much to the dismay of those working at Fox Hollow. The Director promised answers soon, especially for Jake, who had offered to dig into investigation of the Fox Hollow's "guests" while Meg was occupied elsewhere. In addition, he confirmed her suspicion of Derek. How and what Meg's partner had been charged to do was in question, according to Jake's contact deep within the Agency back in DC. That piece of information hadn't set well with Meg and the rest of the core of her team.

Last night had been intense and coupled within the last several days, between her duties at the beach club and her briefings at the inn, Meg slept very little. She'd catnapped, trying to make the best out of every waking moment.

From the boardwalk, Meg heard a voice yell for help just as Matt suggested his mother would approve Meg going out and about to the North Fork. Turning to face the water, she caught the bobbing head of what looked to be a small child just past the barrier reef. Although the water was calm, the child was struggling to make it to back shore. Whoever it was hadn't anticipated the drop off of the ocean floor.

Meg's feet pounded the sand as fast as her legs could carry her, knowing Matt was trailing after her. But how far behind was questionable. Trained, her eyes never left the bobbing head. Ripping off her windbreaker, she made her way to the nearest lifeguard tower. Timing it just right, Meg snatched the orange rescue tube from its hook on the tower's leg and sprinted into the surf, diving into the water.

The calm water made it easy to spot her target when she surfaced. With the tube slung over her left shoulder, she swam using broad, swift strokes, reaching the little boy in minutes. He lunged for her neck, but she managed to position him in a carry which would bring them safely to the water's edge.

"Easy now, buddy." Meg spoke soothingly to him as she carried him on her back, swimming through the small waves to shore. "We're almost there. Hang on. You're doing fine." Meg felt his body shiver, his hold weakening, the sign that shock was about to set in. Meg gripped his arms more firmly.

Matt met her at the water's edge, first aid kit in tow.

"Is he okay?" Matt asked worried.

Meg nodded, "Yeah. Help me."

It had been an easy rescue to in part to the tranquil sea, but Meg needed Matt's help in carrying the boy out of the water and onto the beach. As Meg took a minute to catch her breath and unwrap the recue tube from her body, Matt toweled the boy dry, wrapping him in a red fleece blanket taken from one of the lifeguard stands.

As she reached for the radio to call for the paramedics, the little boy's arm shot out to stop her.

"No! Por favor! I'm fine. Really." The boy's teeth chattered. His deep chocolate brown eyes sent a pleading look her way. "Mi madre…my mom. She will be mad if she finds out I went swimming."

"What's your name?' Matt asked, squatting down eye level with the young boy.

"Jose."

"Where do you live?""

Jose pointed to the large, modern home adjacent to the club. "I don't really live there. My mom works for the Tabers. She's their housekeeper and nanny for the summer. Por favor, senor…." Josh begged. "She'll lose her job. The Tabers…They weren't happy that I couldn't go stay at my grandmother's for the summer. I don't want Mom to lose her job. It's all we have."

Meg's eyes softened and looked over Jose's shoulder hoping for Matt's approval. Meg had seen first hand his soft spot for kids. She had often seen him talking and playing with the kids both on the beach and in the pool, even though he had his business to run. One of the first things Matt had done, according to Sarah, was institute summer evening camps to teach water safety, first aid, and safe surfing practices. Meg was starting to realize he was a caring, compassionate individual—much more than the "one-night stand" man the "townies" called him in the village.

"Bien" Meg ruffled the boy's hair, pointing to the house. "Head on home."

As Jose turned to go, Matt laid a hand on his shoulder to stop him. "Tell you what, Jose. You bring a friend to my classes tonight…*after* you tell your mom what you did here this morning. I'll give you and your friend passes to swim for the summer." The boy's eyes widened at Matt's generous offer.

"Wow! Could I even take those surfing lessons?" Jose stopped. "I mean if I'm invited."

"Yes, you can. And I'll introduce you to Tyler." Matt sat in the sand and smiled at Meg. She reciprocated. How could you not be drawn to man who liked kids? With the adrenaline no longer rushing through her body, Meg shivered, realizing she was chilled.

"Can I go now?" Jose looked over his shoulder at the house beyond the dunes.

Meg spoke up. "One more thing. You do know the most important rule about swimming, don't you?"

Jose stared blankly at her. "I guess I don't."

Meg stood up and tipped his chin up so that he would gaze into her eyes. "Never, ever, swim alone. No matter where. Here at the ocean or over at the bay. Swim with a friend. The buddy system. Got it?"

"Got it." Jose dropped the blanket to the ground and scampered off. He waved at both Meg and Matt as he climbed the staircase to the home where he lived, disappearing behind the tall beach grass.

Meg shivered as another chill overtook her.

"Come here." Matt said. He shook out the blanket which had engulfed Jose moments earlier and wrapped it around her. "I'll warm you up."

For the first time, Meg didn't question the man's motives. She allowed Matt to lay the blanket over her shoulders and rub his hands up and down her arms. That simple gesture warmed her in seconds. She didn't complain when he tucked her under his arm to absorb his body heat as they walked back up the beach.

Meg halted, digging her feet in the sand. "I've got to get the med kit and lifeline back in place."

"No." Matt said, his hand on her lower back pushing her towards the stairs. "You're going to up to the clubhouse, change out of that suit, and take a hot shower. I'll tend to things. I can manage something as simple as making sure the stations are equipped. You go get warm, and, if you don't mind, Sarah's late. Could you check the message tape?"

"Sure, no problem."

"And Meg?" Meg gripped the blanket more tightly around her since he'd let her go. "I brought some Earl Grey tea from home. Hannah bought some at the store yesterday. I thought you might like to have some here…you know, for when you have a break."

Great. Just when I want to dislike the guy, he goes and does something nice.

"Thanks, boss."

"Oh, so we're back to that now? Well, next Friday we'll be back on a first name basis."

What was the man talking about? Meg temporarily forgot but suddenly remembered their conversation before she'd run off to rescue Jose—Matt's proposed trip to the North Fork. Well, she'd plenty of equipment she could carry along that would allow her to record anything unusual without making Matt suspicious. She definitely could outfit herself into looking like a tourist.

But somehow Meg still needed to find a discreet way to broach the subject of what she'd found when she'd arrived at the club that morning. There wasn't any doubt someone wanted Sarah's thumb drive. What information did it contain? Would the contents verify that the Director was correct in her assumption the DC money trail had indeed led to the Sunfish Beach Club?

The bigger question was how her team was going to move forward. Meg couldn't just walk up to Matt and say, "Mind if I take a look at your recent cash deposits and club's private spreadsheets? I've got a thing for serial numbers on one hundred dollar bills in circulation."

After Meg radioed Jake and Samantha that morning, she made her way carefully back down and around the footsteps left behind, taking pictures with her IPhone, emailing them to a source at Langley. When Jake and Samantha arrived, the trio decided to take a different approach with the knowledge of the break-in and what they would relay to Reggie, Victoria, and the Director. After the scene in the inn the other evening, Meg trusted no one to give her accurate intel except for Jake and Samantha.

Having received a follow-up text from her contact, Meg was now positive the footprints were from Coast Guard-issued terrain shoes. The boots were of a make and model used for rock climbing rescue, waterproof and the soles were designed specifically for dealing with slippery surfaces.

Glancing at the clock, Meg saw she had a little less than thirty minutes to get showered and changed. She needed time to finish and relay her report. Disrupted by Matt's peace offering of tea and saving Jose, she needed to finish vetting the people at the Hallock function. The people Jake pointed out by the dance floor weren't employees of the club. And Meg had found through her research the two individuals had no affiliation to anyone remotely associated with the workings of the club or the farm. Her laptop pinged when the Agency's facial recognition database identified one man with ties to the Russian mob, and the other a Saudi Arabian businessman named Al-Dossari.

The time had come for answers from the Eagle and the Black Swan. Meg's gut told her the two knew more than what was being laid on the table for her team to use as intelligence. Elizabeth had sent her on a job with an agenda to be accomplished. There was no way to do the job without everyone knowing all the cards on the table, to paraphrase Sam Tanner. And Meg wanted to know what exactly what hand she'd been dealt *now*!

CHAPTER NINE

Peconic Bay

Meg couldn't remember the last time she felt so free. She hadn't had a day off in over a year due to her assignment in Paris. And she could truly say she never experienced being pampered to the extent she and Matt had been by the crew of the ship once they boarded the *Golden Rod*.

Spending the morning cruising the southern coast of the North Fork and skirting Shelter Island, the boat finally headed out into the open waters off Orient Point. The captain's planned route fit perfectly into Meg where wanted to go without asking. Clicking away with her high power camera, Meg took as many shots of the surrounding scenery as possible. Standing on the bow, she released her grip on the camera, leaving the strap to dangle around her neck. Closing her eyes, she opened her arms wide, and breathed in the fresh, salty sea air. As an agent, she was always pretending to be somebody she wasn't. But in that moment, with her hair flying behind her, the wind in her face, Meg felt like Kate Winslet in the movie *Titanic*. That is until she heard a husky, deep chuckle coming behind her. How foolish she must seem to Matt and the crew manning the boat.

"Please don't think this ship is going to sink, fair maiden. Trust me. With a twin keel, there's no way we're going to flip over. And certainly not with Captain Chuck at the wheel."

Meg swung around from the bow. Matt sat on a red plaid blanket that lay on top of the cabin, a Sam Adams in one hand. As he saluted her with his beer, his eyes roamed the length of her body. Even on that hot summer day, Meg felt the heat of a blush under her suntan.

Trying to get Matt to focus his attention elsewhere, she gestured back to the sea. "Don't you think the view is captivating? I've never seen anything like it."

"Neither have I," Matt replied, wiggling his eyebrows playfully, his eyes never leaving hers.

"Matt…" Meg didn't want to spoil what had been a delightful morning, but the sensual tone in his voice made her stomach do summersaults. "Don't. You'll ruin a perfectly good time. We made a deal if you remember."

Matt's wide smile disappeared. Good. She didn't need to be distracted by his obvious interest. She really should have thought more carefully about what she'd wear. But the temperature was predicted to surpass the ninety-degree mark and, even with the sea breeze, she wanted to be cool. Meg had donned the only other bathing suit she'd brought with her—a hot pink strapless one-piece bathing suit with a matching flowered sarong that tied around her waist. She'd brought a change of clothes for the lunch at the club, but everything was neatly packed away in her bag in the cabin below deck, including a beach coverall which would serve a useful purpose from keeping her body exposed to Matt's roving eye.

"God, Meg, you really have a knack for taking the fun out of things. I finally get you all to myself…no wait." Meg took a step in Matt's direction and he reacted by holding up his hand to ward her off. "I promised Mother I'd be the perfect host…and gentleman." Matt drank his beer and choked on the liquid as it went down the wrong way. "Give a guy a break. I'm simply giving you a compliment. Nothing more."

Cautious, Meg responded. "Apology accepted." Suddenly, Meg's balance shifted, forcing her to grab for the railing. The boat was turning, away from where she thought they were headed, away from Plum Island. "What's going on? I wanted to head over there." Meg pointed to the rocky island that rose like a mountain from the sea.

Matt looked at his watch. "We need to head back in order to make our reservation. Besides, how many pictures do you need to take? You must have well over three hundred by my count. That's one pretty sophisticated piece of equipment you have around your neck. Most average people carry a digital one, maybe orr they take the photos with their phones. I know you have one. No offense, but that thing looks like it could see right through whatever you're taking a picture of…" Matt's voice trailed off. "How about I grab a few pictures of you in that hot pink bathing suit?"

Meg's patience about her outfit or lack thereof came to an end. She cut to the chase. "Can't you ask Chuck to make one pass by? *Please*? Taking photographs is kind of a hobby of mine. I could get some great wildlife shots. The island can't be that far away that we couldn't get back to the club for lunch."

Matt reached into the cooler by his side and popped the tops off of two beers, motioning for Meg to come and sit beside him.

"No can do," Matt stated.

Resigned to her fate, she walked over and sat, taking the cold bottle from his outstretched hand.

"Why not?" Meg was determined to change his mind, knowing there was a good chance she'd be shot down, knowing the rules of water around the facility. But she really needed a few close up shots of the west side.

"That's Plum Island."

Playing dumb, Meg asked, "And we can't go because…?"

"I don't want to have to call my brother and ask to be bailed out of jail because I was boating in a restricted area."

"Restricted? Why ever would it be restricted?" Meg probed for what he knew of the facility nestled high up on the top of the rocks. If Matt had sufficient knowledge of the lab, Meg would have to report that back to headquarters and the team. And the Director…Meg couldn't even begin to imagine what Elizabeth Hallock would want to do if Matt knew the inner workings of the research facility. From what she'd gleaned so far, she doubted he did.

"Hell, if I know. I have several friends who do a great deal of fishing and trapping of lobsters. They've been warned a time or two by the Coast Guard not to get any closer to the shoreline. Something is over there. There seems to be an imaginary line no one can cross. I just don't know what…" Matt's voice trailed off and he shot her a questioning look. "Why are *you* so curious?"

Trying to avoid Matt's scrutiny, Meg took a long swallow of the ice-cold brew. As the liquid slid down her throat she warned herself to tread cautiously. "Just idle curiosity. From that map you showed me, there seems to be a wealth of great places to explore around here via the waterways. Block Island, Shelter Island. I'd love to see them! I may never get a chance to come back. You know I head back north come Labor Day weekend."

Shifting her gaze away from Matt, Meg sipped the remnants of her beverage and placed the empty bottle back in the cooler. She lay on the blanket to soak up the warmth of the sun which beat down on the white deck. She closed her eyes in an attempt to temper the whirling thoughts traversing her brain. As the boat cruised through the bay, the sea breeze wafted over her, cooling her hot skin.

A warm stroke lightly skimmed down her arm, surprising her. She couldn't help but shiver at his touch. Even with her eyes closed, she was aware of a shadow blocking the direct heat of the sun she'd been relishing only moments earlier. Meg opened her eyes to find Matt intently staring down at her. She sucked in a deep breath as he raised his sunglasses. She hoped he couldn't see how his nearness affected her. Her heart started to raced and increased to the point where she thought Matt might be able to hear it. No matter how hard she tried to keep her distance, Meg was drawn to this man no matter how hard she tried to stop the errant thoughts she had of him, especially at night. How could this be possible? He was her polar opposite. And in her playbook opposites didn't attract.

"Matt…"

"Shhh…" Matt lightly glided his fingertips over her lips. "I just want one kiss."

Meg knew very well that with Matt there was going to be no such thing as "just one kiss." Her body betrayed her. He'd become a magnet, drawing him to her whenever he was close by. As his lips descended on hers, Meg attempted to tilt her head away, but he captured his prize before she could completely turn her face away. The briefest touch of his lips sent a bolt of heat coursing through her. Meg had never felt such a burning desire as deep as this for anyone. The kiss, which started off sweet and delicious, grew deeper. And, heaven help her, Meg wanted more. More than the kiss. More of the man. Her hands touched his glistening chest, rising up to loop around his neck. After running through her hands through his sun-bleached hair, she intertwined her fingers and pulled him to her. She ran her tough over her lips and smiled at him, opening her mouth just slightly. It was her invitation for him to deepen what they started. Matt had no problem obliging her request. Their tongues locked together, the taste of the richness of the ale they drank moments earlier still present. Matt's caressing hand slid down her neck and came to rest on her breast. The minute his finger swirled around her nipple, Meg bolted into an upright position, practically smacking Matt's head with her own.

"No!" Meg tried to put distance between them She gulped in deep breaths of air trying to shake the lustful feelings that had overtaken her. "You promised. You…you told me…"

A small grin formed at the corners of Matt's mouth. "Whoa. Slow down. It was only a kiss, Meg. And a rather nice one, I might add. *You*, my dear lady, took it further than a mere kiss." He again reached for her, but she batted his hand away.

Think fast. "My God, what am I going to tell Derek?"

"You're thinking about Derek, *now*? After you gave me a kiss like that?" Matt leaned back on his arms, placed his sunglasses back on. How she wished she could read his mind. What was he was thinking? Shaken by her loss of control, Meg's only recourse was to take a defensive posture and glare at him. Matt Hallock was turning her orderly world upside down. Not to mention her mission.

"I shouldn't be thinking about…my boyfriend?" Meg spat out the last word as if it left a bad taste in her mouth. "You must think very little of me…and my character, if I didn't."

Matt grunted. "As a matter of fact, dear lady, I spend way *too* much of my time thinking about *you*, if you want the damn truth. But I made a promise. And I'll keep it…grudgingly. But I'm not sorry I kissed you."

"Don't do it again." Meg's mind blurred. She couldn't think straight. "Maybe it would be better if we passed on lunch and going crabbing tonight. Better we just call it a day."

As Meg rose wanting to get as far away from Matt as possible on deck, he wrapped his hand around her wrist and tugged her back onto the blanket. "No. We'll share the blame. I can honor my promise if you can."

The man was daring her. And Meg had never been one to back away from one in her entire life.

"I didn't make any…" She saw merriment coupled with yearning in Matt's eyes. It was taking a great deal of self-control on his part to make things right. And Meg really needed to see the activities around by the beach club by night. "Okay. I'll go below and change." Taking her eyes off Matt, she saw the captain signaling to them. "Uh, Matt. Captain Chuck looks like he wants to talk to you."

As Meg picked up her belongings to head below to change she saw the ship's crew scurrying about readying the ship to dock. Meg blushed realizing she'd been totally oblivious to the others on board when Matt made his play for her. Captain Chuck had had a bird's eye view. And she could have sworn he was winking at her right then. As Matt rose and grasped the handle of the cooler, Meg couldn't reach for the blanket fast enough, wrapping it around her shoulders to cover her body from everyone on board, especially the man at her side.

Meg made a beeline for the stairs that led to the cabin below. She kicked herself. Meg violated every rule she'd set for herself in regards to relationships and life. Number one—there would be no time for men. Number two—her career would always come first. But she hadn't planned on Tropical Storm Matthew brewing above board.

* * *

Jessup's Bridge
Midnight

"That a girl! Easy. Don't bend over too far. Let the crab come to the light." Meg braced herself, feet apart, on the bow of the Boston Whaler anchored under the bridge. As directed, she followed the beam of light on the water off the bow of the boat. The crabbing net's pole was large and cumbersome but she had managed to scoop twelve crabs into the bushel basket which sat on the floor behind her.

Looking over her shoulder, with the moonlight lighting up the darkness on a perfectly cloudless night, she could make out the gleeful look in her teacher's eyes. After their tender moment on the deck of the *Golden Rod*, Meg was glad she hadn't bailed from the afternoon's lunch and evening's activities.

"I'm the one having all the fun here. Don't you want to change places?" Meg called to Matt as he directed the spotlight to a different side of the bow.

"No. I caught five showing you the ropes. You're doing just fine. You're a natural. Quite frankly, I'm just enjoying what's left of my day off. I know we got off to a rocky start today, Meg. But I'm glad you didn't jump ship on me. No pun intended." Matt and Meg both laughed. "It's been pure heaven for me to have a day like this. I can't remember the last time I've felt this relaxed. I haven't given the club one thought all day long."

Meg knew he was telling the truth by the peacefulness that was mirrored in his eyes for most of the day. Even though his blue eyes followed her every move, he surprisingly had kept his promise since they left the boat to lunch at the Bay View Yacht Club's restaurant. No more innuendos, strictly two friends enjoying a pleasant outing.

"I don't see any more crabs, boss. I think you scared them away with all your chatter." Watching Matt lean back against the windshield of the boat, Meg saw the corners of his mouth turn into a smile. It warmed her insides to see him like this.

"Turn around." Matt motioned for her to get back to crabbing. "Lean over the rail." Meg did as instructed as Matt adjusted the light once more. "Yup. Bend over a bit more. That's it. The net's perfectly placed in the water. Those crabs will take the bait for sure now." Only then did it dawn on Meg that Matt had a bird's eye view of her long legs and her backside.

"Matt…" Meg warned. The man made it impossible to concentrate. His deep chuckle resonated through the night air. Once again his contagious laugh turned her insides warm. He was getting to her.

"Now *you're* taking what I said completely out of context, Megan Spears. I was simply telling you what to do." She didn't need to look back to know Matt had a shit-eating grin plastered on his face. "Get your mind out of the gutter, woman."

Ready to respond with a smart retort, she spied two crabs popping to the surface. Leaning over with the net in hand, she swooped in to nab them. Turning her back to the bow, she shook out the net, the crabs dropping into the basket with the others. What she would give to have one crab miss its intended target and land on the man's foot. Serve him right for baiting her.

She admonished herself. *Girl, stay focused.* Thinking back on the day's events, Meg was more than pleased with the progress she made in subtly asking Matt questions regarding his friends and the club. The better part of lunch was spent probing how Matt had met his investors and what he knew about their respective backgrounds. Some details she'd already known from the Director's briefing, but hearing how Matt had hooked up with his old friends gave her a fresh take on each candidate on her list. Several needed vetting a second time around. And she'd gleaned some valuable information for Jake and Samantha to use in the process. Meg hoped she didn't sound overly interested or too eager for information.

Matt had answered all of her questions truthfully, she believed. He hadn't seemed bothered by the topic of conversation. He seemed happy to talk about the Sunfish and his voice rang with pride when talking about his accomplishments. There was no doubt Matt had everything riding on the success of the beach club. Meg would give anything to be able to tell him that one, or possibly more, of his investors had designed a well planned out scheme to topple his world. And Draper was definitely one of the men whom the team had their eyes on.

From Meg's observations, Matt and Sarah Adams had a strong handle on everything going on at the surface level in the operation of the club's daily activities. Jake, Samantha, and Meg believed he and Sarah knew nothing about the money being filtered through the deposits.

Jake had heard from his sources that the last twenty-thousand-dollar deposit had indeed had serial numbers from the money in the DC drop, but, this time, not in any kind of numerical order. The Director would be pleased to read that in the next morning's report. Matt would be devastated, when the time came, to know he had been deceived by a man he trusted. However there was one problem. Although Jake had found some of the missing bills, the forensic lab had informed him they were unable to lift any fingerprints other than those of the employees at the village bank.

Matt's voice broke through her thoughts. "I think we've got enough crabs, Meg. Time to head back, get these babies boiled up and have a beer. Morning's going to come soon enough."

Meg yawned, shaking her head in agreement. "Sounds good. It's been a great day, boss. You were right about seeing the sights by boat. I can't thank you enough."

"Here. Give me that pole." Meg handed over the long rod. He grabbed the pole and secured it in place on the side of the boat. "Time to haul anchor."

Matt pressed a button and, within minutes, Meg heard the sound of the anchor locking in place. Out of the blue, a boat's engine roared to life from the marina of the hotel located next to Jessup's Bridge. A large quantity of boats had passed by on that beautiful summer evening, but all had slowed to the five mile per hour speed limit when passing through the channel. From the gunning of the motor, Meg senses were on red alert that this particular boat had no intention of paying attention to rules and regulations. Within seconds, it darted out from a slip located directly across from the Sunfish!

"What the hell?" Matt reached for her, but missed, as the boat sped past them. "Meg!" Matt shouted, "Grab something! The wake could swamp us!" Just as Meg reached for the handle by the passenger's seat, Matt fired up the engines, put the Whaler into gear and took off. Thrown off balance, Meg's elbow banged the windshield and she landed with a thud onto the leather passenger seat. It was obvious Matt intended to try to trail after the speeding boat and try to out run it.

"Matt! What the hell do you think you are doing?" Meg cried out over the roar of the boat's engine. She couldn't believe he was crazy enough to outrun the cruiser.

"We're going to find out who the hell that is and report him to the harbor master."

"Are you nuts?" Meg screamed back in disbelief. "You think you can outrun *that* boat and get its number *in-the-dark*?"

Regaining her equilibrium, Meg made her way to stand at Matt's side. She spread her feet for balance as she grabbed hold of the windshield. The Whaler bounced and rocked in the wake of the boat ahead of them. But the driver was obviously used to dealing with high speeds and picked up the pace. Consequently, its running lights dimmed as the distance widened between the two boats. If Matt wanted to catch whoever was on that cruiser, Meg knew she had to take control. Her past experience in dealing in with a water chase would have them close to the cruiser in no time. Meg was equally determined to find out who the driver of the boat was that had shot out of the slot near the Sunfish. It could be the break she and her team needed.

Meg yanked the steering wheel Matt's hands. Her first attempt to do so was unsuccessful.

"What the hell?" Matt wrestled the steering wheel away from her. "You don't know how to drive a boat!"

"Believe it or not, I'm quite good at it. " Meg pointed ahead, her ponytail flying in the air from the wind whipping in her face. "Do you want to catch that fool or let him get away?" Matt stared down at her, shocked at her temerity. Meg could see he struggled with his need to be in control. He looked out over the water, squinting to see the fading running lights. Meg had only seconds to convince him she was right. "Whoever shot out of the slip came from over by the Sunfish!" Matt's head whipped around and his eyes locked on hers. *Now* Meg had his attention. Matt relinquished his grip on the wheel, no questions asked. "Sit down!" Matt did as she instructed. "And for God's sake, hang on!"

Her hand reached for the throttle and shifted into high gear. Meg placed her hands at ten and two o'clock on the wheel, readying herself for the action she was about to take. Matt wasn't going to know what hit him.

She flipped on the spotlight in order to illuminate the wake ahead and utilize brighter lights for a view of the water in the dark. Aware that if their boat got caught up fighting the cross-wake of the cruiser their progress would be impeded, Meg steered for the flat open water where the waves already had dispersed. She desperately needed to pick up speed. Speed equated to time. Timing was critical to whomever at been at the Sunfish. She'd bet her paycheck on that assumption.

"Where the hell are we?" Meg shouted. "Give me some landmarks, Matt! " Meg was frustrated for not having familiarized herself with the body of water she was trying to navigate. She'd half listened in on Reggie's briefing, caught up in the issues of the other day.

"We're coming to the entrance of the Hampton Beach Marina." Matt shouted over the roar of the engine. "Meg, be very careful. Don't drive out of the channel!"

"Why?"

"We'll run aground."

"Is this where we came out tonight?"

The boat rocked dangerously to its right. "Yes! Damn it!" Out of the corner of her eye she could she see the ashen look on Matt's face as he hung onto the edge of the passenger seat for dear life. "Are you trying to kill us? Where the hell did you learn to drive like this?"

Had he been with her in Venice six months ago, Matt would know she could handle the Whaler perfectly, but he'd be puking over the side from the way she'd navigated the canals.

"I'm turning in, Matt. Where's the boat launch? Right side? Left side?"

Meg peered ahead, her mind anticipating her next move. From the speed of the boat ahead, the only plan that made sense was to run the dock and make for land. She had no idea how many people were onboard. Were there accomplices waiting onshore? She instinctively placed her hand inside her jacket to draw her weapon only to remember she was unarmed. The new Glock, she recently acquired from Reggie, was locked away in her room at the estate. Stupid. From now on, she wouldn't "play it safe" around anyone, including Matt and Sarah. She had been caught off guard twice. In the Director's book three strikes had an agent working a desk job… forever.

"Meg…" Matt's voice was tinged with warning and worry. "The marina entrance is tricky. "We've got a problem."

"What's that?" Meg's peered into the darkness in front of them.

"Low tide." Matt made a move to stand up. "Let me steer us in."

"No." Meg said emphatically, taking her eyes off the water. Matt sat back down. "You'll follow my lead. Understood?"

Her use of evasive boating techniques she'd learned at the naval base last year had her gaining on the boat faster than expected. The red and green buoy lights highlighted the entrance into Moniebogue Creek. Meg turned off the boat's running lights.

"Turn those back on!" Matt yelled, but she ignored him. "It's illegal to drive without them."

"Sorry, boss. We don't have time to worry about being legal." *And the element of surprise is just what we need right now.* Even in the moonlight, Meg could read the dread on Matt's face. She also saw the uncertainty mirrored in his eyes that she could not pull this off. Meg needed him calm if she had to take evasive action. "Matt, you've got to trust me. Use the windshield to shield yourself, but you've got to be my extra pair of eyes. Keep track of anyone on that cruiser when I get close. Tell me if you recognize anyone. If you see any movement, anywhere, yell out the position. Just like on a clock, okay? Do you understand?"

Matt looked shell-shocked, but said, "I've got no choice but to trust your judgment. Take it from here."

"Listen, I'm going to have all I can do to bring this boat in without crashing." Meg and Matt swayed to the right as the Whaler bounced up in the air and landed back onto the calmer waters of the channel. "Talk me in."

The red and green lights blinking, Meg peered over the windshield, squinting to find her target in the dark. What she wouldn't give to have her night vision goggles. But even without them, she made out two men standing on the dock, dressed in black, hoods drawn up to shield their identities. Her suspicions had been right. They were there to pick up whoever was in the boat. The cruiser headed straight for the boat launch with no intention of stopping. Whoever was behind the wheel was insane!

"Matt! The boat's going straight for the launch ramp! Hold on!" Meg quickly calculated the speed of their boat and assessed how long it would take to stop and get on land.

"Watch out!" Matt cried at out the same time Meg issued her final instructions. The crunch of the mysterious boat hitting the launch had both Meg and Matt cringing as its bottom ripped apart coming in contact with the stony gravel ramp. The explosion echoed through the still of the night.

"Hold on!" Meg threw the Whaler into reverse, engines grinding, steered the boat around a sharp corner and docked. It was imperative she find out who she was dealing with.

Quickly assessing the evolving situation, she threw the throttle into neutral. With the engine still idling, Meg poked her head above the dock. The two men, who'd been waiting were in the process of helping two men from the smoking remains of the damaged boat. Feeling Matt's breath on her neck, Meg reached for and squeezed his hand. She whispered, "Do everything I say."

For once the man didn't argue. Matt placed his hand on her shoulder. "Ready on your count."

"We move on one."

Meg ticked off the count on three fingers then yanked Matt up onto the cushioned driver's seat. From there both stepped out onto the dock. Trying to make a better vantage point her number one priority, Meg didn't dare ask the logistics of the marina afraid her voice would carry. She and Matt were too close to their prey to let their whereabouts be known.

Sirens sounded in the distance. It was then the unexpected happened. The four men, one with his arm wrapped securely around a wounded boater, turned directly into Meg's line of sight. Meg had miscalculated...badly. The light pole at the corner highlighted their position.

Meg placed her hands on both sides of Matt's head forcing him to look her in the eyes. "We're going to get wet."

A dazed, questioning, bemused look passed across his face.

Meg reacted as soon as she saw the glint of the steel flash in the light.

"Jump!" Meg pushed then followed Matt into the cool water, hearing the popping sounds of the gunshots as they both hit the water. A whiz of bullets passed by her ear as they plunged into the dark canal. Coming up for air and looking about, Meg shoved Matt back below the surface once more as she listened, waiting for more rounds to come their way. But nothing happened.

"What the hell?" Matt came up beside her, choking on the water he'd ingested. The sound of police sirens drew closer.

"Stay here." Meg directed. "Keep you head down." She left Matt to swim to a ladder nearby. She didn't want to leave him floundering in the cold creek, but she had no choice. It was too dangerous to drag him with her. Climbing to the top of the dock, she peered over the ledge in time to see a black Escalade peel out from behind the harbor master's quarters. Damn! Was that the same car from the club? If so, the pieces were fitting together. She needed to get to Fox Hollow. But as she glanced down Library Avenue, she saw two police cruisers, lights on, sirens blaring, headed for the marina. Someone had called 911. Great, just freaking great. Just what she needed—a police report with the Hallock name attached to it. The Eagle would *not* be pleased.

She nearly lost her grip on the ladder as a pair of arms encircled her waist. Feeling a shivering body nestle against her own, she relaxed. Matt. With her mind thinking possible strategies to employ, she'd almost forgotten about him treading water.

"You okay?" Meg turned and reached for him. "Come on. Let me get you out of the water. We're both going to need to be seen by the medical team and talk to the police."

Meg helped Matt climb up the ladder, but when he reached the top, he collapsed, falling face first onto the grey dock. Rolling him over, Meg knelt at his side to check him over. Matt's eyes fluttered open. He was alert, but in shock. A confused look registered in his blue eyes.

Meg felt for injuries. No broken bones. Running her hand through his hair, she checked for the possibility that a bullet might have grazed him as they hit the water. Nothing. No blood. No bumps.

Matt grasped her wrist with his hand. "Who… are… you?" he stammered, teeth chattering.

"I beg your pardon?" If Matt was implying what she thought he was, Meg wasn't ready to answer him. She needed to maintain her cover at all cost. "What do you mean, who am I? I'm your chief lifeguard. I didn't think you hit your head. How many fingers am I holding up?" She held up three fingers and wiggled the middle one.

Matt swatted her hand away and sat up slowly. His eyes pierced hers. "No… You're not."

"I'm not what?"

Holding his hand to head, Matt seemed to be trying to shake off the fog of shock. "You're my lifeguard, but you're like…like some kind of superwoman. Only in real life, not like in the movies."

Meg had to look away, play her role. She was sure he'd read something in her eyes. She spotted two police cars pulling into the parking lot, followed by an ambulance and fire truck. Good. Maybe she'd be able to make a quick statement and get out of there. It was imperative she get to Jake and Samantha. "Matt, let's get checked out and get you back to the estate."

This time it was Matt who grabbed Meg's chin, forcing her to look at him. "Stop with the commands for one minute, will you? Someone shot at us. And *you*, Megan Spears…*you* didn't even flinch. I watched you move as if you'd been trained to do so. Who the hell are you?"

Meg didn't know what to say. But the one thing she did know was that Matt deserved the truth. The Eagle had to tell her nephew what was going down at the Sunfish Beach Club. And on Meg's watch that would happen tonight.

CHAPTER TEN

Fox Hollow Inn

"Tell me you have a lead, *anything* for us to run with," Meg eyed Jake over the rim of her coffee mug. She grimaced as the vile taste of the beverage met her lips and slid down her throat. The caffeine in the rock gut liquid was the only thing that was going to keep her awake until she and her team finished talking to the Director. After filing a police report at the marina, Meg ducked out on Matt, taking advantage of the appearance of his two brothers, Thomas and Ethan, who showed up unexpectedly.

"I wish I had better news." Jake stood next to her as she leaned against the wall. "Sammy and I have been over those marina tapes three times. Those guys were good. Pros. For a small town dock, there's a hell of a lot more cameras than I would have expected for security. Probably due to the clientele the place serves. Whoever we're chasing had to know exactly which cameras to dismantle."

"Were you able to ID the license plate to that Escalade?"

"Nada, Meg." Samantha walked over from the monitor to join the duo. "Want a refill?" She pointed to the coffee cup, her eyebrows arched, knowing full well Meg despised the stuff. Tea being Meg's preferred beverage of choice.

Meg shook her head. "I don't suppose the crime scene unit got a partial print from anything?" When no response was forthcoming, she stomped the heel of her boot into the floor. "Shit!" When were they going to catch a break? It was becoming evident tonight was going to be an all-nighter.

"Meggie, girl!" Meg turned her attention to Reggie, who called to her from the conference table. "The Director's been contacted. She'll be on the speaker in five minutes. Come." He waved Meg over to the table. "Go over this map one more time and outline the chain of events."

Meg did as she was asked with Jake and Samantha following close behind. Reggie and Victoria sat at the conference table along with several other team members. Jake and Samantha took up their positions in their normal seats while Meg pulled her notes out of her backpack. Taking her place at the head of the table, for what seemed the umpteenth time, Meg reiterated had taken place.

It dawned on her someone was missing. Suddenly, Meg stopped, looking around the secure room. "Where's Derek?"

"Working on something for the Director." Reggie replied.

"What? Why wasn't I informed?" Meg shot a glare in Reggie's direction, but the man's eyes were downcast. He seemed "distracted" by a pile of papers on the table in front of him. The man knew something she didn't. She was positive of it. *Again*, her "partner" was MIA during a serious point in the investigation. What the hell was going on? "Reggie…"

"Now, Meggie. I know what you're thinking. But let's get our ducks in a row before the Eagle calls." Reggie covered her hand with his. "You couldn't have handled the situation at the marina any better. It's imperative we make Elizabeth realize Matt needs to be told what has gone down at the club in recent weeks. From the onset, she hasn't wanted him involved. I believe Matt deserves answers, especially after what you two went through tonight. You've come to know him. After the incident at the dock, he's going to want to know exactly who you are and what the hell is happening. There is no way the Eagle can keep her nephew in the dark any longer. I think it's hindering our investigation. What do you think?"

"I agree. But how do I tell him? Having Matt keep the information we share with him under raps is my biggest fear. We're used to role playing. He isn't."

The red light on the speakerphone blinked.

"Ready?" Meg looked at the faces sitting around the table. All were nodding. Ready to rock and roll. "Let's hope we can convince her." Meg pressed the red button. "Director, Agent Spears. You received our communication?"

The normally soft southern drawl was laced with sharpness. "I don't like where this is heading. Nor what ya'll are asking me to agree to. I made that very clear from the start. I don't want Matthew involved. I certainly didn't plan on the scope and scale of what has evolved. Considering the amount of time that's passed, I thought we'd know where or who the trail the DC money had led to by now, and for what reason. You should be in clean up mode by now."

"But, Madam Director…" Meg interrupted but was cut short.

"Let me finish." The Director was unusually curt. "Since this is more complicated than we imagined and some pieces have fallen into place, I'll go along with your plan, Agent Spears. But Matthew will be given intel on a need to know basis."

Meg sighed inwardly. She could see from the looks of those around her, the team was relieved as well. "Thank you for your confidence in us to get the job done. It won't take long to find and contain the men. But how should we proceed in regards to Plum Island? We've gotten nothing from Ranger."

"Sources confirmed there's been unusual activity in the area, especially with the Coast Guard vessels. I've talked to Homeland and the DOD. They're looking into tracking the training activity paperwork. If what you sent me pans out, I'll have some news for you tomorrow. Reggie?"

"Yes, luv." Meg almost burst out laughing when she saw the look on his face. She knew Reggie's position on dealing with the island and heartedly agreed.

"Make your nightly rounds as always. If there's something amiss, question whoever you need to, citizens, Coast Guard staff. If something seems strange report anything and everything to Sam Tanner. He'll let me know ASAP. Don't go storming the beaches!" There was a distinct pause. "The rest of you, stick to the assignments Agent Spears hands out. Megan, it's up to you to handle my nephew."

"Agreed, ma'am."

"Good. Now, go make your plans. It will no doubt produce the beginning to the end if we play our cards right. Eagle out."

Chatter began as soon as the red light went off. Meg pulled several slips of paper from her bag and handed a page to each team member.

"Here are your personal assignments. You will see you have been repositioned but with a definitive target to tail. Jake and Samantha. Your absences from the club will be explained to Matt as personal and nothing more that way you can focus on incoming intel and the North Fork.

"I'll deal with Matthew in the morning. By now, I think he's astute enough to know I working for some federal agency. The less he knows the safer he and his family will be. For those of you who don't know there was a similar crisis with his family two years ago. Last time, Kate, his sister, fled Hampton Beach to the Director's compound and wound up getting kidnapped in the process. This operation impacts the family in their own backyard. I want it contained. Minimal damage. Understood?"

Jake yawned, looking down at the paper he'd been handed. "I see we're changing the time to report."

Meg nodded. "Yes. Cell phones on at all times. Find one thing that seems odd, I want to know about it—someone sneezes the wrong way—shows up in what seems to be an out of the way place—I want to know ASAP. Now go. Get some sleep."

Meg glanced at her wrist; her watch read 0300. The caffeine from the coffee had kicked in. She hadn't planned on getting much sleep; there was a lot to accomplish, especially providing an explanation for Matt that contained minimal details.

Chairs scraped across the concrete floor. Her team rose and headed for the door, leaving her alone.

"Meggie!" Meg's head snapped up to see Reggie standing at the foot of the basement stairs waving for her to join the group exiting the secure room. "Come on, lass. 'Tis time for some shut-eye."

Meg waved him off. "I'll be there in a minute. Let me put my stuff back in my bag."

As Meg pushed her papers into her backpack, she noticed a pink Post-It note lodged in its inner pocket. She hadn't noticed it earlier. Pulling the thin slip out, she read the simple sentence written in black marker. Shocked, she quickly glanced up, but no one was left in the room except the two men operating the property's security monitors. Her eyes fell back on the note:

LOCKER ROOM – 0600

Meg tucked the pink note into the back pocket of her jeans and exited the room. Not even two hours left to do what needed to be done. She might as well head back to the estate and pour over her notes. Her report was due in three due hours.

* * *

Walk away from him, would she? Push him into the water while bullets flew through the air? File a police report and sneak away into the dark of night? Megan Spears had another thing coming if she thought he was going to wait until they met up again at the club for answers to the questions he'd wanted answered on the docks. Meg had evaded everyone. And, to top it off, Matt surmised he was right. Megan Spears was trained to act just like his aunt.

Where the hell had she taken herself off to? Matt came home from the marina and searched the house from top to bottom to find Meg MIA. He'd even knocked on the bedroom door adjacent to hers. When no reply came, Matt opened it to find Jake and Samantha snuggled under a mountain of covers in the chill of the air-conditioning, the soft sound of water playing from the IPod alarm clock. He backed out trying to be as quiet as possible, realizing he'd invaded their privacy. It was a known fact the two guards were in a relationship—a summer fling. Bravo for them! At least somebody was getting laid this summer. He sure wasn't.

Matt grew more uncomfortable in his present position the longer time passed. He could have taken the easy way out and simply sat in Meg's room to confront her when she finally arrived back at the estate. But he had decided not to go that route. The room was very easy to access by another means. Meg's room had been his during his younger years. Matt spent many nights climbing out of the window and onto the roof ledge. From there it was extremely easy to climb down the tree to escape. He had often done just that for a night out with his beach buddies, making sure to be back home before his parents, or Hannah, found out.

After tonight, he had no doubt Megan Spears would be making her entrance in the untraditional fashion. She wasn't about to rouse the household. Matt prayed he was right and that Meg wasn't out with that jerk of a boyfriend, Derek. Her facial expression at the dock led him to believe Meg was *not* who she portrayed herself to be, especially after the hair-raising chase of the cruiser. She had maneuvered his boat as if she was a female version of James Bond.

Hearing the crunch of tires on the drive, Matt shimmied farther up the tree. As the Beetle Bug turned the corner into the back parking lot, its driver shut off the headlights, pulling into one of only spaces left.

From his high hidden vantage point, Matt watched Meg open the car door, get out and wrestle a huge bag from the trunk of the car. The duffle bag was added to a backpack that was slung over her shoulder. He watched as she took a moment to scan the parking area by the paddocks. Seeing no one, she did exactly as he predicted. Meg made her way toward the tree where he waited. How many times had she repeatedly come and gone like this late at night since she'd arrived in Hampton Beach? And why? Matt was a betting man. He'd stake his next paycheck she had not visited Derek Taylor tonight or any other night.

Leaning his back against the main trunk of the tree and bracing his feet on the branches below him for balance, Matt ducked under a leafy bough. Meg strapped the duffle bag to her body and effortlessly started to climb up the oak tree.

As her head poked through the branch where he sat, Matt kept his voice low. "Fancy meeting you in a place like this."

He heard her swift intake of breath. Meg didn't cry out, but he could tell from her face he had caught her off guard.

In a hushed and controlled voice, Meg retorted, "What the hell are you doing here? It's 0330! The doctor told you to go home and rest." She climbed up and perched on the same thick branch he had been squatting on for the last several hours.

"I've been waiting for you...and the answers I didn't get."

"Let me get this straight. You've been sitting in a tree, outside my bedroom window when you have a perfectly good bed in that back cottage? You couldn't wait until morning?" Meg snorted, "You look like my father when I came home way past curfew. I'm a big girl, Matt. I can take care of myself."

Matt grunted, not only in response to her question but because he had slipped, causing a shift in position. A sharp branch jabbed into a certain part of his lower anatomy, which always seem to harden whenever Meg was around.

"What's wrong?" Meg asked. She eyed him quizzically. "You look...

uncomfortable." Even in the dark, he could see the twinkle in her eyes.

"Nothing." Matt bit his lower lip as the branch nudged the bulge in his pants. He was getting nowhere. He wanted Meg to tell him what had gone on… not tomorrow morning…*now*. And he wanted out of the damn tree!

"Listen." Matt pointed to the bedroom window. "I've been waiting for more than two hours. I'm tired and I'm not going anywhere until I get what I want." Meg's eyebrow arched. "Let's take this inside. Don't play the 'I don't know how to do this' crap on me. Get on the ledge and go through the window. We're going to talk."

Meg put a finger to her lips to silence his tirade. "Okay! You'll get the brief version… for now. I've got to get work done and some shut-eye. It's almost time to get up."

Amazed at her agility, he watched in fascination at the short time it took her to jump onto the ledge and enter the house. He was out of practice and prayed he could do the same. He'd been thirty pounds lighter the last time he attempted a get-away. Slowly he measured the distance, stood, and moved cautiously to the end of the sturdy limb. He heaved himself onto the ledge. Surprised that he had landed on his feet, Matt made his way to the open window and climbed in, only to get his belt caught on the window sill. His upper body tumbled into the room while his legs dangled out the second story window.

"Oh, for God's sake, Hallock!" Meg hissed.

Matt felt the tug on his belt as Meg grabbed it, heaving him up and over the sill. Matt found himself face down on the braided rug on the floor. Not quite the way he'd planned on entering her bedroom. He had pictured rose petals, a turned down bed and champagne.

Getting up off the floor, Matt was mesmerized by her programmed movements. Meg was all business. She stowed away the duffle bag in the closet and sat down on the queen size bed with her back to him. Matt walked over to stand at the foot of the bed.

"What are you looking at?" Meg never looked up at him.

"You." It was all he could muster. In the past hours, Matt struggled to reconcile the woman and her behavior of the last several hours with the woman who'd manned his beach club, blowing a whistle to get someone's attention or when things were amiss. She had practically taken out his eardrum once to make a point when he'd gotten too close for comfort.

Like a robot, Meg unhooked her black Agency-issued vest and went through the process of cleaning and stowing her weapon. Seeing her unload the clip from the Glock and place both pieces in the nightstand by her bed sent a chill down his spine. Only then did Meg turn to face him. Her eyes, in the dimly lit room, showed no emotion.

"Out with it." Meg said. "You first."

"You're CIA, aren't you?" Matt asked.

"Well, boss," she said sarcastically. "Considering what you and I have been through tonight, I sure as hell am not from the Culinary Institute of America."

CHAPTER ELEVEN

The transom window above the four-poster bed let in the remnants of the moonlight. Matt stood, arms crossed, waiting for Meg's explanation. His clothes were wrinkled and grass stained, his shirt torn. The man did not look happy. He looked as drained and tired as she felt.

Having stored her gear and gun carefully away, Meg plumped up the pillows and leaned back against the headboard, her legs crossed, eyes closed, trying to find the words to tell Matt his world was on the verge of imploding—unless he could fill in the blanks. Her gut told her he couldn't.

The floorboards creaked. At the sound, she opened her eyes. Matt stood on her side of the bed. She could see in his eyes he had every intention of parking his butt on the mattress next to her. There was no way *that* was going to happen. Lately, Meg was disturbed how his presence affected her ability to think and act objectively. The mere fact she might be drawn to a man like him was a puzzle for another time.

Meg held up her hand to ward him off, "What do you think you're doing?"

"I was going to get comfortable. If I sit close, we won't wake up the rest of the household."

"You're kidding, right?" Matt's startled look told Meg she'd read his motives right. He wanted details. But he also wanted her. She pointed to the end of the mattress at the foot of the bed, "Down there. Prop yourself up on this."

Meg tossed a pillow to him. Matt caught it and reluctantly did as she asked. He kicked off his boat shoes, sank onto the mattress, and put the pillow behind him, propping himself up against the skinny bedpost. He stretched out his long legs, his toes touching her knee on the blue quilted comforter.

"Judas Priest!" Meg tried to back up but the headboard stopped her. "It's four o'clock and I told you I'd fill you in. But you're only getting the abbreviated version."

Matt crossed his arms and moved his legs off to the side. "Spit it out, then. What the hell have you gotten me into and who are you?"

"First, it's not what I've gotten *you* into. It's the opposite."

"What are you talking about?" Matt whispered, his voice challenging hers.

"Your business."

"What about the Sunfish?" Matt inquired. "What's my business got to do with that shooting down at the docks tonight?"

Would the man just let her talk? She said in a hushed tone, "Could you just shut up and let me tell you? Twenty questions is a waste of valuable sleep time in case you hadn't noticed. Do you think you can manage to keep quiet so I can get you up to speed?"

Matt simply said, "Go for it."

Meg drew in a deep breath to calm her rising temper. She wasn't use to explaining to anyone outside the Agency what was transpiring or giving out sensitive information until a mission's conclusion was declassified. "I'm Agent Megan Spears, CIA. I was sent here by the Director...."

"Aunt Elizabeth sent you..." Meg glared at Matt. "Sorry. The floor is yours, *Agent* Spears."

"About a month ago there was a money drop in Washington. Some of the sequences of numbers on the series of bills have showed up in your club's bank account. What do you know about a man named Jeff Draper?"

"Jeff? We've known each other for years. Met in high school. He's an investor in the club. We've been having a few problems..."

"What kind of problems?"

"I don't think..."

Meg lobbed a pillow in frustration in Matt's direction hitting him squarely in the face. "Listen. Don't think. Just tell me about the problem."

"God, you are relentless!" Matt looked up at the ceiling. Now it seemed Matt was the one uncomfortable with the direction the conversation was going to head. "Jeff's been off schedule with his payments of cash into the start up fund for the club. Two investors had me speak to him a couple of times. He got pretty pissed. Not at all like him."

"Who does he hang around with?"

"A lot of people. He's a regular in the Coast Guard Auxiliary in Hampton Bays. He's also certified in SAR, which flies out of Gabreski."

"SAR?" Meg had never heard of the abbreviation.

"Here in the Hamptons we have the National Guard base. SAR is Search and Rescue. They deal with all sorts of sea rescues on the ocean and Long Island Sound. Even fly backup to downed spacecraft in the Atlantic." Matt paused and frowned. "You can't possibly be thinking Jeff's involved in...what did you call it? A drop?"

"How many times has he been late with payments?"

"Three. And, to be honest lately, I've been wondering where his money's been coming from."

"Why?"

"Because after getting out of his Coast Guard commitment, Jeff went to work for the family business, which took a major hit financially last year. I was surprised he wanted in when we went looking for capital."

As Matt relayed the information about Jeff Draper, Meg whisked her encrypted laptop off the floor, logged in and began typing. "So you have no idea where he's getting the money?"

"No."

"What kind of car does he drive?" Meg typed as fast as she talked.

"A red Audi. That's new, too, come to think of it."

"Know anyone who drives a Black Escalade?"

Matt's head snapped up. He leveled a knowing look at her. "Like the one tonight?"

"You saw it? How the hell could you? You were in the water."

"Meg, you filled in the police report. Since Red Rogers is an old friend, he let me read your write-up when you disappeared."

"Matt, listen to me. I've seen that car twice now. The first time was the break in at your office. The second time was tonight. It may be a total coincidence that it's the same car. My gut says it's not. Tonight, the Escalade pulled away with the two guys who rode in that boat. Now, I'll ask you again, do you know anyone who drives that car?"

"Jeff Draper's got a friend named Baker. Steven Baker. He owns one. I've only seen them together a few times. There's a new bakery with Wi-Fi on Main Street. I was walking up the steps and Jeff was getting into Steve's car."

"Do you know Steve very well?"

"Not as well as I know Jeff. But Steve belongs to the auxiliary. I used to be a member a few years ago. But I never really had an occasion to train or work with him. I had to drop out because the club takes up too much of my time. But the group meets Wednesday nights at the old CG station in Hampton Bays near the Pontquogue Bridge. That's over by the Shinnecock Inlet."

"Can you access the Sound or the waters of the North Fork from there?" Meg's mind reeled with multiple "what if" scenarios given the new information.

"No, not unless you went out the inlet into the Atlantic. But you'd have to make your way around Montauk. It would take forever. You'd need a pretty powerful boat to make good time."

"You sure?"

"Positive." Matt yawned. "I don't like the sound of where this is heading. Are you telling me my club is being used to launder money? And I'm being betrayed by one of my closest friends?"

"It's looking that way. But, Matt," Meg snapped her fingers to get his attention as his gaze had drifted off again. "Hey! I can't impress on you the need to keep a lid on this. You can't tell anyone. Not even Sarah. The Director didn't want you involved. But after tonight, she and my team felt you had to be on a "need to know" basis. My main concern is you being able to pretend nothing is amiss when you come into contact with Draper again."

"There's more isn't there?"

"A few things. Nothing that can't wait until morning."

Matt picked up the pillow that had been launched at him plus the one he'd been leaning on. Uninvited, he shimmed up on her left side, laid down on the mattress and faced the wall.

"What the hell do you think *you're* doing?" Meg poked him in the side and tried to nudge him off the bed, but to no avail.

"Look at the damn clock. If you think I'm going out that window and down the tree to find my bed, you're mistaken. You're the spy, put the clues together. I'm spending the night."

"You are not sleeping in my bed!"

"Goodnight, Goldilocks."

Muttering and cursing under her breath, Meg suddenly realized she was talking to herself. Matt was sound asleep.

"Urghhhhh!" Meg punched her fist into her pillows and turned her back on him. The man was impossible! Sleeping with the nephew, even platonically, could not be included in her report to the Director in the morning.

CHAPTER TWELVE

Liar's Club

Mike Kranepool and Steve Baker walked into the run down shack after docking their boat. It was their second visit to the there that week. But tonight, given the wind and the rain, it had not been possible to attempt crossing by kayak. Both men decided to take a chance and arrived in Mike's twin engine C 260. They were cold, wet, and aggravated the meeting could not have taken place on the mainland. Docked safely, they walked the sandy trail from the marina at the Shinnecock Restaurant to the club. It was a miserable night. Mike hoped the weather that night wasn't an omen of what was to come.

Entering the dilapidated building, Mike's eyes adjusted to the dimness of the bar's lighting. Spying Jeff Draper and the "suit," he started for the circular table nestled in the back corner of the room. Personally, Mike hadn't cared for the new team member on sight. The man had done little to win Mike's confidence by his subtle actions and remarks.

The wind slammed the door shut, forcing Steve to bump into Mike from behind. Mike whispered over his shoulder, "Baker, watch where you're going. I can barely see in this god forsaken hole in the wall."

Steve came to stand beside him, his eyes squinting in the dark room as well. "Do you see Jeff?"

"Yup. And that "suit" is here. In the rain poncho." Mike jerked his head in the direction of the corner of the back of the Liar's Club. He paused. "But, who the hell's *that* third guy?"

Steve moved to Mike's left side for a better view. "Don't know. But I can tell you right now, I'm not liking this."

Another man sat at the table, his back to them. Mike pulled Steve into a dark corner by the door. "Me neither. We started with the three of us. I'm not splitting my take with anybody else. Come on. Let's see what Draper's got planned."

Mike and Steve were moving past the bar when a drunken voice called to them. "What'cha drinking, mates?" *Great*, Mike thought. *Just what we need. The village idiot*, Buddy McLean, one of the bar's regulars.

Sitting next to Buddy was a tall, ragged, weather beaten fisherman. From his looks, he was fresh off the boat. Mike waved Buddy's offer. "No thanks."

The old man grunted and wiped his graying beard with the back of the sleeve of his shirt but wasn't going to be deterred, slurring his words. "Come on, fellas. Let the new boy buy ya a drink." Buddy tapped the bar stool next to him. "Park a spell. Haven't seen you two in here lately." *And that's the way we want you to remember it*, Mike thought.

"No thanks." Mike called out and kept walking. "Give those two a drink on me. And keep the change." He threw a twenty dollar bill on the counter of the bar.

The bartender nodded.

Steve whispered from behind, "What the hell are you thinking? We're not supposed to leave a trail. You better hope Jeff didn't hear you. You have no idea who that fisherman could be."

"Your paranoia's showing through again. Back off. Buddy may be the town drunk, but I bet he remembers more than we give him credit for. He probably knows how long Jeff's been sitting here with our two new friends."

"It's about time," came Draper's gruff voice as Mike and Steve arrived at the back table. "What the hell took so long? This meeting could have been over and done with an hour ago."

Mike pulled out a chair and sat, biting his tongue. He was tempted to issue a caustic reply. "In case you hadn't noticed, it's not the greatest night to come across. And there was no way in hell I was letting Steve bring his car. It would stick out big time. But we're here, so would you do us the honor and introduce us to the new guy?"

Steve, who'd apparently gone back to the bar and grabbed two beers, slapped one in front of Mike and sat beside him.

But it before Mike could say anything more that Steve chimed in. "For the record, and you can glare at me all you want, Draper, this plan of yours has started to really tick me off. First it was just the three of us with that Arab… then the other night we meet up with Steeler here." Steve pointed at the man in the yellow rain slicker who sat to Jeff's right. "To be honest, I didn't need to know who the hell he was. Just that he was formatting a second set of books for the club. Then, you inform us, we're not just *paying* him to do the job…Oh, no. You tell us he has become an 'investor.' You've gone against everything we agreed to." Steve paused and took a long swig of his beer, smacking his lips when finished.

If looks could kill, Steve was on Draper's hit list. Mike wanted Steve to shut up, but his buddy continued. "Now...now...you've brought somebody else to the table. Who is he and what's *his* piece in *our* action? Is he going to cost me and Mike more of our share?"

Mike didn't like being included in Steve's tirade, but his friend made several valid points.

"You done?" Jeff asked. "Or is there anything else either one of you want to get off your chest?" He glanced at his watch. "I don't have all night and the later we stay here, the riskier it gets."

Silence ensued.

"Let me introduce you to Jim Fleming." Draper pointed to the main in the orange poncho. "He's going to be our inside man at Plum Island. Jim's a microbiologist with an extremely high level of clearance. He has access to what we need. We just have to figure out how to take the money from the Sunfish to pay for it."

Mike's first impression of Fleming was that he was a stereotypical nerd. Tall, thin, geeky with large, metal rimmed thick glasses. He sure didn't look like the kind of person who'd muddy his hard earned reputation by stealing a strain of the avian flu virus that was similar to the 1918 pandemic outbreak that killed thousands. Surprising what the lure of money can do to human nature.

"Jim, why don't you tell them what we're going to need to do when the time comes?" Draper leaned back in his chair, a smug expression on his face.

The man was too cocky for his own good, Mike thought, as if all the bases were covered and nothing could go wrong.

"First let me say I prefer not to know who you are. And you," Jim motioned at Steve, "I don't want to be an investor. Just pay my fee into my off shore account. I plan on heading out of the states once I get my hands on what you want and I know the money has been wired into my account."

Mike sat up straight more willing to listen.

"Without giving you all the science jumbo, here's the simple version. Plum Island has a research group of which I've been a part for several years. Our mission was to mutate the H5N1 avian flu virus similar to the lethal 1918 version, the one that has the possibility for rapid dissemination. Good news for terrorist groups, bad for anyone else. There's one big problem at Plum Island. Research labs at the facility have different levels based on the agents being investigated—biosafety levels 1, 2, 3, and 4.. We call them BSLs for short. This particular strain you want requires entry into BSL 4, the highest on the list."

Mike noted that everyone at the table had taken out notepads and started to write while Jim was talking. He followed their lead and jotted down several questions that came to mind. "So...if understand, trying to get entry is going to be a problem?"

"Not for me. I've got the clearance. Anyone in that area wears special electronic ID badges that grant us access, but two weeks ago, the security was raised. Entry is now done by using swipe cards, fingerprints, and iris scanners."

Jeff Draper tipped his chair back against the wall behind him. "So where does our problem lie in getting the virus out? You *can* do it, right?"

"I can. But someone else has to be a decoy inside so I can get the canister to whoever you're sending up those steep cliffs on the north side. You have a logistical nightmare at the moment. Not one of you has any security clearance at any level. Your military levels don't count in this scenario. It takes months to acquire and have the simplest of background checks done for a BSL 1."

"Shit!" Steve banged his fist on the table. "I knew this was too good to be true. Here we are with all the connections to make a run at the island on a supposed "drill" for Homeland and we can't get access."

John Steeler had been quiet while Jim talked. His pensive expression turned into a sly grin. "What if I could hack into Homeland's database to get a simple BSL 1 clearance. Wouldn't that at least get somebody in the door? That person might be a new hire? Help me out here." John sipped his drink, then said to Jim, "What kinds of jobs are posted at the moment?"

Jim began to tap his fingers on the side of his beer glass. "I think you're on to something. As a matter of fact, since you're the IT guy, I know there's a position opening up next week because of a maternity leave. Albeit a short one. But if we could take advantage of the window of time, we might have a shot at making this work. The head honcho goes ballistic whenever he's left with an opening and no one to fill it. Hacking the database would allow us to move someone up to the top of the list."

Jeff Draper dropped his chair into its upright position. "Sounds like a plan. What do you think, Steeler? Can you pull this off?"

Mike watched as John's eyes twitched. The man was nervous. He scratched at his hands as he thought. It was obvious to Mike that it was one thing to play around in computer systems hidden away from the rest of the world until an IP address was located. It was another to come out in public and portray the part of an IT specialist in a real job. Mike had a few concerns on that score, knowing John Steeler never left his office. He was a loner. Rumor had it in town he probably was agoraphobic. Hell, the man hadn't even hired a secretary for his busy accounting practice.

"I'm in." John stated firmly, shocking Mike, and apparently, by the look on Steve's face, him too. "I think I can do this."

Jeff eyed him warily. "I don't want 'think', Jim....I need someone who has no doubt he can accomplish the task. We've got way too much at stake.... *Can* you do this, Steeler?"

"Yes." John said, locking eyes with Draper.

"Good." Jeff was satisfied and that was all that mattered.

As much as Mike would back up any decision made, he had strong reservations John could pull off being the point man inside Plum Island.

Steve had been extremely quiet. "There's something else you're not telling us, Draper. Isn't there? What's going on?"

Mike turned to Steve sitting with his arms crossed, a determined expression on his face. The paranoid kid had suddenly developed one very set of large set of balls. And Mike was glad of it. Maybe he had misjudged him.

Jeff twisted the empty beer mug in his hands. "It's the Arab. For more money, he wants us to infiltrate the stockpile of vaccines at the SNS."

"And? Come on...spit it out." Steve wasn't backing down.

"Kalil says the final payment won't be made unless he has both the virus *and* the vaccine."

The table erupted, the shouts drawing attention from the small group of fishermen gathered at the bar. Even Buddy and his new friend looked over.

Mike had had enough. A shiver traveled down his spine hearing the wind howl and the thunder boom overhead. He and Steve were in over their heads. Draper had conned them. Big time. They'd wanted to meet the Arab before doing business but Draper said it wasn't an option. Disgusted, Mike rose, his chair scraping along the sandy, plank floor. "I'm outta here. I've had all the good news I can handle. Steve, you coming or staying?"

"I'm coming." From the look on Steve's face, he was as shocked at the news Draper had delivered as Mike was. "Draper, you better find a way to get us out of that second issue. I came in for the virus. Period. Call us when you have our "drill" mapped out. We need a few more trials to make sure we can traverse that side of the island. So far, we've been pretty lucky no one's asked questions. We've just written it off as SAR training." Steve pointed to the door. "Let's get out of here, Mike."

Mike turned and walked away from the table, Steve trailing behind him. As they passed by Buddy, he actually waved. Strange. The man was usually intoxicated, head down on the bar. Maybe it was his new friend. As he and Steve exited the Liar's Club, Mike had the strangest feeling he needed eyes in the back of his head.

CHAPTER THIRTEEN

Meg's internal clock woke her every morning at 0500. As her eyes opened, she groaned, her mind thinking back on the past evening…and Matt. She'd chosen her words carefully as they talked. Meg was surprised how well he'd taken the news. He had been shocked and felt betrayed. Who wouldn't? But Matt was ready to move on to whatever needed doing.

Contrary to the rumors and innuendos, Meg had become privy to a different side of her boss while working at the club, as well as when she popped into the cafe and bakery in the village. Matt truly had people's best interests at heart. And from what she'd gleaned last night, he was willing to go to any length to protect what was his—his employees, his family…even her. And it was his feelings for her that had her worried.

Shaking her head to clear away the cobwebs of a sleepless night, with no time to re-energize, Meg rolled out of bed only to be grabbed and pulled back onto the mattress.

Eye-to-eye with the man who was foremost on her mind, Meg struggled to return to an upright position. "Matt, let me go. I don't have time for your antics right now. Have you forgotten about your club? I need to go check it out."

"I'll go with you."

This was exactly what she'd been afraid of. Matt wanting to be a part of whatever she did and wherever she went. If he would just take his hands off her. She couldn't think straight when he touched her.

"What did I say last night?" Meg poked him in the chest. "Weren't you listening? You *have* to play your part. Have you any idea how important it is that you maintain your presence at the club as if you know nothing? You could blow my cover. All of my plans will go to hell if you can't hold up your end in all of this. You'll create a danger for everyone at the club, not to mention your family. If you can't do as I ask, I'll pick up the phone and you can talk to your aunt—"

Matt placed his finger to her lips and tucked a stray tendril of hair behind her ear. The minute he lightly brushed her cheek, she lost her concentration. Her body tingled. "You've got time. Come here." Matt tugged her closer. "You felt good snuggled against me last night."

Meg had to set the record straight before he had the wrong idea. "I did *not* cuddle up against you. You had your side of the bed and I had mine."

"You most certainly did curl your body into mine, lady. I know when I've got a woman in my bed. You snuck your arm around my waist and…"

Meg wouldn't give Matt the satisfaction of knowing he was right. She remembered how wonderfully safe it felt to have him near. Her Agency life left no time for relationships. No check that. *She* had refused to carve out a dual life as some of her fellow operatives had done. It wasn't in her to lie and say she was on a business trip, when she was really tracking two art thieves through the streets of Paris. She'd made the Agency her career—and her family.

"Stop! I did no such thing. Now let me up! I have to find out if anything is missing before the rest of the club employees arrive."

"And I can help you. But first…"

The man was positively frustrating! "Remember that boat from the marina across from the Sunfish? Those men may have broken into your office. For all we know they may have gone back." *And I need to get to that locker room.*

But Meg wasn't winning the battle of getting out of bed and onto the tasks at hand. Meg felt the evidence of Matt's arousal as he wrapped his leg up and over her hip, securing her to him. He nuzzled her ear. "Just fifteen minutes. Last night was a lot to take in. Don't you dare tell me, lady, you can't feel this connection we have. You know as well as I do it's been building since we met."

Meg was losing ground rapidly. "Matt." Her voice came out in a husky whimper, not as the stern warning she wanted to convey. She pushed against his chest but he entwined his fingers with hers and locked them in place above his heart. "You promised."

"I want a good morning kiss."

Meg saw the raw desire in his piercing blue eyes. She couldn't help but be sucked into the heat of his gaze. Matt leaned his head toward her and she met him halfway. But this kiss wasn't like the one on the boat. This time she didn't admonish him for going over the line. If the truth be told, it felt glorious to release the pent up emotions she'd bottled up for the last weeks. Her arms snaked up around his neck. Curling her fingers into his hair, she pulled him to her and as their lips met, she whispered back, "Just one. Make it good."

Meg nibbled at his lower lip lightly, hoping he would take the hint she wanted more. Matt obliged and locked his lips to hers. When she opened her mouth, his tongue slid in and found hers. Meg's body was consumed by the banked passion she had hidden away. Throwing caution to the wind, she savored the memory of having her body melt in his arms. Heaven help her, but she couldn't get enough of the man.

Meg was so engrossed in showing Matt how she felt, she hadn't realized he had pinned her to the bed. As Matt ran feather light kisses along the side of her neck, his hands brushed the under sides of her breasts, the mere touch sending a bolt of heat to her inner core. If he took her now, she would never regret it. Meg was ready to throw rational thought out the window for once in her life.

Matt sat up, his hips straddling her. He tugged his tee-shirt up and over his shoulders, flinging it onto the floor. Meg did the same, her eyes riveted on the solid muscles of his torso and abdomen. Her shirt hadn't landed on the floor when she froze, suddenly realizing the mistake she inadvertently made in the heat of the moment.

Her eyes shot up to take in Matt's reaction, knowing from past experience what she expected to find—a startled, shocked, disgusted look, eyes opened wide in surprise. No matter how feminine Meg attempted to be by wearing lacey underwear, it never erased the thirteen-inch gash that crossed from beneath her left breast to her lower right abdomen. Her hands couldn't react fast enough to cover up the hideous scar.

Meg's eyes captured Matt's and swallowed. He didn't turn away as others had done in her past. God, where was her shirt?

She tried to push herself up, but Matt rested his hand on her chest. "Don't."

"Please," Meg pleaded. *Oh God, please don't cry. Not in front of him* . "Please don't look at it."

It was then she felt the light touch of his fingertips. For the very first time, hands lovingly explored and caressed her hated scar, a reminder of a mission gone sour. A secret buried by the Director herself for the risk Meg had taken on her behalf.

"Not look at you?" Matt asked, his voice sounding as if in awe of her. "Megan, you're beautiful." Matt bent over to drop kisses along the ridge of scar tissue. Butterflies fluttered in her stomach. He stopped, reached for her chin and brought her eyes to meet his. If she had thought the man pitied her, she was sorely mistaken. There was only pure raw desire…for her. "Don't *ever* think your scar defines your beauty. I find it a real turn on. Now I know the real you. You must have been brave to endure whatever caused this." How like the man to dwell on the positive and never the negative. It was then Meg knew she was falling for him.

A tear rolled down Meg's cheek. "Oh, Matt."

More tears followed as she tried to stop her roller coaster of emotions. She lived her life in a black and white world. Now, totally out of her element, she was allowed to be a woman.

Matt's strong arms lifted her up, changed his position and cradled her on his lap. Her arms instinctively wrapped around his neck. Matt feathered her lips with light, butterfly kisses. "To me, you're a warrior, Megan Spears. You're beautiful, strong, and determined. You take my breath away every time I'm with you."

Meg sat, looking at the man, speechless.

Ding! Ding! Ding!

"What the hell is that?" Matt, tightening his hands around her waist, scanned the room, then eyed her warily.

Meg grinned sheepishly. "It's my fifteen minute warning timer." Meg tapped the face of her watch. "You said you wanted fifteen minutes... so I set my watch."

"You timed our foreplay?" Matt shook his head in disbelief and laughed out loud.

Damn the man. He would wake up the house. The last thing she needed was to explain why he was in her room...and in her bed. She did the only thing she could think of to shut him up. Meg kissed him one last time...for that morning at least.

Meg broke off the kiss and shimmied off his lap. "Now listen, boss." She felt his eyes following her every move. Walking to her dresser, she opened the bottom drawer and pulled out her beach attire. "I've got to get to the Sunfish. But you need to get there later with some sort of excuse."

Meg put her hand up when she saw the glint of a question forming from the expression on his face. She didn't have more time to give him, but Matt won out.

"Meg, will there be some time today we can talk?" For a fleeting moment, a look of alarm crossed Matt's face. Perhaps he was only going to ask to be kept abreast of what went on behind the scenes. Meg prayed it would only be what she was authorized to tell him.

"Yes, but not here at the estate. I can assure you the house, and every inch of the grounds, are being guarded, if that helps. I'll come up with a time and place."

Matt simply nodded, then a broad smile broke out on his tanned face.

"I don't like that look. You're planning on doing something I won't like, aren't you?" Meg asked. Making her way to the nightstand, she opened the drawer and pulled out her pistol. She loaded the magazine into the Glock and secured it in its holster. "Tell me quick. I've got to get out of here."

Matt rose from the bed and came to stand in front of her. "Well, Megan Spears. You and I are going out on our first date."

Meg sputtered. "I can't. We can't. It's not protocol. I have things to do..." Matt's right eyebrow arched as she finished. "...at night."

"We're going to the Marakesh...tonight. No ifs, ands, or buts. It's a bar in the village, full of people. *Interesting* people, if you catch my drift. Very loud, too. No one will be able to hear us talk or make anything out of us being out together. We'll just go from nine to ten. Does that leave you enough time to do what you need to do afterwards?"

For once Meg couldn't fault Matt's logic or plan. Actually, it was perfect for come to think of it. She had wanted to visit the various town's hotspots and see who dropped in, but time hadn't allowed for it. And since the club's break in, coupled with brandishing her gun, she'd wanted to keep a low profile.

"All right. You're on. Now get out of here. And use the stairs." She grabbed onto his arm. "Watch the third step from the bottom. The damn thing creaks... a lot." She smiled as Matt left the room without any argument.

Meg checked her watch once again. No time for a shower. Meg raced to get dressed. As she headed out the door she thought of how she should file her morning report: *Spent the night in bed with your nephew. Nothing happened but, for the record, he's a great kisser. Oh, and BTW, we're going on out on our first date.*

For the first time in her life, Meg was happy at the possibility that her life could exist within two worlds, the real, and the one dictated by the CIA. But, did Meg have a fairy godmother watching over her or would her Beetle Bug turn into a pumpkin at midnight?

CHAPTER FOURTEEN

Sunfish Beach Club

Meg cautiously made her way from the upper deck of the beach club down the tunnel that led to the locker room. She had checked Matt's office. Everything looked untouched, at least from her perspective. But how could she determine what might be out of place if she was never the last to leave? She'd have to point out the need to make a change with Matt without tipping Sarah off.

Hearing the sound of metal clanging on metal, Meg halted. She drew her weapon. She tiptoed slowly toward the room set aside for the lifeguards, praying the wooden planks beneath her feet did not creak. Outside the dark blue entrance door, she paused and placed her ear to the door to listen. Her back against the wall, she looked up and down the hallway. The sound had stopped but Meg swore the noise had come from inside the guardhouse. *Trust your gut.*

Opening the door with her elbow, Meg defensively swung the muzzle of her Glock in all directions searching for a possible intruder. The room was eerily empty. The hairs on the back of her neck rose, memories of what had transpired running through her brain. Making another sweep of the room, she spied a pink, folded piece of paper stuffed into the air vents of *her* locker. Being vigilant Meg approached it, keeping her eyes darting from the paper to the wide expanse of blue lockers surrounding the perimeter of the break room. She pulled the paper from locker and read:

255678924409#8904

What was the meaning of the coded message? She unsnapped her encrypted cell phone from its casing to call Jake. Jake and Samantha already texted her information regarding two items on her "to-do" list: the registry number of the boat that crashed and a partial plate number to the Escalade. Jake managed to enlarge footage from a gas station's security camera at the end of Library Avenue near the marina.

Meg was about to message her team with a photo of the note she'd taken when a familiar voice spoke up from behind her.

"You don't need to use your phone. Jake already has the number."

Meg turned and holstered her weapon. "You're going tell me how you're in on this."

"I am," Sarah Adams said calmly.

"Make it short and sweet. I want to know how you got involved."

Sarah walked to the island in the middle of the room, sat down on one of the stools, pointing to the note paper in Meg's hand. Still taken aback at seeing Matt's second in command, Meg sat as well. Sarah reached for the coffee pot on the white work surface where many of the maps, weather reports, and rotational charts were usually laid out. She poured two cups. Meg hadn't even noticed the pot had been filled. "I know you hate this stuff, but drink it. I've a lot to tell you and not much time."

Meg eyed the woman whom she thought she knew so well. Obviously, Sarah was trained to do her job as well as the others. "So who are you really, Sarah Adams?"

Sarah, a semblance of a grin forming at the corner of her mouth, said, "Believe it or not, my real name *is* Sarah Adams. I went to GW University same as you. And before you ask… Yes, Elizabeth Hallock made plans for me when my parents died many years ago. She saw that my grandparents were taken care of, paid my way through college, and saw that my love of languages paid off. I possess dual degrees in marketing and linguistics. I've been working for the Agency since I graduated three years ago. It was easy for me to go undercover here given the fact most people know me. My appearance working as Matt's assistant didn't need an explanation. I fell into the perfect cover. I can come and go without anyone questioning my whereabouts."

Meg shook her head in disbelief. "I would never have thought…" Meg's thoughts drifted off before realizing, yet again, she had been omitted from knowing pertinent details of Operation Hurricane. "Why wasn't I informed?"

"I don't know. I just do what I'm told. I should score points for getting the Director to rethink your need to live in town, not over on the North Fork. It was my idea to get you invited onto the Hallock estate. It took some major convincing on my end, but finally the Eagle realized she had you and your team spread way too thin." Sarah's infectious giggle echoed in the almost empty room. "I can't believe how miffed you were." Meg joined in, remembering how livid she'd been. "Mrs. H and I are on great terms and with just a little push and knowing it was for Matthew's club, she was willing to let some of the agents live there. Thank goodness, she's not aware she's running a semi-version of a safehouse."

Meg grimaced as she sipped the steaming liquid. She'd had to endure two days of the wretched beverage. "Fill me in. What's with the number?"

"I worked on a case last year where my partner and I tracked off shore accounts to the Cayman Islands and Swiss bank accounts. The minute I saw the number pattern, I knew it was a routing number. I sent it to a few friends at the Agency. They didn't get very far, so this morning, like I said, I passed it along to Jake. I'd stake my job on the fact it's offshore. Swiss accounts normally start with letters. My sixth sense has me thinking Draper's involved. Personally, I think the guy is hanging with a dangerous crowd."

Meg's eyebrow arched hearing Sarah's comments mirror her own. "What was Jake's response when you gave him the info."

Sarah took a sip from the styrofoam cup. "Jake said he'd get right on it. Hoped his contacts would get back to him by noon today, five at the latest."

"Good work. But back track. When did *you* get the number?"

"Draper has been on my radar for the last couple of months. Being manager has me in a good position to notice Draper's comings and goings." Sarah frowned, distaste showed in her eyes. "Jeff's a scumbag. Gives me the creeps. But I digress." Meg took another sip and listened to what Sarah had to say. "Everyone who knows me thinks I'm some kind of techie geek. I keep everything digital when it comes to records. Every account has a file or spreadsheet. All of the club's documents are backed up for security reasons on a multitude of various servers. But for Matt's access, I do keep paper copies of the records for all the investment deposits and transfers for when he's got to report to the board. Matt hates to use the computer. The man only wants access to his cell phone and even the one he owns is archaic. It would make things so much easier if he'd use a Blackberry or IPhone, especially for email and data retrieval. The man won't tweet or use Facebook. He sees no use for powerful social media tools in promoting the club. It's been an uphill battle." Sarah sighed, but then laughed.

"What's so funny?" Meg's curiosity was piqued.

"Matt says he doesn't have enough time in the day to keep up with all the women who would want to "friend" him. And he's not about to tweet about his exploits in the—"

"Stop. Please. TMI." Meg held up her hand. "Anything else?"

Sarah was on a roll. "Matt says he's got his own little black book that half of the single guys in the Hamptons would pay top dollar for at auction."

Meg didn't want to know about Matt's exploits, especially after what had transpired that morning. Meg cleared her throat. Sarah took the hint and moved on.

"Sorry, Meg. Where was I? Oh, yeah. About the time you reported the break in, I got curious and started to compare the digital files with the paper reports. I must have spent four or five days trying to find if some kind of weird accounting system existed. My files for the club are encoded and password secured. I let Matt have copies with a few modifications. Matt made some notes and changes when Draper dropped by with a deposit. That's when I found the investor's monies weren't adding up. I made a few more false changes to see if someone would bite."

"And someone found out."

Sarah nodded, taking another sip of her coffee. "Yup. Too coincidental, don't you think? Somebody is onto what I'm doing. When the Director told me that some serial numbers on the first deposit into the club's account were from the drop in Washington, we knew Draper was definitely involved. The big question is who he's working with?"

Meg retrieved her laptop out of her bag and booted it up. She wanted to access what she had typed into her notes from her discussion with Matt. "There's a strong likelihood his friends in the Coast Guard Auxiliary are. My interest was piqued when Matt brought the group to my attention. We need to vet the list of men and women on the membership list. Look at their financials. Cell phone records. It's imperative we find a link to anybody with ties to the Middle East."

Sarah rose, walked to and opened her locker. She took out a manila envelope and came back to the table. "I got this via secure mail from the Director. I was told to give it to you."

Meg took the envelope from Sarah. "Is this for my eyes only?"

"Is it stamped? Open it up."

Meg reached in and drew out a dark brown file folder. The formal imprint of "CLASSIFIED" wasn't stamped on the front so she proceeded to draw out its contents—a pile of surveillance photographs, a list of cell phone records, and the number Sarah had already gained access to typed on a blue piece of paper.

"Looks like we've got some digging to do. There's a connection somewhere. We're just not seeing it." Meg held up the photos, squinting at blurry images. "I can barely make out these out. Whoever took these, didn't or couldn't bring the best equipment." Meg placed each photo on the worktable for a better overall view. "Got any idea on the location? Looks like a hole in the wall."

Sarah leaned over the table to carefully scrutinize each picture. Meg moved out of the way, letting Sarah arrange them. She seemed to be putting the pictures in some sort of a time-lapsed, chronological order. The young agent worked intently as she studied the photographs, placing several side by side.

"If I'm not mistaken," Sarah tapped the clearest of the five, "this was taken at the Liar's Club in Hampton Bays."

"The what?"

"It's a dive bar frequented by the local fishermen near the Shinnecock Inlet. I've only been there once. It's pretty seedy." A look of satisfaction passed across Sarah's face as she topped off her coffee from the pot. She smiled at Meg. "I think we've just found the four corners of our puzzle."

"Why? What's so significant about this place in particular?"

"The Liar's Club is located by the Pontquogue Bridge."

"And what's that got to do with anything?"

Sarah seemed to be pondering her choice of words as she looked down at her watch. Meg, too, had noticed the passing time. Guards and employees would be arriving in the locker room soon.

"The Liar's Club is directly across the bay from the Coast Guard Auxiliary's base of operations. Meg, this could be really big… And…" Sarah dragged and placed the pictures of four of the men in front of her on the island, leaving the other untouched.

"What is it? Have you any idea who these men are? Can you make out anything that might identify them?" Meg wanted Sarah's input before she added her own. She was almost certain she knew who the three were, but she didn't want to bias Sarah. The trio Meg recognized were the men who broke into the club the morning of her run. Now all she needed were names.

Sarah dragged the first photo in front of Meg. "Jeff Draper. Not dressed in his usual dapper attire. Homeland's had their eye on him because he's got an Arab friend named Kalil. You mentioned a Middle Eastern connection. Kalil, or someone near him, could be the person you're looking for.

"This guy," Meg eyed the next picture Sarah showed her, "is John Steeler, a local accountant. He's weird. Amazing how he runs one of the most successful accounting firms in the area all by himself, no help, no secretary. Makes me wonder what he's hiding. He's mostly a loner. In that he went to MIT, I'd stake my reputation he's trained in IT specialties."

Meg drew a third photo across the island to study it and the other two carefully. No doubt about it. They were the three men who'd been trying to find something in Matt's office. Particularly, the thumb drive.

"Why did you pull that third picture out of the pile?" Sarah asked. "Have you seen him before?"

Meg held up her hand. "Finish what you wanted to tell me. Then we'll talk."

Sarah looked at her suspiciously, but continued, "We need to check into John's background. Bet the guy knows a thing or two about hacking into computer systems." Sarah moved another photo from the remaining pile into view. "This guy's Steve Baker, ex-Coast Guard, but an auxiliary member. He drives a black Escalade."

Meg simply nodded. "Matt mentioned Baker drove one. What do you think the chance is his plates were on that fleeing car last night?"

"Personally, I think Baker's too smart to get caught. But, from what I've heard about town, he's always paranoid about something or other. However, when you're in a hurry to get something done, you get sloppy. Might have done just that."

Sarah reached for the photo Meg had placed in the pile in front of her. "And this guy…I wouldn't want to meet in a dark alley. Name's Mike Kranepool, ex-Coast Guard, now working with the auxiliary staff. He has a first-degree black belt. Just a plain, mean SOB. I say we search their military records. Look for commonalities. Something might pop up. The auxiliary seems to be the common denominator running through their relationships."

Meg totally agreed with Sarah's assessment. She didn't know if Sarah was privy to the fact that the Director had mentioned she was going to look into the activity of recent SAR training sessions out by Plum Island. There'd been more than the usual requests to use the Coast Guard vessels. Eyeing the clock on the wall, Meg pointed to the last image from the envelope. "And him?"

Sarah picked up the picture. Meg wondered why the Director simply hadn't scanned the photos. It would have given her team the ability to manipulate the pictures via enhancement software. The arrival of the photos and documents told Meg perhaps now she was operating within a very inner circle of the Director's confidants. Perhaps the Director embedded an informant somewhere in the area?

Sarah shrugged her shoulders when she looked at the photo. "Have no idea. I'll get working on it. Maybe there's somebody at Fox Hollow who can make a better sketch for us to take to facial recognition."

Rapidly assessing her to-do list, Meg knew she had to delegate her agents' times wisely now that four men had been identified. It was best to send Sarah to Fox Hollow. Meg would alert Reggie with what she needed and put in a call to Jake and Samantha to step up surveillance on the four individuals, tracking down whatever they could.

But Matt was going to be the issue. With what he now knew, Meg believed he was going to question every move she made. She would have to have a plausible plan and explanation regarding Sarah's disappearance on a busy work day if this was going to work out.

As Meg went to put the photos back into the manila envelope, a small folded piece of paper fluttered to the floor. Meg bent over, opened it and read the hastily scribbled message:

Best I could do given the circumstances. I'll make contact soon. DT.

So that's where Derek had been! So this was the "new" assignment Reggie had alluded to. That explained the state of the photographs. Meg slapped the folder on the island, her anger getting the better of her.

"What's the matter?" Sarah asked, concerned. "Did I do something wrong?"

Meg took a deep, calming breath. She smiled genuinely at the young woman who stood patiently waiting Meg's next set of instructions. "No, Sarah. Nothing's wrong. You and I are good. I think we're more than good actually. Let's get upstairs and get things set up. Then I want you to head out. What do you know about Fox Hollow?"

"It's the base of operations…but," Sarah paused.

"If you've got something on your mind, tell me now. I need you on your way."

"What are we going to tell Matt?" Sarah queried. "He's in a rough jam. I don't want him getting hurt."

"You leave Matt to me. Someone is shadowing his every move. The family is well protected, but I think you already know that." Meg made a mental note to check with the Director on exactly how deep Sarah was immersed in Operation Hurricane. "The more in depth we probe, the more Matt will need to fill in the blanks. The Director is adamant for now on limiting what we tell him. You're with him most of the time in his office. Be sure his time with Draper, in any capacity, is done with a witness. Radio me the next time Draper comes by."

"You got it. I'll be back as soon as I can. Oh, and there's one problem beyond our control today, Meg."

Meg drained her cup. "What now?"

"Major storm's brewing. The weather channel says it should hit here mid-afternoon. The surf will turn really rough from the north winds sometime around noon. It's starting to churn pretty good even now. We need to talk to Matt about shutting down. The surfers will be out in droves if we don't. We don't need them on the grounds risking our guards. Post the red flag for undertow and riptide."

"Will do." Meg said. "I'm on it. You just get things rolling." Meg handed Sarah the original folder. "I've made some notes and tucked the note page inside. This is for Jake's eyes only."

"Copy that." Sarah left the locker room with the Director's envelope under her arm.

Due to the impending storm, Meg needed Matt at the club sooner than she'd told him to report. The storm couldn't have come at a more perfect time. With the club shut down, it would allow Meg time to talk to him about the individuals in question and have extra time to meet with her team at Fox Hollow. Meg hoped there was news about the connection between the men and the Coast

Guard drills being performed in the vicinity of Plum Island. But she was still stumped as to where the Russian fit in. If Interpol had answered Jake's request perhaps she'd know better how much longer it was going to take before the last pieces of the puzzle clicked into place.

CHAPTER FIFTEEN

Scanning the beachfront from the office window, Meg saw only the lone manned lifeguard tower left with a skeleton crew. The rest of the beach was deserted. The storm clouds had blown in from the north as predicted. The waves crested and crashed onto shore devouring the shoreline as the water crept up the beach toward the club. Dark ominous clouds made the late morning seem as if dusk was about to fall.

Where was Matt? She'd left a message on his cell phone over an hour ago saying it was urgent he get in touch. It was unlike him not to respond. She couldn't believe, with the stake he had in the new club, he wasn't monitoring the deteriorating weather conditions.

Hearing the door to the office open, she turned and said, "Finally. I need to talk to you about..." Meg stopped short seeing Tyler, not Matt, standing just inside the entrance.

"You expecting somebody?" he asked.

"Yes. Our boss. You haven't heard from him, have you?"

Tyler shook his head. "No. I don't understand why he isn't here to close up the club. Maybe something's happening on the mainland."

"Like what?"

"I don't know. Can't be anything at the farm. There's a multitude of workers who prepare the horses for storms like this. Don't worry. He never shirks his responsibilities. If Matt said he was coming, he'll be here. I came to tell you I made the decision not to wait to close. The storm's coming faster than we anticipated." Tyler pointed to the windows behind where Meg was standing. "I need to screw on the hurricane shutters."

"Oh. Sure. Sarah said you had a key to close up." She moved out of the way for him to do his job. "When you're done here, can you radio the guards to pull the stand up to the dunes? Then, tell them to take off. What do we do tomorrow?"

"Depends on how bad the damage is here and in town. Matt probably will open a bit later. Gives us time to get things up and running. That's if there's no major flooding and the weather is good. Sure am glad it's going to hit at low tide."

"Why's that?"

"There's a slim chance the water will break through the dunes. Don't know if the beach can take much more erosion." Taking a screwdriver out of his pocket, Tyler looked at her questioningly, "You look anxious, Meg. Anything I can help with?"

Meg uncrossed her arms. Body language meant everything and the last thing she wanted was for Tyler to think there was something going. Her mind, however, had been off on a tangent, thinking Matt might be in the process of doing something stupid after their talk last night. She hoped he'd understood the protocol he had to follow and hadn't gone snooping into things he knew nothing about. Her biggest fear was Matt would tip Draper off that he was under investigation.

"No." Meg sat down and leaned back in the captain's chair behind Matt's desk. "Just a bit nervous I think about this kind of storm and its ramifications to the club. Living up north we deal with tons of snow and blizzards. But you know best since you've been through this before. Let me know what to do."

Tyler smiled as he reached for the crank to pull the shutter closed. "Take my advice. It's a good night to hunker down. I've got a scanner in my car. I'm heading over to see if anybody needs help mooring boats at the marina. If the main man shows up that's where he can reach me. Have him call my cell." Tyler patted Meg on the shoulder reassuringly and walked out the office.

"Take care." Meg called after him, but Tyler was gone. She studied the office layout one last time. She'd spent that morning memorizing where things were and what remained under lock and key. She also made sure Sarah had taken the club's laptop, passwords, and insurance records Meg had found in a file folder inside Matt's desk when she'd left for Fox Hollow.

Meg shut the door behind her and made her way down the stairs to the entrance of the club. Looking up, she saw that the navy blue and white striped awning that said "Sunfish Beach Club" had been removed in anticipation of the impending windstorm.

Eyeing her Bug in the parking lot, she was surprised to see Matt leaning against the driver's side door looking none too pleased. Why hadn't he come into the club?

Meg strode up to her car. "You don't look happy." Not seeing his car nearby, she said, "I take it you need a lift?"

Matt retorted sarcastically taking her by surprise. "As a matter of fact,

Einstein, I do. My BMW… over there," he pointed to the emergency lane of the bridge, "is d-e-a-d. Dead. I think someone siphoned the gas out."

Meg's ears perked up, alert. "What? Surely you're mistaken? Maybe the gauge is off and you didn't keep track when the light came on." Matt glared at her. Backtracking to break the tension, she said, "Well, I guess you are sure. Do you think this might be related to what's been happening?"

"It crossed my mind now that I know. But right now I can't think about the car. It's going to be towed back to the estate. With the storm coming, I need to run over to the yacht club to check on Ethan's boat. I knew you and Tyler would close up, so I told him I'd take care of it. But I just wanted to check on the club first, just in case. Ethan's at the country club and can't get away. He's got as much riding on that place as I do here." Matt kicked at a clamshell with the toe of his shoe. "So given the circumstances, can I hitch a lift over there?"

"Like I'm going to say no?" Meg tossed Matt the keys to the Bug. "But you're going to have to drive. I always get lost along that stretch of Oneck."

Buckled into the passenger seat, Meg watched Matt try to fold his large frame into the small car. He started the engine and headed for the bridge. The drawbridge rose for an oncoming sailboat headed in the direction of the marina, putting the fleeing beach traffic at a virtual standstill. Large rain drops began to pelt the car's windshield.

Meg pointed out the driver's side window. "What's going on over there? Looks like something's happening on the water." There was a beehive of activity in the distance she couldn't make out.

"That's weird." Meg saw Matt's furrowed brow.

"What is?"

"That's over by the Medina residence. The National Junior Women's Sailing Competition was supposed to start this afternoon. But I can't believe the boats are out on the water given the wind and approaching storm."

"Isn't that dangerous?"

"Yes. It's irresponsible to put anyone on the water today."

The drawbridge lowered and Matt drove past the flashing lights.

"I wish I'd unhooked my scanner from my car. I'd know what was going on. Hold on."

Within minutes, after passing three cars by crossing a double yellow line and careening around one very sharp curve, Matt turned the Bug into the drive of the Hampton Beach Yacht Club. Cars lined the drive, most parked askew, not in their designated parking places. Meg became alarmed when she saw that the parking lot was chaotic. People were rushing toward the front of the clubhouse, which overlooked Moriches Bay. A Hampton Beach rescue truck pulled up next to her car, red lights flashing. Out jumped Sam Johnson and his crew, who pulled rescue ropes and flotation devices out of the back of the vehicle.

Matt called out, "Sam, what the hell is going on?"

The rush of the wind in the reeds and the pounding of rain on metal made it hard to hear. "Boats are overturned," Sam called out. "Couple girls were able to swim to the buoys, but somebody's injured. Grab our backboard, Matt! Bring it to the dock. The Coast Guard chopper has an ETA of two minutes."

"Where's the police boat?"

"Stuck at the marina. A boat capsized coming in from the bay. Damn, we're stretched thin." Sam hurried off to catch up with his men.

"Come on. Help me with the board." Matt tugged hard on Meg's arm and led her to the truck. The wind worked against them as they struggled to maintain their grip on the long board as they pulled it from the back of the rescue vehicle. "We've got to get bayside," Matt called out.

Buffeting the winds, she and Matt managed to get the board to Sam's crew. Meg estimated the sustained wind speed to be around thirty miles per hour. Neither of them was dressed appropriately for the soaking they would obviously get from the black rainclouds overhead. Concentrating on weaving her way to the crowded dock area to drop off the backboard, Meg noticed people scrambling for lawn furniture that had blown into the club's pool.

However, the main action that drew Meg's, and everyone else's attention, was out on the water. Trying to see through the light fog, Meg could barely make out the three buoys set up in a triangular formation. From the shoreline, she could make out the five sailboats, all capsized. Two female sailors clung to one of the buoys waiting for rescue. Two others bobbed up and down in the choppy waters, holding onto a lifeless form. The farthest buoy bobbed and weaved in the choppy wake of the water, tossing its rider like a cowboy on a bull ride.

Chaos reined everywhere. Parents searched for missing children as the rescue squad made announcements over the public address system. As Meg followed Matt to the dock, she barely heard the commands being relayed to the crowd. The people surrounding her were obviously distressed.

"Korey!" One distraught woman screamed as she stood at the shoreline looking out towards the buoy. Another woman tried to offer the woman comfort in the time of crisis. Oh no, Meg thought. Her child must be one of the girls in peril and need of rescue.

Suddenly, the roar of a helicopter coming into the airspace overhead had all heads turning in its direction. She watched the crew of the SAR chopper set their position for the rescue of the two people trying to aid in the rescue of the lone swimmer.

"Matt!" Sam called to Matt over the roar of the noise around them. He motioned Matt to the Boston Whaler that rocked back and forth from the turbulence of the waves hitting the dock.

Meg stood motionless, watching Matt run to where Sam was making his way down the dock to the boat. It was then she saw Matt gesture at Sam toward the bay.

"No!" Meg silently cried. An irrational fear for what she thought he was about to do overtook her. Her heart lodged in her throat. What was wrong with her? Meg herself had been in far more dangerous scenarios. But it was her fear for Matt, that he was putting himself in harm's way, that got to her. She knew rationally he could handle himself. Why was she so afraid? Why? Because Matthew Hallock had gotten under her skin and into her heart. He'd invaded that space she closed a long time ago.

Meg's natural instinct was to aid in the rescue effort. Considering all of the agencies in place to do their assigned jobs, she was better suited to help in whatever capacity she was needed.

But her legs wouldn't move; she stood rooted in place. Matt donned his life jacket and jumped into the boat. Sam quickly motioned to the driver and the boat sped off towards the buoy where two young sailors held on for dear life.

With Meg's rain-soaked clothes melded to her body, she watched as the boat crested and rolled with each wave that came its way. One extremely large surge of water broke across the Whaler's bow. The wind's velocity forced more and more white-capped waves to roll across the open water. The rain was now coming down in sheets, at times horizontally.

"Meg! Meg!"

Meg spun about hearing the familiar voice call for her the second time that day. Sarah. What was she doing here? Meg specifically gave her an order to go to Fox Hollow.

Meg swiped her windswept, wet hair from her face. "You're supposed to be on the North Fork!"

"I know. I stopped to check on my grandparents. That's when my scanner picked up that the rescue squad put out an all points bulletin for help for water rescues. I'll head out as soon as I'm not needed."

Meg pointed to the helicopter hovering above. "Is that the SAR crew? Sarah nodded. "Could those men be up in that chopper?"

"Maybe. Two crews cover this territory. But you and I aren't going to be able to see anything without binoculars."

Meg looked up as two SAR divers lowered themselves into the water and draped flotation devices around the two swimmers, who'd been holding onto the lifeless girl. Now hooked to ropes dropped from the chopper, one of the divers tugged on each line. Each girl held tightly to the guide rope as they were raised up and out of the water. Reaching the open door of the chopper, the girls were whisked safely inside.

Meg wasn't just going to stand there watching. She headed for the shoreline of the sandy beach with Sarah following close behind. "Can you identify anyone?" Police keeping the crowds back knew Sarah and allowed both of them closer access to the water's edge than the other spectators.

"Not in the chopper. But that diver," Sarah pointed to the man treading water with the lifeless form draped across his neck, "I could swear that's Jeff Draper."

Meg and Sarah watched as the two divers strapped the unresponsive body into the waiting basket that had been lowered. Sarah reached for and squeezed Meg's hand. The basket rose slowly swaying from the billowing wind but made its way to the waiting helicopter. The rescuers followed soon after. The chopper dipped its nose and took off heading north. The crowd burst into applause. Feeling an overwhelming sense of relief, Meg hoped the girl had only been knocked unconscious by the boon of the sailboat as it had inadvertently swung about in the rough seas.

"Where's the chopper headed?" Meg queried.

"Peconic Hospital. Then back to Gabreski." Sarah replied. "Do *not* think you're going there."

"What do you mean?"

Sarah eyed Meg warily. "Gabreski's off limits. You can't go there. If those SAR divers saw you, they'd wonder what your business is, especially if you're asking questions. If they're suspicious about anything at this point you would blow your cover." Sarah nudged her, bringing her attention back to the remaining rescue. "Look, Meg!"

"Sam and Matt got to the buoy!" Meg was caught up in the moment of the next rescue.

Sam eased himself over the side of the Whaler and was in the process of handing the girls up and over the side of his boat to Matt, who struggled to keep his balance. It wasn't an easy task, as the boat fought the rolling of the waves. With Sam safely back in the boat, the Whaler turned back toward the yacht club dock.

Sarah squeezed her hand tight. "See. I told you Matt would be fine. Matt's done a ton of ocean rescues, Meg. Never doubt his ability to get the job done."

Meg didn't hear Sarah's last comments as her eyes became fixed on the third buoy. Wasn't Sam planning to swing about and bring in the last girl? Why weren't he and Matt headed to her while the chance presented itself? Even from shore, Meg could tell the girl was growing tired and losing her grip on the green water marker.

Meg reacted the only way she knew how.

"Wait here, Sarah." Seeing a shocked look on Sarah's face, Meg took off on a run, her eyes in search of the Jet-Ski she'd seen sitting half in and out of the water earlier. She hoped the owner had beached the craft in a panic from the storm and had left it.

"Meg! No!" Meg heard Sarah, but she was determined to get to the girl. Matt was not going to be happy when he returned to shore. He'd told her specifically to wait for him where he'd left her.

As Meg approached the watercraft, she said a silent thank you. Wrapped around the handlebars was an adult lifejacket. Meg righted the Jet Ski, donned the vest and started the engine. She took off looking back over her shoulder at the shoreline. Now back at the dock with the rescued girl taken care of, Matt had come to stand next to Sarah who was pointing in the direction of the water.

In any rescue operation, time was a precious commodity. Meg couldn't stand idly by while the last girl clung in desperation waiting to be rescued. Meg took an oath to save lives, at any level, at any cost. Assessing the wave action and the path she needed to maintain, Meg thought fleetingly of the man on the shore. She'd just have to deal with the wrath of the "one-night-stand man" when she was back on shore.

CHAPTER SIXTEEN

Matt clenched his fists in an effort to maintain control of his temper. He didn't want Sam or Sarah to notice how furious he was with Meg's decision to ride the Jet-Ski to the outer most buoy. He had come to terms with her driving his boat chasing down criminals. In reality, though, knowing what she really did for a living still didn't make the thought of putting herself in danger any easier on him. Matt had to admit to himself that he was scared, even in a scenario like the one unfolding before him.

Thinking he could take Sam's Whaler and aid Meg in the rescue, Matt tried to make his way back to the dock but he was unsuccessful. Several members of the rescue squad who stood nearby spied what he was about to do and restrained him.

"Stop, Matt!" Sam Johnson barked at him as he struggled to break free from the grip of two firemen. With one eye on the water and one eye on Matt, Sam reprimanded him. "Meg's your chief guard. If she gets into trouble, we'll go out. I'm not risking anymore lives today." Sam pointed to where Meg approached the buoy on the Jet-Ski. "Meg is a professional. She has everything under control contrary to what you might think. Trust me. I have every faith she can handle what she's doing. If you haven't figured that out by now, you're dumber than I thought."

"Sam, you have no idea..." One very strange look from Sarah had Matt stopping what he was going to say for some unknown reason. "I'm going to wring her neck when she gets back on dry land." The rain hit Matt's face, blurring his vision. He wiped the water from his eyes and shoved his hands in his pockets otherwise he might be tempted to haul off and hit someone. Normally cool, calm and collected, Sarah stared at him as if he'd grown four heads. "What?" Matt glared at his manager. "I'm not happy. *You* could have stopped her."

"Oh yeah. Like that would have worked." Sarah smirked. "You don't know her as well as you think you do, boss."

"Oh? Then, why don't you tell me? What don't I know about Megan Spears?" *Besides the fact that she's a trained CIA agent.*

No response was forthcoming. Sarah went so far as to look the other way. After rapidly scanning the water, she dropped her head and stared at the ground. What was with her? Did she know about Meg? No. Matt couldn't believe she did. It was impossible.

Sarah glanced up and glared at him. Placing her hands on her hips, she spat out, "For your information, Meg's performed at least ten Jet-Ski rescues with the Lake Placid Fire Department. And she won two commendations for bravery in the process." Sarah bobbed her head at him as if to say 'beat that.'

Matt arched his eyebrow knowing full well that wasn't true. Where the hell had she dug up that resume? "And how do you know that?"

"For heaven's sake! I read her personnel file and references. Why do you think Tyler pushed hard for her to be chief guard? So, with all due respect, I think you should trust she knows what she's doing."

So that's what they all think. Great cover. He was relieved to find out Sarah knew nothing about Meg's true role at the club. With his eyes still following her movements on the water, Matt imagined Meg jet-skiing her way through the rivers and canals of Europe, aka James Bond. He just shook his head thinking of what they'd been through the other night.

"Here, Matt. Take this." Matt's rambling thoughts were interrupted by one of the firemen offering blankets retrieved from the rescue truck.

"Thanks." Matt shivered as he wrapped the wool blanket around himself and helped Sarah into hers. The elements were getting to him. If the rain, wind, and cold breeze were taking their toll on him, Meg was taking it head on out in the water. Hypothermia could set in if she didn't get back to shore soon. God, this day needed to be over. Matt wanted Meg safe. And safe and secure meant was to be with him.

When had the relationship with Meg come to mean more than a summer fling? His dreams were filled lately of long evening walks at Jetty Four every night at sunset walking hand in hand with her. Were his brothers right? Was Meg his soul mate?

Sarah gasped bringing everyone's attention back to the buoy, its red beacon flashing. "Look at Meg! She made it!" Sarah jumped gleefully up and down adjusting her blanket, which was falling off her shoulders.

Matt watched mesmerized as Meg rolled the Jet Ski with the waves. She masterfully rode the watercraft, like a surfer in competition, calculating the exact moment to catch the curl to make her way to make a pass by the buoy. She circled the marker twice, sizing up the water, the wave action, and wind direction. Sarah had been right. Meg had done this before.

"Sam!" Matt called out to his friend. "Get that boat ready to go."

"Calm down, Matt. Meg's doing fine. Hell, I wish I had her on the department's roster."

Matt told himself when Meg returned to shore, they would have a long talk about *his* risk tolerance. Hell, she was CIA. He was *not*. Matt had zip, zero, none, nada.

On her final approach to the marker, Matt's heart hammered in his chest. One wrong move and Meg would be hurled into the buoy. Meg managed to maneuver close enough for the girl to lunge onto the back of the Jet-Ski. Seeing a large wave start to form behind the craft, the crowd on shore let out a collective gasp. The curling wall of water seemed as if it would crash onto them. But, Meg instinctively turned the craft at the right angle. Riding the jet ski as a surfboard, she rode the crest of the wave bringing her and the young girl closer to shore. The teenager clung to Meg's waist, her head burrowed in Meg's back. Meg gave a "thumbs up" signal to the waiting crowd.

Within seconds, Sam Johnson's crew met them at the water's edge. Meg beached the craft, handing her rider off to the rescue personnel. Matt panicked when both Meg and the girl disappeared from his line of sight.

Grabbing Sarah's arm, Matt said, "Come on! I've got to talk to her."

As they came around the side of the yacht club, Matt saw the rescued girl being strapped onto a stretcher. A waiting ambulance was in place to take her to be checked out at the hospital. A tearful, but grateful mother hugged Sam and his crew. Matt's eyes scanned the onlookers, but Meg was nowhere to be found.

Spotting Sam, he called out, "Sam! Where's Meg?"

A familiar voice popped up from behind. "What are you fussing about now, boss? Sam tells me you're not very happy with me. Says you were ready to punch out a few of his men."

Matt spun around and stared down into a pair of twinkling brown eyes. As mad as he was, Matt was never so happy to see anyone in his entire life. Meg stood wrapped in a fire department-issued blanket, shaking not only from the cold, but because she was laughing...at him!

Matt's temper got the better of him. "Get in the car!" he bellowed. Everyone within earshot stopped to stare.

"What?" Meg stood, stunned. "You can't be serious. I need to be checked out." Her face reddened as she checked her temper. No doubt she was fuming at his "take charge" attitude. But this time, *she* was going to listen to *him* for a change.

Matt grabbed her elbow. There was no way he was letting her have her way or get away. "I said... *get-in-the-car*. We're going home. Mother can check you out."

Meg struggled to release herself from his firm grasp, but was unsuccessful. She glared up at him. "I'll hitch a ride with somebody else. I'm not going anywhere with *you*. Not the way you're acting." Meg pulled the blanket more tightly around her. "I'll go find Sarah. She'll take me."

"Uh, Meg…" Sam spoke up. Sarah stood next to him.

"What?" Meg barked sharply at the fire chief taking Matt by surprise. "Why can't Sarah give me a ride home? I'm not going anywhere with…*him*."

"Please." Sam pleaded. "Just go. Make our lives easier. We've got a lot more important things to tend to. Get him out of here."

Matt saw the disgusted look on her face. Meg spun on her heels and headed for where he had parked the Bug. Matt hurried after her and tried to open the passenger door, but she batted his hand out of the way. She opened the door herself, trying not to lose the grip she had on the blanket, slid into the passenger seat, and slammed the door so hard he thought the glass of the window would shatter.

Matt ran to the other side of the car and jumped into the driver's seat. Starting the car, he turned to her, "Meg…" He wanted her to know how much he cared. How he had worried. But, most importantly, how proud he was of her for saving that young girl's life.

As he was about to speak, Meg shot her hand up to ward off any conversation between them. "See this hand, Matt? Talk to the hand. Drive the damn car and get me back to the estate so I can dry off and warm up. I've had enough for one day."

"Meg, you've no idea—"

Once more the hand shot up. Matt knew when to quit. For now. He'd have his say eventually. He gunned the engine, taking off down the drive headed toward Hallock Farm. With one glance at the woman beside him, Matt thanked God for small miracles. Home wasn't too far away.

* * *

Word of Meg's heroic effort had reached Hallock Farm before Matt pulled in the driveway. Both his mother and Hannah rushed down the steps of the veranda and onto the brick pavement, waiting under a golf umbrella for Matt to steer the Bug into the circle in front of the house. Scared and thoroughly convinced Meg was in shock, Matt had reached for the OnStar button to call his parents to have Doc Davis on call.

Matt wasn't angry at Meg any longer, only with himself and his actions. He should have listened to her. But had he? No. Matt knew full well what appropriate medical protocol was called for when dealing with a water rescue and now he prayed he hadn't jeopardized her health because of his need to be in control…of her.

He couldn't fault Meg for being irate, but he would yell at her all over again if it meant she would know how important it was that she was safe at his side.

A sharp rap on the car window brought him out of his musings.

"Matthew! Matthew!" The look on his mother's face told him she was livid he wasn't paying attention. "What are you waiting for? We need to get Megan inside!"

Matt unlatched his door, shimmied out from behind the wheel, and raced around to the passenger's side door. Meg sat, shaking in her seat, her teeth chattering. Ducking his head, Matt reached in and gingerly scooped her up into his arms and made for the front door.

Helen Hallock and Hannah were right on his heels. "Come, Matthew. Take her upstairs. She needs to get out of those wet clothes." Issuing orders like a drill sergeant, the matriarch of the family continued, "Doc Davis will be here at any minute." Helen opened the door for Matt to enter the house, turning to speak to their housekeeper. "Hannah, usher Doc upstairs when he arrives. Bring me some of Robert's good strong brandy in that special storage cabinet you don't think I know about. We need to get this girl warm and dry."

As his mother held the door, Matt strode through to the foyer only to come to a dead stop. Standing at the foot of the stairs was a surprise Matt hadn't counted on. Derek Taylor walked toward him, arms outstretched...for Meg. Matt took a step back, not wanting to relinquish his precious cargo.

"I'll take it from here, Hallock." Not wanting to make a scene, Matt carefully placed Meg in Derek's care. "Thanks for seeing her safely back."

Interesting, Matt thought, that the "smile" on Derek's face wasn't reflected in his eyes. To be honest, it was more of a steely glare. And how had Derek known to be at the house? Things didn't add up. Now Matt was the thinking like a spy.

It was then Matt made a major decision he wasn't going to stand idly by while Derek whisked Meg away, taking his mother with him. If Meg called for him, he wanted to be there. Matt took a step forward. "I'll go with you, Mother. Doc will need to know what happened at the yacht club, how long she was in the water."

"Matthew," Helen came to stand between Matt and Derek, placing her hand lightly on her son's chest. "Get changed and have a brandy with your father in the study. You've been out in the rain and cold as long as Megan was." Matt's eyes dropped to where his mother's hand lay on his chest. He felt a subtle nudge, her signal for him to back away. "Everything here is under control."

"When can I talk to her?"

"When Doc says it's okay." His mother turned to Derek and said somewhat abruptly, "Mr. Taylor, follow me with Megan...*Now*... Then *you* may leave as well."

Matt felt a small sense of satisfaction at the uninviting tone in his mother's voice. It seemed to him, she hadn't planned on the man being at the house either. Matt hoped Derek Taylor would take the subtle hint and make a speedy exit. And knowing his mother, if Derek didn't leave, she'd be escorting the man out the front door personally.

Matt watched as Derek followed his mother up the stairs to the second floor. When the trio reached the landing, he heard his mother giving terse instructions for what Meg's "boyfriend" would do when they reached the bedroom and when Derek would be able to return to the family compound.

Chalk one up for his mother, Matt thought. Over the years, Matt had had serious differences with his father, but his mother had always been in his corner. She made sure he hadn't let the broodings of a bitter man force him from the family fold. If it hadn't been for the support he received from her and Aunt Elizabeth, Matt would have left Hampton Beach a long time ago and never looked back.

But times were different now. His sister, Kate, had married Special Agent John Clinton two years ago after a horrendous time the family never wanted to relive. But out of the horror of the events that led up to a happy ending came the apple of Matt's eye, his niece, Elizabeth Katherine Clinton. Life at Hallock Farm had changed for the better for everyone. Matt was no longer looked upon as the black sheep of the family. Robert Hallock earned back some of the respect he had lost within the Hampton Beach community and their society circle. Consequently, Matt actually could stand being in the same room with the man.

Hannah cleared her throat. "You're going to form a pond on my nice clean floor if you don't get out of those clothes."

Matt looked down to see the puddle at his feet. "Sorry, Hannah. I guess I better get a move on. I'll get changed and have that stiff drink with the old codger."

Hannah started walking toward the kitchen, Matt following behind her as the shortest way to the cottage was through the back door. "Your father's really not that bad. I'm more worried about that man upstairs." She glanced at Matt sending a suspicious look in his direction.

"Me, too, Hannah." When he made it to the back door, he turned and said, "I'll be back as quick as I can."

Matt left, running through the downpour, making a beeline for the back cottage. He would return to make sure Derek Taylor, like Elvis, had left the building.

* * *

Meg's head felt as if it was going to explode. She was dizzy, nauseous and momentarily unaware of where she was. But when Meg opened her eyes, she saw the look on Derek's face that told her he had something to tell her and the memories of the day came flooding back. But, how were they going to have a conversation with Mrs. H fussing over her? As Derek laid her on the bed and reached to take off her wet blanket, he attempted to whisper in her ear.

"Ahem!" Helen politely coughed. "I'll take things from here, Mr. Taylor. You know your way out." Matt's mother pointed to the door. Derek abruptly stood up. Looking down at Meg, he blinked twice—the signal they'd talk later. Helen moved closer to the bed. "I'll call when Megan can have visitors. Doc Davis will want to give her a thorough physical and see she rests."

Derek backed away as Meg motioned for him to leave. She said in a raspy voice, "It's okay, honey. Mrs. H will take good care of me. I'll call you soon."

"Call my cell. We need to make our plans for the weekend." Derek leaned over and kissed her on the cheek. Meg cringed at his touch and prayed Helen didn't see the expression on her face.

Meg was growing increasingly concerned about her growing dislike and mistrust of the man. Feeling isolated, she had no one to share her inner most thoughts with. Yes, there were Jake and Samantha, but she needed a sounding board in the upper hierarchy of the Agency. Hearing the door finally close, Meg's mind reeled with the possibilities of how she'd meet up with him later and who she'd sent to Fox Hollow… Sarah.

"Seems to me, you should have given your man a more proper kiss."

Matt's mother didn't miss a thing. In the time Meg had spent with Helen Hallock, she'd found out the woman was one strong-willed, determined lady. She ran the house with an iron fist and even though her kids were grown, they came running when she told them to. God help anyone who went after her five children for any reason. She protected each one like a lioness protects her cub.

Meg pretended not to hear. Weak, she struggled to sit up in bed but fell back onto the pillows. Helen was immediately by her side. Within seconds, Helen had changed Meg into a flannel nightgown and covered her with several blankets and a heavy down comforter. But the cold still ran rampant through her bones. Nausea and dizziness overwhelmed her. Meg knew the symptoms of shock. Her body had taken a pounding from the water and the elements during the rescue. It was so unlike her to feel this way. Her body had been through worse. But every joint and bone ached. It took every amount of effort to try to move.

Meg looked up into a pair of caring, brown eyes as she felt soft hands helping her get settled. "Mrs. Hallock, I'm so sorry," she whispered in a husky, hoarse voice.

"Whatever for, dear?" The woman continued to fuss.

"I won't take another chance like that." Meg was rambling. "Please tell Matt not to be too mad at me."

Helen sat on the edge of the bed. "Oh Megan, you've got it all wrong. Matt wasn't mad. He was scared. Frightened, really. Everything will be all right. You'll see." Tears formed at the corner of Meg's eyes. She tried to swipe them away but Helen had seen them. "Shush now. You need rest. The doctor will be here soon. He'll look you over better than the vet checks out those horses over at the farm."

Both women chuckled at the small joke.

Helen plumped her pillows and Meg leaned back, pulling the downy comforter up under her chin for warmth. The shiver and chills started to subside. But Meg still couldn't think straight. She fought the urge to fall asleep as her eyelids drifted closed.

"Drink this." Meg's eyes popped open to find Helen standing by the side of the bed, a brandy snifter in her hand. "Don't sip it. Take one big swallow. 'Down the hatch' as the saying goes. Your insides will be warm in no time."

Meg followed orders. The liquid left a burning sensation from her throat to her stomach. Meg sucked in her breath as the brandy worked its magic. Warmth spread throughout every extremity. It was like the zing she got from eating her major stash of dark chocolate, only better. Mother Hallock sure knew the perfect medicine to take the chill away. Meg smacked her lips together, holding the glass out for a refill.

Helen laughed. "No, my dear. Not unless the doctor says it's okay. Lord, it's been awhile since we've had a heart pounding day around here." Meg watched Helen take hold of Meg's glass, fill it with another shot of the brandy and down it in one gulp. She, too, licked her lips. "Robert's secret stash sure hits the spot." Helen placed the glass on the nightstand.

Helen clasped one of Meg's cold hands in hers. "Here's my take, Megan, on your... dilemma. Matthew was scared for one very simple reason. My son is falling in love with you, if he hasn't already. Believe me when I tell you I've seen him with many women over the years. You're the only one who brings out the best in him."

Meg knew what Helen was telling her was true. Her feelings mirrored his, but she didn't need an affirmation from someone else. She needed her mind on her mission and on the life she'd carved out for herself within the Agency. Her dreams of what she truly wanted died the day her parents had been killed. Helen's take on Matt's behavior of the day's events was too much. Meg broke down, a torrent of tears, matching the rain pelting on the bedroom windows, coursing down her cheeks.

Helen did what she did best by embracing Meg in a motherly hug. The harder Meg cried, the tighter Matt's mother held her.

Meg would have been surprised to know the Hallock matriarch had no doubt in her mind that Megan Spears was falling in love with her son as well. The young woman just didn't know it yet.

CHAPTER SEVENTEEN

Matt struggled to put on his sweat pants and flannel shirt as he body stiffened from the cold and chill. He donned a pair of running sneakers as he briefly looked out the window. In the brief time he'd been gone from the main house, the storm had intensified. Trees twisted and bent from side to side, rain blasted the windows. Visibility to all parts of the farm was limited.

Not caring about the wet clothes he'd left in the bedroom, and not wanting to be miss out when news came about Meg, Matt pulled on the rain slicker he kept hanging on the back of his front door. Hoping, but doubting, the coat would keep him dry, he made a run for the back patio steps and launched himself through the back door and into the kitchen. He took Hannah by surprise when the wind slammed the door shut. As usual, in a moment of crisis, the woman had pots and pans strewn over every counter and figuratively cooking up her own storm.

"Heard from your siblings?" Hannah asked as she moved from sink to refrigerator to stove. During any major storm she was always concerned about those on the island. She'd been with the Hallock family for more than forty years. She'd come to the estate as a young maid when Helen and Robert had married. It had been a stroke of good "fortune," for the young girl from Ireland, that the head chef fell ill one evening and she was forced to step into the role of cook, saving the dinner party. The night had been deemed a raving success by Hampton society standards and the rest was history.

Matt hung his wet coat on a hook by the back door. "Thomas is hunkered down in South Hampton. Ethan secured the golf course and is praying he's not going to have to close for a long length of time if the trees topple onto the fairways. He may be over later. He asked if you might save him a plate, if that's not too much to ask. Good thing we've still have power, huh?"

Hannah nodded as she lifted a roasting pan from the oven. "Yes. I wouldn't want to listen to your father if I couldn't cook, especially dinner."

"Is Meg still upstairs?" Matt didn't rush out of the room to be with the others thinking Hannah would be kept abreast of any news from his mother.

"Doc just came down." Having placed the pan on the top of the stove, she turned to look at him. Wiping her hands on her apron, she placed them on her hips. From her body language, Matt knew Hannah never missed an opportunity to speak her mind. "From the look on your face, and the number of questions you've asked, I'd say you're mighty fond of that girl, Matthew. For the record, I like her. Very much, I don't mind telling you. She's one tough young woman. Got a lot on the ball. If you ask me, I think you've met your match." The corners of Hannah's mouth playfully twitched into a grin as she returned to fixing dinner. He watched as she mashed the potatoes in a huge tin pot atop the kitchen island. If Hannah knew anything regarding Meg's condition, she wasn't going to tell him. "Best head to the study. Your mother ordered up hot toddies."

"Who's here?" Matt approached the door leading to the hallway. *Please do not let Derek Taylor be waiting around.* He hoped his mother had shown the man the way out.

"Some members of the rescue squad…and Sarah. Your mother insisted Sarah bring her grandparents here for the duration of the storm but they wanted to stay in their home." Hannah shooed him away with her kitchen towels. "Go! I've got to serve supper."

Matt left thinking of Hannah's comments. Meg had ingratiated herself everywhere at Hallock Farm, from Hannah, to his parents, to the people who worked the thoroughbred racing facility. As Matt reached the study, the cacophony of chatter came through the open door. Matt took one glance up the grand staircase in the front foyer wondering if he should take a chance and check in on her. Setting aside the idea for later, he entered his father's hallowed chamber. Only in times of emergencies did the man ever let the room be used to entertain visitors.

Standing inside the doorway was Sarah. "Matt! You're here!" She lunged at him, wrapping her arms around him in a bear hug. *Where had that come from?*

"Whoa." Almost knocked off his feet, he steadied himself, looking down at the woman at his side. Conversations ceased. Breaking the silence, Matt asked, "What's going on with our patient?" He didn't care if his question sounded a tad impatient.

Matt eyed Doc helping himself to a hot toddy from a tray on the coffee table. Doc looked quite comfortable sitting in one of the black leather wing chairs.

"Doc? Meg's going to be all right, isn't she? No bad after effects?" Matt badgered the older man with his questions.

Doc simply smiled and sipped the hot liquid. Doc Davis was a true Hampton

Beach legend. The man didn't own a car and practiced out of his home. All he had to do was call and someone would take him to wherever he needed to go. He'd even been seen hiking the twenty-five mile stretch of highway from Hampton Beach to Peconic Hospital, but never had to walk the entire way. Every one knew him, invariably picking him up along the main road what lead from Hampton Beach to Riverhead, making sure he got to his patients. East Hampton, Southhampton and Bridgehampton all had their concierge doctors, but Hampton Beach had Doc. And that's the way the villagers liked it.

Doc brought Matt into the world and saw him struggle to become a man in his own right. Doc was one of the few people who fully understood his life had not been easy living in the shadows of three very successful brothers and one over bearing father.

The elder gentleman took another long sip of the toddy and finally replied, "Megan's going to be fine."

Matt didn't realize how tense he was until he heard the doctor give him the good news. He sighed in relief. "Is there anything we need to do to make her more comfortable?"

Matt missed the look his father gave his mother who winked at his wife, a knowing smiled on her face.

"Come on, Doc. You're not giving me much to go on."

"Matt, you know the rules about doctor-patient confidentiality. I'm not allowed to discuss Megan's health. Those damn HIPA laws." Doc eyed Matt over the brim of his mug. "Come to think of it, I've never seen *you* so concerned over a woman... maybe an injured surfer or a farm employee." Matt took in the gleam in the man's eyes.

Doc was baiting him. Matt chose his words carefully. "Surely Mother knows what we need to do for Meg over the next day or so?"

"Yes." Doc Davis replied and continued to sip his beverage. Matt grew frustrated with the man's one-word replies.

Matt turned to his mother who stood by the fireplace. "Mother, what's Meg's status?"

Helen eyed him thoughtfully. "Megan is exhausted. She needs rest and a good hot meal." Addressing the small group, she said, "I hope you will all think about staying for dinner before you head back out. Hannah's prepared a Yankee pot roast." His mother looked to where he stood with Sarah at his side. "As for Megan, Matthew, she's tucked up in bed, per doctor's orders. When she wakes, Hannah will be sure she eats."

"Mother," Matt lost his patience and ground out, "Isn't there anything *we* can do?"

"Don't you mean what can *you* do, dear?" His mother grinned slyly back at him. Touché. His mother had figured out his ulterior motives in regards to the woman who lay in his old bed upstairs. Matt blushed. Seeing the crowd glance at each other, he knew they suspected there was more behind the sparring of comments between mother and son.

"Did Doc forget to mention that Megan asked to see you? You must be hard of hearing… Or perhaps with all the commotion, it slipped his mind."

Matt bolted from the room the moment he heard "see you." Those left in his wake snickered as they heard his footsteps pound up the main staircase. The man was a goner.

* * *

Matt lightly tapped on the bedroom door. If Meg had awakened, she would answer. If she hadn't, he would quietly check in on her anyway. Meg had asked to see him, *not* Derek Taylor.

Matt gingerly turned the doorknob and opened the white six-paneled door, poking his head inside the room. The only light came from a small hurricane lamp sitting on Meg's dressing table. It cast a soft glow throughout. Meg lay propped up on the pillows of the wide double bed, her eyes closed.

Matt promised himself he would only check on her if she was sleeping, but he found himself whispering, "Meg? You awake?"

Meg's eyelids fluttered open. His instinct told him the look on her ashen face had to be from worrying about something.

"Get in here." Meg's hoarse voice commanded. Matt was beside her in an instant. "You've got to get me out of here, Matt. The sooner the better." She held out her hand to him, the other clutched the downy comforter to her chest.

Matt enfolded her cold, clammy hand within in his own. "Meg, honey, you don't look good." There were dark circles under her eyes. "You can't go anywhere right now. Your body's recuperating. Hypothermia can hit hard even when someone is in great shape."

Meg's eyes darted to the doorway. "You don't get it. I've got to go to work. *Tonight*. It can't wait."

She's got to be delirious. If Meg thought she was leaving to go off and play spy given her health and the weather outside, she had another thing coming. He'd personally see to it.

Matt noticed she was shaking beneath the large, down comforter. His professional first-aid training kicked into high gear. "You still cold?" Matt asked, alarmed. "I can't believe you haven't warmed up. Did you take a hot shower?"

"No." Her teeth chattered as she answered.

To hell with what was proper or not. Matt didn't have time to wait. Pushing the blankets to the end of the bed, he scooped Meg into his arms for the second time that day and headed for the private bathroom adjacent to his old room. Having opened the shower door, he adjusted the shower's temperature as he struggled to balance Meg within his grasp. He tested the temperature as

Meg sagged against him.

Gripping her waist firmly, Matt instructed, "Get in this hot water. Now."

Meg's only reaction was to stand and nod meekly.

"Can you take your clothes off?" Matt tried to hold her upright but the weight of her body worked against him. Was she able to make sense of the urgency of what needed to be done?

Meg shook her head, looking up at him, her brown eyes pleading for help. If Meg couldn't help herself, he'd have to do it for her. He whisked off her flannel nightgown. His breath caught at the sight of her. Tamping down the yearnings he felt just by looking at her naked body, Matt proceeded to pull her under the spray of the hot water. Holding her upright, he did the only thing that made sense before he dropped her. Stepping in behind her, still fully clothed, he anchored her to his body, allowing the hot water to work its magic on the woman in his arms.

Meg leaned back, resting her head on his shoulder, mumbling, "Soap."

Meg was coming around. He prayed she had enough strength to lather herself, if not, Matt was going to need to beat a hasty retreat in search of a cold shower when he finished tending to her.

"Do you think you can take it from here?"

Meg nodded. Matt took the lavender scented bar out of the soap dish and placed it in her hands. Knowing she had a hold on it, he felt it was safe to back slowly out of the stall. But he was too sure of himself and was totally prepared for what came next.

"Stay," she whispered, the steam whirling around them. "Please." Meg's smoky dark eyes locked onto his, her husky voice reeling him in.

Check yourself. Keep your mind out of her pants, or lack of.

"Meg, honey. You're okay. Hold onto the towel bar. I'm going to get some towels to dry us off."

Meg's hand shot out, grabbing his wrist, her grasp much stronger than he imagined for a woman in her condition. What was she thinking? He was only human, a flesh and blood man with a hard on who'd do anything if tempted. But with Meg? Now? Meg was special. Not like any of the other women who'd walked through his life.

Matt came out of his dream like state as it became impossible for him to keep his eyes from wandering over her naked body. Her breasts were full and plump, nipples pert and pink. Water trickled over the firm mounds to the triangle of hair between her thighs.

An image of a baby suckling at his mother's breast flashed through his mind. The baby was Megan and the baby was his. Feeling like he'd been punched in the solar plexis, he tried to pull away, but her previous dazed look changed into one of smoldering desire.

"Come." Her voice seduced him.

Matt lost his internal struggle to stay away from the temptation she posed. This woman was no damsel in distress. With one steamy look, Meg lured him in—hook, line, and sinker. Throwing caution to the wind, Matt took a deep breath and stepped back into the shower stall.

"Can you lather my back?"

Matt totally forgot he was still dressed and took the soap she offered, doing as she asked. His hands glided over her sculpted body, starting at her shoulders, moving down the small of her back and cupping her trim buttocks, pulling her up against his hard erection. It was useless to try and concentrate on anything but the feelings this woman evoked in him. Meg was perfection, inside and out. She wormed her way into that special place in his heart where no other woman had been before.

Meg had to be aware by now how her nearness affected him. As she finished washing herself in the most intimate places, his arousal strained against the front of his wet flannel running pants.

"Are you feeling better?" Matt asked, his voice wavered as he clung onto every ounce of control before things got out of hand. "Let's dry off. Get you back in that bed."

Meg abruptly turned one hundred and eighty degrees and faced him, catching him off guard, her naked body pressed against his chest. They fit together as if by design. Matt swallowed hard as he met the smoldering gaze of her deep brown eyes.

Meg reached up, her hands stroked the sides of his face.

"What are you doing?" *You know perfectly well what she's doing.*

"I think *you* need to get out of those clothes before *you* go into shock." Meg's voice was raspy, husky. Then, she winked. Color had returned to her cheeks, the twinkle of something yet to come danced in her eyes.

"Meg…" Matt still tried to be the gentleman. "We need to talk."

Meg shook her head and slid her arms around his waist, resting her head on his chest. He could hardly hear her when she whispered, "No. I have a better good idea."

Releasing one hand from his waist, she slowly slid her fingertip along the bulging ridge of his pants. Matt groaned, placing his hand over hers showing her how he liked it.

"Meggie, you know where this will go if I don't go now. I have feelings for you. Do you *really* want this?" Matt tipped Meg's chin up with his forefinger. "Tell me…yes or no?"

Meg didn't need to say the words; her eyes spoke volumes. "Stay." Matt's heart melted.

Meg had complete power over him. He stood mesmerized as she slid his pants to the shower floor. When she rose, Matt stood naked having rid himself of his shirt. His mouth dipped down, swiping his tongue over her lips. She playfully bit his lower lip and opened her mouth. As her body nestled against his, her breasts brushed his chest. Matt had wanted Meg since he met her. He gave himself over to her ministrations. Meg's right finger traced a path down his torso through the light sprinkle of chest hair. An electric sizzle raced through his body as Meg pinched his nipple, traveling on, circling his navel as she neared her ultimate destination. When Meg wrapped her hand around his erection, Matt sucked in his breath knowing he had to stop her.

"Honey, it will be over before we get started if you don't stop. Come to bed."

"No." Meg bit playfully at his ear lobe. "No bed. I need you inside of me… here… now."

Matt needed no further encouragement. He lifted Meg off her feet and placed her against the shower wall, her long, tan legs locked around his waist. Nestled between her thighs, the tip of his penis brushed against her. "Can you feel what you do to me?"

Meg brought his mouth to hers for a scorching kiss. At his breaking point, Matt plunged into her. She was tight. She was sweet. She was slick. More importantly, Meg was his.

Firmly grasping her buttocks, he slid in and out of her, each time pushing deeper and deeper, thrusting, the feeling of utter desire made his body hum.

"Faster," Meg moaned as she bit his earlobe.

"Meggie." Matt suckled her breast.

The wind, lightening, and thunder unified in an explosion as the two became one. Meg shuddered as he spilled his seed in her. It had *never* been like this. Never. How could he tell her? Would she believe him? Could he convince her of the plans he had for them? Matt didn't want to share Megan Spears with her country. Life in the fast lane of the CIA was no place for her. Her life was with him. Here in Hampton Beach. Matt had to convince her.

"I think the time for that cold shower was ten minutes ago." Matt looked down to see Meg's eyes sparkling, a devilish, satisfied grin on her face.

Matt suddenly realized he'd been totally oblivious as his backside took the brunt of the now tepid water. It would only take a second to shut off the shower and dry off.

"Meg, we need to talk." But by the time Matt finished toweling himself dry, he realized he had been talking to an empty room. Meg had left him behind, dropping her towel on the bathroom floor. She'd made a run for the warmth of the quilt that lay on her bed. Sitting beneath the covers, she seductively curled her finger, inviting him to follow.

"Later." Meg folded back the edge of the comforter. "Doc says I have to stay really, really warm. And I think you're the perfect cure. Care to join me?"

Matt didn't need a second invitation. He dove under the covers, taking her in his arms. "About what you wanted me to do…"

Meg snuggled into his shoulder. "Later. Not now." A soft jab of her elbow met his ribcage. "And don't forget my date, Hallock."

Matt kissed the top of her head. Pretending he had forgotten, he asked, "We had a date?"

Meg sighed. "Men! Remember? You said you would take me to see the village action at the Marakesh."

And there it was. The job. The woman had a one-track mind. Had what they'd just experienced meant nothing more than sex? God, he hoped not.

Matt wanted to make Meg forget everything but him. The moan that escaped Meg's lips the second time he kissed her had nothing to do with the clubbing and dancing he'd promised. It was from the sensation of his nibbling a trail of kisses on what was now a very warm body. He was determined to do so way into the night.

As Matt and Meg lay safe from the storm's fury being unleashed outside, he felt confident that all was well for the night. But Matt had seen the look on her face before he'd turned out the light. The one that told him Megan Spears was plotting and planning. Matt had news for her. He had no plans for her to blow out of his life now that she was truly his.

CHAPTER EIGHTEEN

Fox Hollow Inn

"Aren't you a sight for sore eyes, lass." Reggie stood up from the kitchen table as Meg walked in the back door with Sarah trailing close behind. "Hang up your coat and I'll get you something hot to drink." After the last twenty-four hours, Meg had little energy to argue. She had a job to get done. "Victoria and I were mighty worried. Sarah said we wouldn't be seeing you tonight." Meg noted the fatherly look of concern etched across his brow. "Says you were told to stay in bed. Doctor's orders."

Sarah obviously had been in touch. Funny, Meg thought. Reggie didn't seem at all surprised or question the younger agent's present involvement with the Sunfish and Operation Hurricane, much less showing up at Fox Hollow.

"Yeah, those were the doc's orders. But there's work to be done that should have been accomplished this afternoon." Meg glanced over her shoulder at Sarah, who looked up at the ceiling.

"Don't even go there, Reggie." Sarah's warning tone had Reggie looking from Meg to Sarah and back again. Sarah shook her shoulders out of the yellow rain jacket and hung it on a hook by the back door. "I was sound asleep in my bed when Meg woke me to come here. Scared the living crap out of me. Nothing like opening your eyes to see your own Sig Sauer pointing down at you."

"Weren't you scheduled to be here earlier?" Reggie asked as he put a teapot on the stove.

Sarah nodded. "Yes, but with the storm I got stuck over at the farm. Mrs. H wasn't going to let me go anywhere except to check in on Gramps and Gram."

Reggie retorted, "Then I'm surprised you couldn't convince Meg to stay put on a night like this."

"You try it someday." Sarah sat down at the table and cast a glance in Meg's direction. Meg merely stared back.

Meg finally took a seat, not wanting to nit pick the details of why she'd showed up at Fox Hollow in the storm against doctor's orders. She'd lost a ton of time and it needed to be made up. "Well, it certainly was a hell of a ride. Good thing Sarah thought to take the Jeep. We were off the roads more than we were on them."

Reggie placed mugs on the table. "When Sarah called to tell me the two of you were on your way, and what you needed done, we started the research on the backgrounds of those men on your list. There's a buzz of activity downstairs."

The tea kettle whistled as Victoria entered the room that smelled of freshly baked scones. "Oh, thank goodness!" She embraced both Meg and Sarah in a motherly hug. "You two finally got here! My heart's been racing since we knew you set out in this storm. Reggie and I have been watching the radar. The forecasters are predicting the storm may make its way off the coast by mid morning, if it continues on track off Montauk."

"Pays to have a place running with generators to help us access what we need," Meg stated.

"Couldn't afford to be without them," Reggie said. "Too much at stake. We can't afford to lose the use of the equipment."

Victoria let her hand drop away from Meg's shoulder and got to work pouring the hot water into the mugs. "I was sent up to tell you both Jake and Samantha have something of interest." Victoria looked at the clock over the stove. "Go and get to work. I'll bring down something to eat. It's going to be a long night. It won't take but a few minutes."

Meg watched as the woman methodically moved around the kitchen. Grabbing her own mug, Meg nodded in the direction of the secret staircase hidden behind a fake kitchen cabinet. "Let's get on it. We should have had our plan in place for the Director's approval hours ago."

Reggie and Sarah grabbed their cups and followed Meg to the secure room. The room, normally quiet and focused, was buzzing with a sense of urgency.

Jake and Samantha stood at a large fifty-inch video screen, watching pictures of faces rapidly click by. Both took copious notes from the information the split screen provided.

Jake turned as Meg walked up to the table. "Well, look what the cat dragged in." She returned the warm smile he sent her way knowing everyone had been overly concerned since the incident at the yacht club. "Seriously, what the hell made you think you had to come? Word has it you had a pretty rough day."

Meg set her mug on the table along with the manila folder she'd given Sarah that morning. "The Eagle, for one." She tapped the folder. "I think we may be onto a link between the money at the Sunfish and the Coast Guard drills at

Plum Island." Dangling her conjectures had Jake and Samantha's full attention. "I have a theory. I want to know if you think it's plausible, and, if so, what action are we going to take to close up this operation once and for all."

Samantha pointed at the map of the eastern end of Long Island laid out on the table. "I've got an idea as well. If our minds are headed in the right direction, we can finally set up the sting." Samantha paused and said, "Do you know if the Director is calling?"

Meg looked over her shoulder to see Reggie deep in a conversation with one of the agents at the security monitors. She tried to capture his attention but to no avail. He was deeply entrenched talking to the two men manning the screens, pointing at a visual. A notepad was in his hand as he scribbled furiously on it. What could have him so engrossed?

Meg turned her focus to the agents around her and busied herself withdrawing the photos from the folder. She spoke to Jake, "As soon as Reggie is finished, I'm sure he'll tell us. In the meantime, what have you been able to dig up from the info Sarah gave you?"

Jake motioned for her and Sarah to come and stand in front of the video screen. "Sarah was dead on with those four photos and the location."

Jake clicked the remote and brought up Jeff Draper's military ID. "Jeff, Steve, and Mike work with SAR along with the operations within the auxiliary. Steelers' MIT resume shows he does indeed have training in computer programming—hardware and software. I find that intriguing if we're dealing with someone accessing Plum Island and its research lab."

Meg's eyes searched the records displayed before her. She scanned the full-blown files for the first time. Her eyes darted from file to file as they whisked across the screen. "Haven't you found anything unusual? There's got to be something that links…"

Samantha laid a hand on Meg's arm.

"Jake! Stop! Back up two frames." Samantha pointed at the box in the left hand corner, circling it with the laser pointer she'd taken from his hand moments earlier. "See? Look…under 'specialties.'" Meg silently read the records as Samantha read out loud to the rest of the team who'd gathered around them. "There! Kranepool is trained and certified in climbing high mountain terrain and rescue operations. Click back to Draper's file."

Jake did as instructed. Meg saw immediately what Samantha was searching for. Jake then clicked onto Steve Baker's dossier, bringing up his military experience. Bingo! Bingo! Bingo!

Sarah let out a low whistle. "Well, would you look there? All three attended a tactical training program in Stone Mountain, Georgia several years ago. At the same time. What a coincidence. Huh, Meg?"

Meg knew at that moment it certainly was *not* a coincidence. "Perfect training for anyone planning to climb the sheer cliffs of Plum Island if they can manage to get to that side undetected." Meg was satisfied at having made a positive connection. "And a Coast Guard boat wouldn't be held back in the restricted waters, would it? The crew would have filed the appropriate paperwork to be there."

Sarah, who'd been silent since entering the room, responded, "Works into the theory the three might be the ones asking for the authorization for SAR training. We still need that confirmed. Did we find out who signed for permission to take the Coast Guard training vessel into restricted waters?"

"No. The DOD is still working on it." Jake said. "The paperwork's in the system. Personally, I think they're taking their own sweet time."

"Well, maybe the Director can hustle their asses a bit given the circumstances." It was then Sarah walked to the map Samantha had put on the table earlier. The girl traced her finger along a blue water pathway. "What are you doing?" Meg eyed her young agent curiously.

"Give me a minute. I'm thinking," Sarah replied.

Meg glanced back at Reggie, who had finished his conversation and was making his way toward them. But something was awry. His face was flushed. His eyes flashed daggers, not at the team, but something had him furious.

Meg continued on, fascinated by Sarah's interest in the map. "Flip through one more time, Jake. Slowly."

The three men's profiles, blurred in the surveillance photos the Director had sent, were perfectly clear due to the use of the military database. Jake had managed to find a driver's license photo of John Steeler thanks to the New York State DMV. There was no mistaking that she had indeed encountered the three in Matt's office: Jeff, Steve, and John.

When Reggie arrived at the table, he stood beside Meg. She waved her agents to gather around. Ready to move on, Meg said, "We've got what we need, except for that last photo." She eyed the Scotsman beside her who looked as if he were about to blow. "Reggie, what's going on?"

Normally the one who was cool, calm, and the voice of reason, Reggie was clearly agitated. "Seems we've got unwanted company... again! Finish up!"

"The Director put more agents in place around the property. How could there possibly be a breach in security?" Meg tensed thinking she and Sarah were followed. With the weather as bad as it was, she'd done her due diligence in monitoring the mirrors while Sarah navigated the treacherous roads, making sure no one had picked up their trail when they'd left out the back entry road of Hallock Farm.

"Ted said they've caught two intruders, coming in from two different sides of the property. One came from the woods near the Sound, the other parked in the Stevenson's driveway around the corner. That one never even made it through the hedge before we nabbed him. The other gave my men a good chase through the woods. I tell you, Meggie, if we don't…"

The pocket door to the secure room slid open making everyone in the room turn towards the commotion.

"In!" came the command from the Special Ops agent in charge. Both men bound in Flex-cuffs were shoved bodily into the room.

Meg reached to steady herself using the table behind her, shocked beyond belief at who she saw. Her jaw dropped as she gasped out loud, "Matt!"

Jake moved toward Matt the same time Reggie bellowed, "What the hell is *he* doing here?"

Matt's eyes fell on Meg. "I guess I know now where you go when you leave the estate at night, don't I?" He put his hand-cuffed hands out in front of him. "Really? Handcuffs? Take these off. You know I'm perfectly harmless."

Meg glared at him. Did the man not see the seriousness of what he'd walked into? "Matt, this is no time to joke." She had a job to do, damn it. What possessed him to follow her? She'd warned him he had a role to play while she completed her mission. "You're treading on serious ground. FYI, you've trespassed on government property, which, BTW, is a federal offense."

Meg tried to imagine Elizabeth Hallock's face when she had to report Matt's appearance at the base of operations. There would be hell to pay and as lead agent it would be her neck on the chopping block.

But it was the man to Matt's right who eliminated all thoughts of dealing with Matt and the Director for the time being. Standing in a puddle of water was a sleazy, shaggy, gray bearded man with a battered cap on his head. Even from where she stood the smell of rancid fish emanated from his wet clothing. He stood, head hanging down, his jaw resting on his chest, eyes directed at the floor. Hand-cuffed like Matt, he stood silent. But it was the way he stood, the way he kept his eyes from meeting those around him that piqued Meg's interest.

"You! Look at me!" Meg snapped her fingers under his nose as she moved in. The smell of his body and clothes rank with the odor of dead fish made her want to back up to the other side of the room.

Reggie came to stand behind the man, knocking the man's filthy cap to the floor. "Do as the lady says."

The man still stood motionless, standing his ground. But Reggie was in no mood for their captive to play games and she winced when Reggie shoved the man in the back. The man tumbled to the ground, hitting his head on the cement floor. Now he couldn't help but look up.

And when he did a wave of recognition flashed through Meg's mind. No, it wasn't possible! Could it be? Leaving momentarily to retrieve the blurred photo she and Sarah had not been able to identify, she returned to compare the face of the man to one in the photo she held in her hand.

"What is it, lass?" Reggie asked curiously. Jake, Sam, and Sarah moved to stand around the intruder. Less of a threat, Matt had been dragged off to one side and placed in a metal chair by one of the guards. He'd be dealt with later.

Meg held the picture up, turning it so the image on the photo lined up with the man in question. She felt the eyes of every one of her agents on her.

"This!" Meg spat out in disgust, her tone taking everyone by surprise. "This is *you*! *This* is where you've been?" Meg was so tempted to rip the photo into pieces, giving into the frustration she felt.

A smug look appeared on the face of the old man. What Meg wouldn't give to slap away the arrogance she saw in those beady eyes boring into hers.

"I was undercover." The man rose to his feet and held out his hands in front of him. "Could you cut me loose? I'm on your side, if you remember."

The voices in the room rose as they recognized identity of their captive.

"I'm not doing anything of the kind until you tell me why the hell I'm not being told what your role is in *any* of this." Meg's voice rose in incremental levels at Derek Taylor. She was losing control of the situation. And Agent Megan Spears never lost it. *Never.*

"How could I not have put two and two together?" Matt's voice came from out of nowhere, rising above the chatter that engulfed the room after Derek's identity was revealed. "He's CIA. Boy, how could I not see that coming?"

"Shut up, Matt." Sarah chimed in. The look Matt gave Sarah was priceless when she appeared from out of nowhere. The shock of Matt finding out who Sarah was would be forever imprinted in Meg's memory. It was as if the world he'd known had turned itself upside down. Matt definitely had not planned on seeing *his* club's manager standing in *her* command center for Operation Hurricane.

"Sarah, what the…You…? What the hell has been going on at my club? A sting op?" Matt struggled to break free from the grasp of the agent who held him down. "Can someone just uncuff me? I want some…"

Meg was ready for him. "Release him, Sarah." Sarah did as directed, cutting him loose. Matt glared at Meg as he rubbed his wrists. "*Don't… move.*" Meg dared him to counterman her orders. "*Sit -in–that-chair.*" Meg enunciated the last four words. "Do what Sarah said. Shut up."

Taken aback, Matt's jaw sag in disbelief; Sarah had never spoken to him in that tone before. Hours earlier, they'd been making passionate love in a shower. But right now, he was on her turf and there would be no way he would hinder her investigation.

Reggie unlocked Derek's handcuffs. It was time for Meg to focus her attention back onto her partner. She'd been waiting days for a chance to take the ass down a peg or two.

"Get out of that ridiculous get-up," Meg commanded. Derek pulled off his fake nose and ears and tugged the now drenched beard from his chin and the gray wig off his head. Meg didn't need to look around her to know they were the center of attention. "Somebody get this asshole a cup of coffee. We need to get to the bottom of this, this…*mess.*" Once again she flashed the blurry photo in front of his face.

"I gave you what I could get." Derek dropped his disguise to the floor and crossed his arms in a defensive stance. The man was infuriating. Sarah may not have wanted to be in a dark alley with Mike Kranepool, but Meg would give her life savings to be alone for ten minutes with her "partner" and her Glock.

"You better give me more of an explanation than five photos and a note. I want full details on your undercover assignment. Everything! I'm lead agent and you and the Director have dangled me on a string long enough." Meg drew in a deep breath. "This…this…subterfuge you're involved with ends tonight!"

Reggie stepped in and tapped Meg on the shoulder. "Are we calling the Eagle?"

Derek's large frame tried to block Reggie as he moved passed. Derek warned, "The Director's not going to discuss our arrangement with anyone. I don't need to tell you that, Meg. You're well versed in protocol."

Derek Taylor didn't know her at all. When she did the job she was given, she saw it to completion. Meg didn't allow any obstacles to stand in her way. She and the Director butted heads over issues in Paris, but when she completed her assignment successfully and delivered not only the art thief, but also several well-known art forgers and long lost stolen paintings, Elizabeth had been impressed.

"Well, the Director doesn't have a choice anymore." Meg snapped back. "Reggie, my team and I will be ready in fifteen minutes. We just need to tie a few pieces of new information in with what we had gathered. Do *not* tell her Matt is here."

She didn't like the look Derek sent her way. "I always thought you liked your job, Meg. If you interfere here, on something you don't know anything about, you'll be gone. Kaput. Out on the street."

"You think so, do you, *Agent Taylor*?" Derek knew how to push Meg's buttons. But this time he'd erred. She'd have her answers tonight. Derek Taylor was going to be shocked at what Meg had been able to dig up over the last few days. When summoned to the compound, Meg had been able to cement her relationship with the Director in a way no one at the Agency knew about.

Meg gave a nod in Reggie's direction. "Place the call."

Reggie's eyebrows arched, "You sure about this, lass?"

"Don't tell me *you're* siding with him?" Meg put her hand on her hips.

"No, I'm not going over to the dark side. But, Meggie, I think it's best Matt be removed during our conversation."

"He's staying."

Derek's looked shocked by her decision. "You're crazy if you think the Director is going to allow her nephew to become intimate with company secrets. I say he goes."

Meg marched over to Derek and stood toe to toe with the man. "I make the calls. There hasn't been any change in my status that I'm aware of." She poked her finger into Derek's chest. "I say he stays and hears what his aunt's got to say. He needs to hear the seriousness of what surrounds him. Then, we deal with him."

Derek batted Meg's finger away. "You mean you'll be dealing with him. I want a career at the Agency and I'm not about to agree to anything you're going to do. Got that....*Lead* Agent?"

Derek's black, stony eyes pierced hers and a shiver ran down her spine. She would bet her last dollar he was hiding something. He hadn't laid all his cards on the table with her or the Director, which had Meg suspicious of the movements he'd been making. How could she convey that to the Eagle? Her gut told her Derek Taylor was up to something besides what he's been assigned to do. And her sixth sense never failed.

Meg glared back. "I don't give a rat's ass what you think. The fact that you've been acting covertly in this operation makes me wonder what you're up to. But you'll do what I say and when I say to do it or so help me there will be hell to pay. You're—"

Jake stepped between Derek and Meg. "Enough!" Frustration was written all over Jake's face as he pushed Meg away from Derek. "Your bickering isn't getting us anywhere. It's late. We need direction. And answers."

Meg saw the look Reggie gave Derek out of the corner of his eye as he turned to make arrangements for the encrypted call to DC.

Never one for letting things get so out of control, Meg was grateful to Jake for stepping in. Her eyes turned back to those standing around the table, the speakerphone at the ready. Calmly, she gave instructions. "Be ready to answer any questions she or Agent Tanner may ask. I'll outline the plan we're going to put in place."

Then she glanced at Matthew standing off to the side. She pulled up an extra metal chair and, as she sat, she motioned for him to come sit next to her. Matt did as she asked.

Meg turned to him. "Keep your mouth shut and your ears open. You may not take notes. Just take it all in. Say nothing. Do you think just this once you can follow those few simple rules?"

Matt shook his head in the affirmative. He glanced around the table. For once, Matt looked intimidated. Meg saw that her agents had taken out the needed materials for the briefing, their eyes glued on both her and Matt, awaiting his response. *Oh, please, for once in your life, Matthew Hallock, take this seriously.*

Matt folded his hands and placed them in his lap. "I'll do whatever you need me to do."

There was a small shred of doubt in her mind regarding the man next her. He could plot and plan as well as she could. Only in a different way.

It was going to be a long, long night. Or at least what was left. The all too familiar red light lit up. Meg pressed the button. "Madam Director, I apologize for waking you, but we have news."

CHAPTER NINETEEN

So far things had gone well with the conversation between the team and the Director. As each member of the team contributed their respective piece of intel, Meg felt confident the Director would accept their plan to launch the sting at Plum Island within the time frame laid out.

Much to Meg's satisfaction, Matthew had managed to stay quiet for the entire duration, as the people around him hashed out technical details. Out of the corner of her eye, she saw a variety of emotions play out across his face as information was divulged about his friends and as the plot thickened to take the men down emerged. It was a lot to take in. It saddened Meg to see the world Matt had built crumble on false lies and promises by those he trusted. But now was not the time to reassure him that all would be all right in the end. She couldn't offer a one hundred percent guarantee that all would go right. But the Sunfish would survive if she had anything to do with it. Contrary to the "village gossips," Matt was a man of great character and integrity. Meg had no doubt he would rebound. He was as strong minded and determined as she was. Maybe that's what had drawn her to him in the first place. That's what made them a perfect match.

"Your team is to be commended for their fine work."

"Thank you," Meg replied. She gritted her teeth knowing she had to acknowledge the work of Derek in the accumulation of the intelligence gathering. "We couldn't have pieced the who, what, and where had it not been for Agent Taylor's help at the Liar's Club."

"Ah, yes." The soft southern spoke with a tinge of sarcasm. "Agent Taylor finding out about the old hangout and infiltrating the locals certainly was a plus." She paused momentarily. "Luckily, Agent Taylor was in the right place at the right time. Correct, Agent Taylor?"

Derek said nothing in return.

"I asked you a question, Derek."

"Yes, ma'am," he responded, "very advantageous."

Meg could have sworn she had heard a slight questioning edge in the Director's voice. Meg shook her head to clear what had been reeling through her head over the last half hour. Perhaps she was reading into things because her mind was on overload. Meg and her team had been going at the investigation for more than twenty-four hours. Glancing at her watch, Meg noted the time. A new day would be dawning soon.

"So what do you want to us to do regarding your nephew?" Derek suddenly interjected. Meg's head swiveled around to the end of the table. Derek sat with a sly grin on his face. She could throttle him for bringing up Matt. Meg knew he was baiting her.

"Keep him and the family protected as directed, Agent Taylor," came the reply. "I told all of you from the very beginning I want him safe and out of the loop. When we bring his friends down, the less Matthew knows, the better it will be for everyone."

A loud cough caught those sitting at the table off guard.

"Is there a problem?" Meg knew from past experience not to question Elizabeth's authority, especially when others were present. "Is there something I need to be aware of?" The Director asked pointedly.

A light tap of a pencil came through on the other end of the phone line. Meg pictured the Director's spectacles perched on the end of her nose, waiting impatiently for her partner's answer. For those who knew the Eagle well, when she tapped said pencil, she was ready to pounce.

Meg held her breath.

However, out of the blue, the all too familiar voice of the person sitting next to Meg spoke up. "It's good to hear your voice, Aunt Elizabeth." Meg froze. No! Matt promised. "How are things in DC? I'm sorry the family hasn't seen much of you lately. Will you be in Hampton Beach soon?"

"Matthew!" Elizabeth cried out. Meg cringed. At first, the Director seemed somewhat flustered, but soon began to fire questions in rapid succession. "What? Why? Somebody...*not* my nephew, tell me exactly what Matthew is doing at our base in the secure room! Has he been there all this time?"

"Now, Auntie..." Meg knew Matt was only trying do his best to calm his aunt but he was interrupted.

Meg poked him hard with her elbow in his ribcage. He winced. *This is on your watch.* She blamed herself. *Just explain. The Director will see reason in all of this...chaos.*

"Madam Director." Meg cleared her throat. Her hand holding the pen started to tremble. She lay the pen down. "I can explain..."

"Somebody better. I'll start with you, Agent Spears. Everything. You have ten minutes to give me the short version of what, if I know my nephew, is a very long story."

The members of the team, along with Matt, turned to Meg. She watched Matt casually sit back, cross his arms, and stretch out his long legs under the table, waiting for her to clean up the mess he'd just placed *her* in.

As rapidly as possible, Meg outlined the chain of events that led up to Matt's presence. "And during the time the team was translating the information we gathered, two intruders were apprehended. Derek came in disguise and didn't follow protocol." Meg smugly looked down the table as if to say 'so there'. "As for Matthew, he followed us from the farm. Sarah and I were very careful at making sure…."

Elizabeth cut her off. "All right. I get the picture. If it's one thing I know about Matthew, it's that he can trail a woman without her even knowing." The room snickered and a low chuckle came through the phone. "Sam Tanner, you know perfectly well I don't like this one bit."

"What should we do?" Meg asked. "Detain him?"

"On the contrary. To do that would only make those involved question his absence. I've no doubt they're watching his every move, which makes me concerned about his being at Fox Hollow. If Matthew changes his daily routine, the people we've identified will likely think we are onto the money scheme. And their plans for Plum Island, if your team's theory is correct." Elizabeth paused, it was obvious she was quietly conversing with her second in command. Meg couldn't make out what the two were conferring about. Back on the line, the Director replied, "No. As much as I don't want Matthew involved, I believe we can work him to our advantage.

"Matthew, remember Katherine's dilemma in Virginia? When she had no choice but to lure Zoya out into the open at the Peachtree Auction House?"

Matthew flexed his fingers and ran his hand over his face, sitting up stiff and straight. The casual attitude gone, something his aunt alluded to hit a nerve. The man was tense, his gaze drifting into the distance as if to recall the memory but the same time seemed as if he was trying to forget.

Jake and Samantha exchanged knowing glances. Okay. Something needed further explanation. Meg made a mental note to talk to both of them later. Right now, the Director had an agenda for Matthew.

Matt replied, "Yes, I do. But Aunt Elizabeth, Kate was a trained agent."

"Yes, she was."

Matt cracked his knuckles. His right knee shook the table. Nervous energy? No. What had him so wound up all of a sudden? Meg placed her left hand under the table and squeezed his knee in an attempt to calm him. Matt didn't flinch.

There was a long pause, but Matt finally answered. "What exactly are you asking of me?"

"You're going to draw Draper and his men out into the open. The beach club's too obvious. Take them to the country club. Wine and dine them. Meg and the team can come up with a way to use the time to get all they need to proceed." Elizabeth stopped, whispered something to Sam Tanner and continued, "Matthew. You've always been very good at drawing in the ladies. I want you to use your charisma and your reputation with some Hampton ladies on your buddies. It will lay the trap to put Megan's plan into place. I have every confidence you can draw out the major players. While they're with you, Megan's team, along with Reggie and Victoria's Special Ops crew, will be able to infiltrate their cars, home, and the Coast Guard venue and set up electronic tracking and wiretapping devices. They won't know what hit them when they head for Plum Island. Do you think you can do that?"

Matt's eyes landed on Meg's as he cracked his knuckles again, looking around the room. His frown and the initial look of worry had disappeared. "Only if I can be armed, Aunt Elizabeth."

Matt's pronouncement took everyone by surprise, Meg included.

Meg was the first to respond. "Madam Director, you can't possibly—"

Matt wasn't finished. "I want my Glock back…then you can count me in. Since I would like to be alive after this fiasco is signed, sealed, and delivered, I'd like a bullet proof vest as well as a enough ammo to help me go along with the team when—"

"Whoa! Whoa!" Meg slammed her hand on the table. "No way! What are you thinking?" She didn't know if she was directing her comment at Matt or her boss.

Elizabeth, clearly agitated by her nephew's demands, echoed Meg's concerns in a stern voice. "Matthew, you will *not*, I repeat, *not* participate in this mission's final stage. Do you copy?"

Matt leaned back in the metal chair, his hands locked at the back of his neck, legs, once again, extended out under the conference table. "Then *they* can go it alone. You're right when you say I can reel in my friends faster than anyone sitting here, especially given what I know about Draper and Baker. So if you don't think I can contribute…"

There was a hurried murmur of voices as the Director and Agent Tanner commiserated. "All right. I'll see your gun is delivered to you."

"What?" Meg couldn't believe what she was hearing. She was dumbfounded. Quite frankly, stunned was a better word to sum up what she felt. She'd been trying to make sense of the conversation between Matt and his aunt. Nothing about having a permit to own a gun had been in his file. She had a sinking feeling in the pit of her stomach. Her worst nightmare was coming to fruition— Matthew would be allowed access into the classified information on Operation Hurricane. And given the clientele they were about to apprehend, Matt could be in harm's way.

The Director's authoritative southern drawl came through loud and clear. "Agent Spears, Samantha, Jake, Reggie… meet Black Sheep." Matt reached out to shake Meg's hand, but she just sat, shaking her head in denial. "Matt may have failed the final training test to get into the Agency, but he can fire a gun better than half the people who work for me. Work it out. *All of you.*"

The red light went out. The Eagle had had her way. And Meg was left wondering who had blindsided her more—the Director, Derek Taylor, or Matt.

CHAPTER TWENTY

Fox Hollow Inn
One week later

Meg had just dipped one of Victoria's blueberry scones into her cup of tea when the kitchen's back door opened and slammed shut with a bang. Reggie, who was sitting along side her, jumped up, his knee hitting and rattling the table. Taken aback by the sound, coupled with Reggie knocking her elbow, Meg dropped her porcelain cup onto Victoria's prized crocheted tablecloth, her tea spilling onto the creamy lace. She knew full well who'd made the angry entrance and turned to face her young agent.

"You!" After throwing her sequined scarf and purse in a chair, Sarah pointed a finger at Meg. "*You* are going to owe *me* for the rest of your life. And so, I might add, will the Director." Sarah was in rare form.

The corners of Meg's mouth curled into a grin, knowing it had not been an easy night. "I take it you had a wonderful time at the country club."

"The party was lovely." Sarah muttered sarcastically. It was that pawing maniac I had to hook up as my "date" with that made my stomach churn. But I did my job. Kept a smile plastered on my face and made out like I was really into him." Sarah shuddered.

Meg couldn't resist, "You made out with Jeff Draper?"

Sarah leveled an angry glare in her direction. "No! For god's sake! Be serious. Let me just brief you on the evening." She rubbed her bare arms as if to rid herself of the unpleasantness she'd been forced to endure. "I definitely need a shower."

Reggie returned to his chair as Victoria mopped up Meg's spill, both chuckling at Sarah's comment.

Meg motioned for Sarah to join her at the table. "Victoria, Sarah could use a stiff drink. A belt of Reggie's Scotch whiskey should do the trick. What do you say, Reggie?"

"Wouldn't mind if I did—I mean, she did." Reggie's eyes fell on Victoria, who just shook her head and smiled. He stood up and made his way to the pantry door. He opened it and walked in. Meg could hear cans and pans being moved about and the "Yes!" when he found what he'd been searching for.

Coming out, Reggie closed the door, reaching for two shot glasses on the shelf of the cupboard to his left.

"Now," he directed his comments to Sarah. "I know you're not a drinkin' lass, but this will blot out the awful memory of being with Draper."

Reggie filled both glasses and passed one to Sarah who, before Reggie or Meg could say another word, chugged down the liquid in one gulp.

Meg's jaw dropped as Sarah winked at her.

Sarah placed the empty glass in front of Reggie. "That hit the spot. I'll have another, Reggie, if you can spare it. It was a very," Sarah rolled her "r" as the Scotsman often did when he was really angry, "long night."

Meg watched in awe as Sarah tipped the glass back and drank the second shot in the same manner as she had the first.

"You sure, you don't have Scot's blood in you, lass?" Reggie asked, downing his drink.

"No. No, Scot's blood. German and Irish. Beer's more my thing."

Meg raised her eyebrows. Since learning her true identity, Meg had taken a lot for granted regarding Sarah Adams. But the young agent intrigued her. Some day, they would have to talk about the life Sarah had led since college. At least, anything Agency rules would allow.

"If you two are done commiserating over your ancestral trees, I think we need to get to work." Meg nodded at the clock on the wall. "It's almost three. Jake and Samantha should be here soon."

Sarah grabbed the remaining scone off Meg's plate and stuffed it in her mouth. Shrugging her shoulders, she practically swallowed the pastry whole and smiled sheepishly. "Sorry. I'm hungry. Didn't get much time to eat."

"I hope that's not your full report." Meg looked at her empty plate, then at the empty baking tray sitting on the stove. It didn't look like she was going to get much to eat either. Oh, well.

"No. I made nice with the guy just as directed. Draper took advantage of his opportunity and stuck to my side like glue. That man has some very interesting friends. Baker and Kranepool, but a few other names were dropped. At dinner, I mostly talked to Draper, but I got a chance to talk to the other quests.

"Draper never let me out of his sight. Hell, I thought he was even going to accompany me into the ladies' room. And you'll be happy to know Matt played his role to perfection. There was one time when I thought he was going to slip up and say something to blow my cover, but he stopped and left the table. Thank God, no one thought anything of it."

"So who else was there?" Meg took her laptop from her bag. She needed to outline notes for her report. Elizabeth had pushed to have Matthew arrange the dinner party with his friends as soon as feasibly possible. Out of the blue, Meg received word the plans were set, the invitations sent out via the help of his mother and Ethan. It was an extravagant private affair for his "friends:" plenty of alcohol to drink, lots to eat, and a private room off to the side, away from club members, in which to sit and converse.

"Baker and Kranepool kept slipping away from their dinner companions between the dinner courses. When I saw them standing at the bar, I made an excuse to get another drink. Jeff was too engrossed in talking to Matt about some renovation at the club so I took advantage of the diversion to see if the two of them would talk to me. They made small talk, but turned their backs when the bartender came to take my order. Quite honestly, I thought they were brushing me off.

"However, I did overhear them mention Steeler, who, by the way, actually showed up. Matt, along with most of the invitees, was taken aback, given John's reputation as the village recluse. But back to Steve and Mike. I was afraid if I pushed my "interest" in having a conversation, they would wonder why. And everyone there who is male knows I'm not the Hampton debutante type given my background. I've never been any good at flirting, Meg. I played it safe and stayed with Draper the rest of the night since he seemed to be the big fish. I wasn't disappointed."

"You did well. When Jake and Sam get here, you can fill in the remaining details."

Reggie's cell phone rang. He kept biting the side of his mouth as he listened to the caller at the other end of the line. Abruptly he said, "Don't! Come in the bunker entrance. Leave the car in the park's lot. Be careful coming down the rock ledge." He clicked his phone shut and muttered an explicative under his breath.

Meg guessed it would be only minutes before she and Sarah would be on the move. Meg closed her laptop and checked to be sure her Glock was secured.

Meg heard the click of the dead bolt on the back door. She didn't need to know Victoria had secured the back entrance and set the alarm. But Meg did see the communicative nod that passed between husband and wife. Reggie motioned for Meg and Sarah to follow him.

As they crossed the kitchen to get to the door that led to the staircase, Sarah pulled a small revolver from her designer handbag.

"I'm ready. This sounds serious." Sarah waited for instructions.

Meg knew she, too, had to rely on Reggie as to what to do next.

"You have everything covered here, luv?" Reggie said to his wife.

Victoria nodded. "There's nothing I can't handle, Reggie Litchfield. You know that." She shooed them to get out to go downstairs. In the dimly lit stairwell, Meg heard a scraping noise as Victoria slid a cupboard across the floor above them as she hid the entrance to the staircase of the secret room.

Meg, Reggie, and Sarah rushed down the stairs and briskly walked the corridor.

"What is it, Reggie? What's going on?" Meg asked.

"Jake and Samantha are here. But I made them come in via the hidden entrance. They're concerned. And they've every right to be."

"Why?" Sarah hopped along the passageway behind Meg, trying to take off her high heel shoes so that she could keep up.

"Derek has disappeared. They were making the rounds in town, putting all the devices in place. I don't know what to make of this. Neither do they. They can't reach him on any frequencies of the encrypted radios."

A lump formed in Meg's throat. She didn't know either, but Reggie was right to be cautious bringing Jake and Samantha into the base via the cove entrance, hidden in rocks on the hillside leading out to the Sound. Only a few members of the team of Operation Hurricane knew of its existence.

So her partner had disappeared? Meg hated the thoughts that raced through her head. Meg doubted to the umpteenth degree that Derek Taylor was a defined MIA case. It would be just like the man to take it upon himself to go it alone. It was his typical MO. But, backing up and assessing what had transpired, Meg had to admit that it was a possibility someone found out about their plan to infiltrate the homes and offices of the men on their list. Derek may have fallen into a trap.

For the first time since Meg and Derek had teamed up in DC, Megan was concerned for her colleague. Call it gut instinct or woman's intuition. His disappearance clearly felt wrong, no matter her misgivings. She anxiously awaited Jake and Samantha's take on the evening's operation. But above all, her concern for Matt and the safety of his family surfaced. Category 2 was now a Category 3.

* * *

"And you didn't see Derek after that?" Meg asked, dumbfounded at what Jake and Samantha reported.

"No." Jake scratched his chin. "I swear, Meg. The guy disappeared into thin air. One minute, he was behind Samantha going through papers on Steeler's desk, the next…gone. Vanished."

"It's just as Jake said, Meg."

For the last twenty minutes, Samantha had relayed a summary of the night's activities to the key team players. She, Jake, and the others assigned to the tasks on the checklist had been able to accomplish all but one item. And to fail to complete that job was big—planting the Agency's GPS tracking device, capable of doing anything under the sun, most importantly blocking radio signals and jamming computer software on the Coast Guard vessel being requested for the SAR rescue drills.

Derek's absence had everyone on the defensive. It was the consensus that valuable time had been wasted trying to locate him, hunting the alleyways and searching the boat dock behind Magic's Pub.

"I can't figure out what triggered him to cut and run. And without a word." Samantha pulled off her Agency-issued blue cap and ran her fingers through her hair. Her frustration and aggravation was tempered by a look of concern. "How could we not have heard him leave the office? At first we thought it was deliberate. That he'd gotten a call in his earpiece from Agent Tanner, but we were all linked. So we quickly sorted through the paperwork on Steeler's desk where he had been standing. There was nothing important. Just typical accounting papers, copies of companies' spreadsheets, which by the way included the Sunfish."

Reggie leaned forward and placed his elbows on the table. "Well, something triggered the man to cut and run. You know I'm concerned he might be trying to go it alone on some clue he may have found in that office. Or…"

"Or what?" Meg asked.

Sarah had been silent for quite some time. "Not to get off topic, but John was pretty damn fidgety at dinner. I just chalked it up to John being John. It was a big step for him to come to the club. Just around the time dessert was going to be served, Baker, who had had a few, said something to John and Mike about a guy named Fleming. John tried to change the topic, but Matt perked up and asked if the guy was new in town. Mike looked as if he was going to blow. He glanced at Baker, then excused himself from the table "politely" dragged John and Steve off to look at the new golf cart waiting area on the first hole. Of course, I knew, as did Matt, Mike was making sure no one asked anything else and that there was something to this."

"Wait!" Samantha pulled out her IPhone and scrolled through a series of photos. "Look. I took a set of panoramic pictures of John's office. See the screen in the background?"

Samantha laid the phone on the table, the photo in question on her screen. She used the zoom feature to enlarge the type seen on the computer screen. The first thing that registered with Meg was that she was looking at an ID photo of an employee at Plum Island. And the name tag was for James Fleming.

Sarah took the phone from Meg. "Check out the guy's security clearance." She whistled and handed the phone to Jake who scrutinized the picture. "BS level 4. That's at the top of the hierarchy. He's into something big in the research lab at the facility."

"And hence the reason for using the CG boats, my friends," Reggie came up from behind them. "I think we've solved the puzzle. But we still don't know what's become of Derek…and *that* has me worried."

"Do you think he saw Jim's picture and took off to report to the Director?" Meg asked.

Reggie shook his head vehemently, "No, Meggie. I don't. Vic and I had a conversation with Lizzie a couple of day ago. We had some concerns. You were right, Meggie. Derek's been conducting a rogue operation of his own within Operation Hurricane. Lizzie was totally unaware of moves he's made."

"So, what's your take?" Jake asked. Meg, Sarah, and Samantha turned to the man sitting at the head of the table.

"Personally, and I hate to say this, but, he's either gone over to the dark side… or he's dead."

Sarah gasped. "You mean he could be a double agent?"

Meg was afraid to concur with Reggie's suspicions out loud. She looked to Jake and Samantha for support. They'd worked cases with her before and had discussed the clues and signals Derek had given off.

"Where do we go from here, boss?" Jake queried. "It's been a late night. What do we do about Derek? Should be put out an APB on him through the network?"

"No, head back to the estate. Reggie, you make the call to the Director and get some direction. If she says what I think she will, we'll be moving in on this crew very quickly. Plus, we planted all the electronic devices and cameras except on the boat. She's got the right connections to get the job done ASAP. We need to give the staff here a chance to put together the final logistical planning of to close out our mission. As soon as we know, we make our move."

Heads nodded all around. Meg rose. Chairs scraped on the concrete floor as the others moved to leave.

"Shouldn't we stay here tonight, Meg?" Sarah grabbed hold of Meg's arm. "If Jake and Samantha came in through the cove, and we leave via 25A, we might be followed."

From the short time Meg had known Sarah was involved in the operation, Meg never gave a thought to the woman being afraid of anything, but tonight was different. Sarah was questioning every move being made, and even Meg, with far more experience, felt she was doing the same.

"No." Meg flung her backpack over her shoulder. "You and I will go back to the farm. Jake and Samantha will stay here. They have some loose ends to tie up. We'll meet up at the estate for breakfast and head to club from there. I'm more worried about Matthew to be honest. I need to find out if he thinks anyone acted strange or said something was out of the ordinary. I don't think those guys would be fools to discuss business in front of Matt, but alcohol can make tongues wag, and they could have baited him."

"Why?"

"Wouldn't you think it odd to be invited in mass to the country club? Matt doesn't socialize with any of them. I hope the invitation Mrs. H made about getting the investors together with friends or a date went over just as it should. Not be a cause for suspicion. But we won't know until we pick apart Matt's conversations word for word."

"I told you I stayed on top of everything." Sarah picked up her shawl and purse. She reached for the revolver she'd placed on the table, tucking it in the designer bag.

Meg smiled at the memory of being a young agent, wanting to impress the lead agent with what she had accomplished. Sarah was no different. Putting her arm around the young girl's shoulder, Meg squeezed hard. "You did your job. You're one fine agent, Sarah Adams. But you said you had more details. You didn't share them."

"I got side tracked when Jake and Samantha came in." The two walked through the door and made their way to the foot of the staircase. Meg glanced up, seeing that Reggie had had Victoria reopen the hidden passageway from the kitchen. Sarah placed a hand on Meg's arm. "*You* need to be very careful."

Meg eyed her protégé questioningly, "What do mean?"

"When I told you Matt almost slipped up? Baker and Mike alluded to the fact that *you* weren't at the party…they wanted to know where the "beauty of the sea" was. Matt picked up on the comment, casually said your boyfriend came to town and you had to pass on the invite. Which prompted Baker to probe him on your "date night" at the Marakesh. You said there was quite the crowd there the night you went. Baker had a wise-ass look on his face when he asked Matt if the two of you had gotten involved on the side. Eyebrows rose when Matt got up and strode off, acting pissed as if it was all about Derek. Some muffled conversation followed that I couldn't catch. But between you and me, Baker and Kranepool have their antennas up.

"Matt did right by walking away. But I got the feeling those two have reasons for asking about you. One, the break-in. They pieced two and two together and know you are more than just our lifeguard. You can identify them. If you'd stumbled into the burglary without the gun, maybe I could see them viewing you in a slightly different light. But these guys are trained military. Kranepool was persistent with Matt; he wanted to know your whereabouts. Your cover's been blown at the club. The two tried to get a pulse on just how important you are to Matt. He's been a thorn in Draper's side over the money issues. Know what I'm saying?"

Meg started to climb the stairs, taking them two at a time. "I agree. The time has come for me to give the reins to Jake at the club and let me work on closing out the mission. Out of sight. Out of mind…I think I could be putting both Matt and his family in great danger."

"How much longer before we spring the trap?' Sarah entered the kitchen behind her.

Reggie and Victoria were once again sitting in their typical places at the kitchen table; it was evident, both heard the conversation in the stairwell.

Meg placed her backpack in a chair and removed her light summer jacket from the hook behind the back door. "If all goes as planned, and we have the proof we need from the monitoring devices to move forward, I'd say by the end of next week. Come on, we've got to get going."

Meg opened the door and heard Victoria calling to her.

"Are you heading to Matthew's?" Victoria asked.

"Yes. I've got to find out about tonight and tell him what I'll do from here on out."

Victoria winked. "Remember all work and no play makes for a dull day, Meggie."

Meg couldn't help but blush, when Sarah and Reggie chuckled along with Victoria.

"For the record…we will be *working*." And with that, Meg pushed Sarah out the door, slamming it behind her. Meg mimicked Reggie's thick Scottish accent, "You say one word, *lassie*, and I'll…"

"You'll what? Fire me?" Sarah laughed as the two women got into the Jeep. "Just remember, I like June the best."

Meg took her hand off the gear shift and stared questioningly at her companion. "June? Who the hell is June? Is she another agent I don't know about?"

"No. I'm referring to the month of June—the prettiest time for a wedding in the Hamptons."

Sarah's reputation as a matchmaker was legendary in Hampton Beach. Marriage to Matt was on Meg's bucket list in her private journal under the column entitled "only in my dreams". At that moment, Meg wished Sarah *was* the GPS. That way she could mute her for the brief ride home.

CHAPTER TWENTY-ONE

Hallock Farm
0430

Sarah dropped Meg off near the back door of Matt's cottage and left. Meg didn't have the option of waiting until the morning to discuss with Matt what his aunt and her team needed from him moving forward. And as much as Sarah had explained the comings and goings of each invitee of the night's dinner party, Meg wanted to hear from Matt's lips his take of the evening down to the minute details he could recall.

The estate was on lockdown after midnight, with guards patrolling the grounds 24/7. Meg reached into her pocket for the lock pick. With a silent click and a turn of the doorknob, she was inside Matt's cottage, her eyes adjusting to the dark interior, the remnants of the moonlight filtering through the windows and onto the braided rugs that lay on the floor.

Unbeknownst to Matt, Meg had done her own reconnaissance of his humble abode several times within the last few weeks. However, one night a few days ago, she'd entered his bedroom to find him sound asleep, face down in his pillows, naked as the day he was born, the air conditioner humming, blowing cool air into the room. She'd been sorely tempted to join him, but Jake and Samantha were waiting at the back entrance to take her to Fox Hollow. Her primary reason for checking on him that particular night was she had to be sure he hadn't gone off half-cocked into town looking for Jeff Draper. Sarah reported there had been another heated exchange in the club's office that afternoon.

Meg kicked off her sandals and made her way down the hallway to his bedroom. The door was ajar. Peeking into the room, Meg could make out the outline of a body under a white sheet, a pillow pulled over its head. A moan came from beneath the king-size pillow.

Meg tiptoed to the edge of the bed lightly nudging the bed's occupant.

"Matt? Matt, it's me," she whispered. "I've got to talk to you."

With one hand on his shoulder, she drew away the pillow with the other. Suddenly, an arm snaked out from beneath the sheet, wrapped itself around her waist and flipped her over onto the mattress. Pinned like a wrestler to a mat, Matt took her down, again. The man had been lying in wait. Clever, very clever, and from the look in his eye, his agenda was not on the evening's party, but on something far more tempting and deliciously seductive.

"Don't go there," Meg licked her lips, trying to keep her libido in check and tamper down her own desire. She felt him harden as his penis nestled between her thighs. "I've...We've...You and I've got work to do." It was hard to catch her breath with Matt lying on top of her. Meg tried to resist his advances, her arms pushing hard against his biceps.

"Where have you been?" Matt nipped her bottom lip and then began to leave a trail of hot, sizzling kisses along the length of her neck.

She felt as if she'd been branded. A moan echoed in the room. Had that come from her or Matt? "Stop. Please. We don't have much time."

Apparently, Matt took notice of the tone in Meg's voice. Matt hugged her to him and sighed. But he stopped, let go, and sat up, wrapping the sheet about his lower torso.

"Meggie..." Meg shot her hand up in the air.

"No work, no play." Meg's voice was firm, or at least she thought it sounded that way. Why had Victoria reminded her that all work and no play led to a dull and unsatisfying life?

There was a devious twinkle in his eyes, but Matt simply replied, "Deal. We work...then we play." He winked playfully at her. "Set your watch." The tables were turned on her.

Meg sat up and shimmied her backside so she leaned against the headboard of his bed for support. "Can't you be serious? Sarah spent the last hour filling us in on dinner. Her impressions of the guests and conversations were more than helpful. We think the team can make the final logistical plan once we hear your take."

Meg reached for the hurricane lamp on the night stand, turning it on. She wanted to be able to read Matt's facial and body expressions as he recalled the night.

"Well, what did Sarah say?"

Meg sat mute, her arms crossed.

"What? You can't tell me?" Matt flung his legs over the side of the bed, dropped the sheet and walked naked out the door and into the hallway. If this was Matt's way of getting her attention, he certainly had it. Her eyes roamed every part of him as he marched away.

"Hey!" Meg yelled out. "Where the hell are you going?" *And when are you coming back so I can get the better view.*

Meg heard a cupboard opening and glasses clinking. "I'm thirsty. Want some iced tea with lemonade? It's Hannah's special brew. She put a pitcher in my frig this afternoon." Hannah was known far and wide for her own version of "Long Island Ice Tea". Meg couldn't resist.

"Are you coming back, or do I have to come to you?" she asked.

"Meggie, sweetheart, you're right where I want you—in my bed. Stay right where you are." There was a husky, deep ring in Matt's laugh.

Within minutes, dressed like a naked butler, kitchen towel draped over his arm, tray in hand, Matt came toward her and entered the bedroom. Meg almost sighed her disappointment out loud. All the great parts of his anatomy she so enjoyed—covered. What a shame! She shook the lusty thoughts from her brain. She could not focus and *that* was an issue that needed to be addressed.

As Matt placed the tray gingerly on the middle of the king-size bed, Meg threw a coverlet at him. "Cover yourself up!"

"Why? It's hot tonight."

"That's exactly my point…I mean I can't concentrate when you don't have your clothes on. Oh, hell! Just hide yourself for ten minutes, will you?"

Matt roared with laughter, but did as she asked, sinking onto the mattress. He poured two glasses of tea and handed one to Meg, which she gladly accepted. They needed to move on, get back to the main topic of conversation. F – O – C – U – S!

"Relax! You can be so uptight sometimes, Meggie." Wrapped in the coverlet, Matt eyed her over the rim of his glass. "Okay. What do you want to know? Obviously, if you're not going to tell me what Sarah said, you don't want to bias my opinion. Am I right?"

Meg nodded and sipped more tea. She motioned for him to keep talking. If she just kept her eyes locked onto his, she wouldn't be thinking of what lay underneath the blanket.

"Well, for one thing, Draper confided in me that he had to force Baker and Kranepool to show up. They didn't want to come. Something about a CG commitment, but I knew otherwise. I was one step ahead of the bastard. I checked. Nothing was scheduled on the docket. But I'm pretty sure Draper knew I knew. He was very direct when Sarah left to go get a drink at the bar."

"About what?"

"He wanted to know where *you* were. I could tell he didn't buy my excuse that, number one, I don't invite my employees to my brother's country club and, number two, that you were out with your boyfriend. Even Steve and Mike were curious as to your whereabouts—"the beauty of the sea," as they called you.

Lots of subtle glances passed around the table every time someone mentioned you, especially the night we spent at Marakesh. Truthfully, the entire night was stiff and formal, until I got Draper to have a few, and Sarah got several of the ladies to get the men grudgingly out onto the dance floor. Meg, as God is my witness, I could have sworn Jeff was packing a weapon. At one point, I thought he was subtly telling me to back off in regards to the club's money. He glared at me when he said, 'The board will see to it that the club's account would be managed wisely. There's no need for you to go digging around every time I make a deposit, Matt.'

"He said that? Those exact words?" Meg sat up straight, her mind reeling. "He actually used the word 'dig'?" Right then, Meg knew she had to get to Jake about the serial numbers on the money, but to make a call with Matt beside her would only put him in jeopardy of knowing information that could come back to harm him later.

"And if looks could kill," Matt raised his right hand. "I swear I'd be a dead man. Steeler, who'd been sitting off to the side and hadn't talked to a soul all evening, came and dragged Jeff away right then and there. Said something about an upcoming IRS audit, and it was the only time he had the chance to talk to Jeff that week. Apologized for mixing my business with his. Off they went. But by the look on Steeler's face, he'd intervened on purpose."

Meg emptied her glass. "Anything else?" *Come on, mention Fleming.*

"No. My gut tells me they're suspicious as to why they were all brought together. Some aren't investors, but have business with the club." Matt refilled his glass from the pitcher and offered Meg more. She shook her head, placing her empty glass on the night stand.

"You're sure there's nothing else?"

"What are you getting at?"

"Anything else you might be forgetting?" *Not good. Breaking rule number ten— leading the witness.*

Matt had a puzzled look on his face. "What more do you want? Personally, my take was the evening, although it had its purpose for what you needed, was a bad, bad, idea. You're not dealing with dummies. I think if the night did anything, it made them more apprehensive about their activities and the possibility that someone is on to them. They'll be more on their guard, looking over their shoulders, waiting for your agents to find them. Hampton Beach is a relatively small town and word travels fast. Besides, I'm worried."

"About what?"

"Not what. Who. Baker and Kranepool. They made me believe you blew your cover." Matt took the tray and placed it on the floor and moved closer to Meg on the bed. "Meg, it's not for me to say," Matt reached out, his hand catching a hold of her chin and tipping it so she would look him directly in the eyes, "but you have to make yourself scarce. Soon. Like in ASAP."

Meg placed her hand over his. "I know. We've got a plan. Matt, are you sure there's nothing else at all from tonight you're not telling me?"

Nothing registered on Matt's face but a blank stare. Meg knew then she had to break with protocol. She had to know if he could he could shed light on the one person he'd neglected to talk about.

"Ever heard of a guy name Fleming?" Meg waited for any kind of reaction and was rewarded with the dawning of a light bulb going off. Matt shook his head in the affirmative.

"Fleming. Yeah. Somebody mentioned him and everyone sitting at the table gave a collective gasp." Matt paused, thinking, his eyes looking through her, trying to remember. "You know his name's familiar. I thought about him on the drive home and remembered when we were kids, there used to be a family in town. All boys, very nerdy. Not into sports, not into much of anything going on in the village. One of them went off to college and studied," Matt kept snapping his fingers as if it would help him recall what was on the tip of his tongue. "Some sort of biology. Well, they all did, really. He's older, about the same age as Thomas. Got his Ph.D and won numerous awards for some sort of scientific discovery regarding viruses."

Meg froze. The final piece of her puzzle clicked into place. Fleming!

"Meg? Meg?" Matt was waving his hand in front of her face. "You in there? Why are you looking at me like that?"

Meg launched herself at Matt, hugging him to her. "You did it, Matt! You found the missing link!"

Meg pushed back but Matt locked his arms around her. "You're not getting away that easily. What link? And don't tell me I'm on a need to know basis. You know damn well I'm worried about the safety of my family, the club, and," Matt looked loving at her, "you. I love you, Meg. Don't shut me out. I don't give a rat's ass about Agency protocol. Go ahead and tell Aunt Elizabeth if you want. I want to know what you're walking into."

Meg couldn't tell him that his feelings were reciprocated. She'd only come to reconcile her own recently. She hadn't come to Hampton Beach to fall in love. She'd come to do her job.

"The lab on Plum Island, Matt. The technicians have been experimenting with some pandemic viruses in the lab. Draper, Baker, Kranepool, Fleming and Steeler were all after the virus. We're got to stop them."

Matt thrust a hand through his hair. The disbelief in his eyes broke Meg's heart. "God, I can't believe it's led to this."

Meg looked up into the eyes of the man who held her close. She hugged him, her concern for what she was about to say to him weighing heavily on her mind. But it needed to be said. And it was her job to tell him. "Yes. And the money to pay the terrorists has been sitting all along in your club's bank account."

CHAPTER TWENTY-TWO

Hot Dog Beach

"Why the hell are we meeting out in the open? And at this teenybopper beach no less! We're so old, the kids are probably wondering what the hell we're doing here." Mike Kranepool snarled at the two men sitting in beach chairs parked in the sand.

At least whoever picked the spot had the hindsight to sit near the dunes, away from the bulk of the beach goers and packed volleyball courts. Ever one to isolate himself, John Steeler sat slightly away from Steve and Mike, a ball cap pulled low over his brow, typing furiously away on his IPad.

"Where the hell is Draper?" Mike asked.

Steve Baker popped opened a beer and pointed to the ocean. "He's catching a few waves before we make the final training run tonight. Said he had a few things to think about." He took a swig of the cold brew. "Sit down and take a load off. You want one?"

"Keep your voice low, Baker. Someone could hear you."

"Relax. Nobody can hear us."

Mike kicked off his sandals and sat down in the sand next to Steve. "Don't you know about the open container law? We don't need a ticket and get on the cop's radar. And before I forget, you, my man, are indeed being followed."

Steve drained his can and placed it back in a red cooler, closing the lid. "What the hell are you talking about?" It didn't take much to activate Steve's panic button. "How the hell do you know that?"

"A friend. That black Escalade you drive attracts a lot of attention. Unwanted attention, I might add, since that night at the marina. Didn't I tell you to park that damn car in your garage and use another until this blew over? My source in the HB police department told me they got an order from Homeland to identify drivers of Black Escalades. That's too high up the chain for my comfort level. Get rid of that car or I'll get rid of it for you."

Baker didn't like it when Mike took him down a peg or two. "I'll take care of it when we leave here."

"No, you won't," Mike countered. "We'll trade cars and *I'll* take care of it. You're becoming a liability. In my book you only get one warning. And just to give you a heads up, Draper is pissed."

"Now just one minute. I've held up my end of everything he asked me to do."

"You have, but it's the small things that are going to let someone set a trap for us if they find out what we plan to do. Wait until I tell Draper someone is sniffing around in the SAR paperwork."

It was becoming clearer to Mike that Baker had no backbone when the going got exponentially rough. He was too young with a lot of money at his disposal. The only night he'd shown any sign of speaking up was the night when they'd been introduced to Fleming, the lab specialist. It was the only night Steve had put Draper on notice. Since then, the jury was out over how he was handling his end of the operation. Mike had been summoned to meet with Jeff regarding Steve and wound up defending his friend, walking away, afraid of what Jeff might have in store for Steve at the end. There was a knot in the pit of Mike's stomach knowing he also had to tell Draper that Baker was being tailed.

Mike glanced up and down the beach. Fourth of July weekend was in full swing judging by the number of people at the popular hangout. He grabbed the binoculars off the beach towel by Baker's foot and scanned the surf. "Draper's got five minutes to get out of the water or I'm going to make *his* life miserable for a change. He's the one always complaining about time being wasted. I don't want to be here one more minute than necessary. For all we know, someone could be watching."

Steve stood up and donned his sunglasses. "Now who's paranoid? Hell, you didn't even dress to blend in, Mike. And for the record, I did not choose to meet here. I'm sick of being the scapegoat." Mike saw Steve glance over to where John still sat typing, seemingly oblivious to both of them. "I'll go find him. You in a hurry or something?"

"Yeah. Or something."

Mike watched the crowd. No one seemed to be taking an interest, at least from what Mike observed. Idiot, he thought, as he watched Steve make his way to the water's edge. He glanced at John, who'd been working diligently on the computer, taking great care not to get sand on his precious piece of technology. The man was never without it.

It was a good thing that Steve had volunteered to go in search of Draper. Mike had business to discuss with John before the two returned. He and Steve were supposed to have met the other morning, but something had come up.

"Well, don't keep me in suspense. Tell me. Did it work out?"

"All set." John typed as he talked. "I was vetted and got my credentials to start on Tuesday."

"Tuesday? Why not Monday?"

"I don't know. Neither does Fleming. But the lab is going to be closed for some reason."

"How long is it going to take before you're able to get into the areas we need you to?"

"Funny you should ask. I was moved right up to the top of the list for the job because of that maternity leave, right? But I got an added bonus none of us planned on."

"What happened?" Mike eyed the crowd, watching for any signs of anyone eavesdropping.

"Apparently there's a lab technician in level B2 that's working on a research project. He apparently got access to a higher clearance level. The powers that be quizzed me about my research skills at MIT and I must have fit the bill. So, not only am I in, but I'm going to have greater mobility and access than we thought."

"Which means in the scope of things?"

"We're going to be able to pass off the virus and data on the vaccine sooner than we planned."

The excitement of hearing the news had adrenaline rushing through Mike's body. His heart pumped wildly. He willed himself to stay calm, to show no emotion, but the elation he felt that the job was nearing the end was overwhelming.

Mike got up and walked across the hot sand and stood next to John. "Does Fleming know about this?" He then looked out in the direction of the ocean.

"Yeah. We met in town the other day. I needed a crash course on the lay of the facility. He came to my office. You know that no one works for me, so it was private. We went over every possible scenario of what could go wrong and how to handle getting the vaccine out of the lab, several ways to pass it off undetected. He put my mind at ease. But you're going to have to tell Draper there's a need to move up the operation by a week."

Mike turned and looked down into a pair of dark eyes staring up at him from beneath the rim of the ball cap. Eyes that warned him there was something not on the agenda.

"And why would we have to do that?"

"There's a storm off the coast of the Africa headed for the Caribbean, quite possibly the Eastern seaboard. The models have it targeted for the Hamptons in ten days, especially the European model, which is pretty accurate at predicting

Atlantic storms. Jim said if this storm is predicted to hit here the lab will be evacuated and what's in it will be moved to a secure location known to only those at the very top. And if that happens…"

"I don't think I want to hear this."

"You don't. And neither will the Arab."

"What's the worse case scenario?"

"The plan is *not* to return the virus to Plum Island *at all.* It will be moved inland. Way inland, possibly to somewhere in the Midwest."

Mike turned away after hearing the dreaded news and looked out onto the beautiful blue waters of the Atlantic. For probably the first time in his life, he prayed. Because if that virus had to be moved to a secure government lab deep within the United States, Steve, Jim, John, and he would be worthless commodities to Draper and Kalil. There was only one six-letter word to describe their situation at the moment—fucked.

CHAPTER TWENTY-THREE

Sound View Marina
Six days later

Wearing his black rain gear and water goggles to keep his body semi-dry and his eyes free to see through the rain, Matt hid behind a stack of newly cut pilings that lay approximately twenty feet from the end of the dock. The *Scottish Lass* was moored, rigged by its crew to ride out the approaching storm.

But it was Reggie and his crew standing on the edge of the dock, braving the elements, that Matt zeroed in on. A Navy cruiser approached, its horn blaring its arrival in some form of code. Reggie motioned to his men to pick up their gear. Everyone shouted as they passed bags from one to the other, while the Scottish voice of their leader shouting directions, trying to be heard above the roar of the wind.

Matt brushed away a feather light tickle by his left ear, his forefinger coming to rest on hard, cold steel. He froze. Click. The sound of the gun being cocked sent a shiver down his spine.

"Hands above your head!" The gun's barrel shoved him forward ever so slightly. "Raise them so I can see and I won't blow your head off."

As serious as the situation was, Matt couldn't help but smile at the feminine voice.

Sarah.

"Stand up!" Matt did as requested, hands held high. The last thing he wanted was a bullet in the head. This was no time to joke. Sarah tapped down his clothing and took the Glock hidden in the back of his pants. Apparently, satisfied he had no other weapons on him, she commanded, "Turn around!"

When he did as she asked, Matt stood stunned. He would never have recognized her. Sarah was dressed in camouflage, face painted black for the night's operation.

"Matt! What the hell are you doing here?" Sarah raised her gun to his chest, her finger resting on the trigger. "Don't tell me you're in on this with Draper and the rest of the crew?"

"What? No! Sarah, you've got it wrong. I can explain." Matt could see she was serious.

Sarah glanced quickly over his shoulder. "Make it quick. We're about to have company." Matt didn't need to turn around to know Reggie and members of his team were making their way in his direction.

"I came to see Meg off. I overheard her talking to Jake and Samantha a few days ago that the operation was going to commence, but she never came to say good-bye."

Sarah lowered her gun and looked at him strangely, "Please don't tell me it's the last time you thought you would see her."

Matt hung his head. "I did." Hearing the clomping of footsteps on the wooden dock, he looked back up and said, "Sarah, I couldn't bare it if I hadn't told her I loved her before she left." Matt paused, "Especially if it was really the last time I ever saw her."

"What's going on here?" Reggie's voice growled. "Sarah? Is that you? You were supposed to be here twenty minutes ago. What have you...." Reggie came up short seeing Matt in the mix.

Surrounded by a team of people all dressed like Sarah, Matt knew he'd walked into the middle of the shutdown of Operation Hurricane. And from the look on Reggie's face, seeing Matt dressed as Black Sheep, he knew there would be hell to pay. If not right then, then later.

"What in God's creation are you doing here in the middle of my operation?" This time the roar of the Scot's voice could be heard all the way back to where the remaining members of his crew were loading bags onto the boat. "Did your aunt put you up to this? I swear, Matthew, I've no time to deal with you right now. We're ready to roll."

"He came to see Meg." Matt saw Sarah flinch, awaiting Reggie's inevitable wrath.

"For God's sake, lad! Meggie's got a job to do! She's out there risking her life to protect your interests because your aunt thought she was just the perfect..." Reggie's jaw snapped shut. The man had been about to give something away and thought better of it, Matt thought to himself. And then he knew why Megan Spears had entered his life. Yes, it was her job. Yes, his club was the focus of the Agency's investigation. But his aunt, Elizabeth Hallock, was matchmaking. Again. Just as Elizabeth had done for Kate, his sister, and John Clinton.

Surrounded by rifles aimed at his chest, Matt could only smile.

"Wipe that grin off your face, laddie, or I'll do it for you! You're impeding a federal investigation and as I said there's been a crisis. That's why the cruiser is here, Sarah. Change of plans, due to what's happened. I've no time to explain it standing here. Get aboard!"

The team under Reggie's command turned and rushed back to the boat. Reggie turned to go as well and stopped when he realized Matt was beside him.

"Where the hell do you think *you're* going?"

Matt pointed to the Navy cruiser at the pier.

"Not on your life or mine," Reggie stated.

"Sarah!" Matt called out. "My gun." She tossed it over Reggie's head to him.

Matt cocked the trigger and pointed the Glock at Reggie. "I say I go. I can be of help. And you know bloody well I can shoot."

Reggie grumbled and muttered. Matt couldn't hear anything except, "Well, get a move on! I'll brief you when we take off. Something's happening on Plum Island."

Reggie headed for the boat on a run, leaving Matt and Sarah staring at each other.

"How bad is it?" Matt asked.

"That's why I was late. The storm's on the move faster than anyone anticipated. We've only a short window of time or Meg and those with her will be stranded. Worst case, we'll be pulled off the water and the hurricane will go right over the island. There won't be much left of the place if we can't pull the mission off within the next two hours. Trust me. Meg's done her surveillance. There's no place to hide from the storm."

Hearing that, Matt started running. He jumped over the mound of pilings, ran down the dock and up the ramp onto the Navy cruiser with Sarah trailing in his wake.

A hurricane was headed for the Hamptons. As the cruiser pulled out into the Sound, Matt stood on deck, watching waves break over the bow of the boat. He didn't care if the storm tore apart the entire Sunfish Beach Club. Nothing mattered more to him than Megan Spears. And he wanted her safe at his side at the very end.

CHAPTER TWENTY-FOUR

Plum Island

Even the scrub pines that surrounded the research lab struggled to stay rooted in the ground in the fifty-mile-per-hour winds. Sand from the beach below swirled in the air like a mini-downspout tornado around Meg as she waited, listening in her earpiece, as each agent checked in. The Director had given the go. The final stage had commenced.

"Sparrow to Robin Hood. Update your status." Meg first zeroed in on Jake, who was located on the east side of the building keeping a watch for any activity on the beach below his position.

"All clear. Do you copy?" Jake responded.

"Roger." Meg looked through her night vision goggles. Hunkering farther down between the two boulders she'd found for shelter, she checked in with Samantha. "Sleeping Beauty, report."

Stationed on the west side, nestled within the pine trees with a view of both Plum Island Harbor and the lab, Samantha was closest to where the action would go down. A scratchy, crackling sound could be heard in Meg's earpiece as the female agent responded, "Same here. I can make out lights on the upper floor. Over."

"It's going to come your way. Stay vigilant. Over."

"Roger that."

The majority of minor level lab workers were evacuated from the facility several days ago due to the impending storm. The first trap had been laid for Steeler and Fleming to stay overnight for the last several days with the mandate that being upper level lab researchers they needed to lock down their stations for safety reasons and pack up whatever was vitally necessary to transport, putting them within easy accessibility to the virus.

It was during that time, she, Jake, and Samantha arrived in the middle of the night to set up the final stage of fleshing out the individuals who could pose a problem to their final plan. Information in hand from the wiretaps of the homes and offices of Draper and his crew, the traps were set. Everything was in place. Looking at her watch, Meg knew timing was everything and Reggie's interception of the Coast Guard vessel was the critical piece. The Director had given the ultimate command that all were to be taken alive unless agents' lives were placed in jeopardy.

"Sparrow, lights flashing." Samantha didn't wait for Meg to respond. "Morse Code. Sending signal to cutter. Over."

"Copy that. CG in position? Over."

"Roger. Requesting directions to move. Over."

"Negative. Follow directive. Over." The adrenaline revved up in Meg's system. The suspects were obviously taking action to move out.

Jake spoke in her earpiece. "Robin Hood moving to west side. Over."

Meg had worried about the developing relationship between the two partners and having Jake and Samantha with her at the end. She worried that one would cover for the other and mistakes could be made. Meg had put in a request for Sarah to stand in for Samantha, but the Director had denied it. "Stand down, Robin Hood. Over."

"Negative. On the move."

Damn Jake! Knowing there was too much territory to cover with the copse of pine trees on that side of the lab, Meg realized what he was trying to do and relented, "Copy that. Over."

Meg, checking the extra ammo she carried was safely secured, rose from her defensive stance in the rocks. She raised her Glock and slowly panned the area, her eyes trained to look for signs of anything that didn't add up. She cranked up the volume of her earpiece in order to hear the chatter over the roar of the weather.

"Robin Hood in place."

Meg didn't let him finish. "Position in regards to Sleeping Beauty?"

"Covering main exit. Sleeping Beauty at harbor. Over." Meg knew that meant that Jake had managed to hide in the bushes opposite where Samantha lay watching the Coast Guard boat. Hopefully, the distance between them was manageable.

"Copy that." Meg had moved from her initial position and was on the run to make her way to the corner of the north side of the lab.

Meg's earpiece crackled again. She dropped to her knees, cupping her hand to her ear trying to hear Jake through her earpiece.

"Sparrow, heat lamp is detecting four, read that, *four* bodies at the upper window. Lights are flashing code out in the direction of the cove." Jake paused.

"Says estimated ETA exit time ten minutes. Over."

"Copy that." This time the team chimed in.

Again on the move, Meg could barely take in the conversation between Jake and Samantha with the increase of the wind whipping up.

Jake came over the earpiece again. "Sparrow, intel's identified three. Any idea on the fourth?"

Now having reached the corner of the north side of the building, Meg responded, "All units be aware. Possible hostage situation. Over." She knew her agents' exchange was monitored on a frequency followed by Agent Tanner and Reggie. They'd step in with alternative directions should it become necessary. Until then, they'd operate on radio silence.

Taking of a hostage made the most sense to Meg. The Director apprised the team four BS Level 4 workers, planted by the Agency, would be the last to leave. It was their duty to risk their lives to stay behind, but would be backup and do clean up should Meg and her elite team need them. The Director had dug deep within Homeland, calling in a few IOUs, to find a source who'd help the team bring the decoys to the island without arousing suspicion. Knowing Steeler had hacked into the databases to obtain his ID and could possibly be monitoring any systems as well, it had to be done.

It was possible that Steeler and Fleming found out about the embedded agents. Their thinking could be to use human shields should there be unwanted company awaiting them outside the facility.

"Awaiting your instructions, Shadow." Meg heard the readying of Jake's weapon through her earpiece.

"Stand down, Robin Hood. Follow orders. Let them go down the cliff, reach the path, and head to the main harbor. Over."

"Awaiting your signal to follow. Over." Meg sighed, thankful Jake would go by the book. Lately, Meg worried about him as she saw the external anger he exhibited over the duration of the operation. She would be recommending to the Director he be given time off after his debriefing.

With her back to the wall of the building, Meg ducked under the windows, coming to stand at the corner that met the scrub pines. If one hadn't diligently studied the terrain and took a step in the wrong direction, he would misstep to topple off the steep cliffs hidden directly on the other side of the trees. Meg memorized every inch of the area from the trips and pictures taken on those ferry rides from Orient Point across the Sound to Connecticut. And in the darkness of the stormy night, Meg had faith she could walk any of the paths blindfolded.

"Lights off, Sparrow. Heat sensor shows them moving in our direction. Over."

"Copy that, Robin Hood. Beauty, stay in position. Repeat. Do not move.

Over."

Samantha broke in from her position overlooking the cove. "CG crew is untying the riggings. Over."

Meg rushed to the scrub pines at the corner of picnic area she spied out of the corner of her right eye. "Off to your left, Robin Hood." She signaled Jake with a flash of her laser.

"Roger. Doors opening." Intakes of breaths and a gasps, as well as a few swear words, could distinctly be heard throughout the earpieces. "Sparrow, do you have eye contact? Over."

Meg whipped off her night vision goggles, tossing them to the ground, knowing she would regret the move later. But she needed clearer vision from her vantage point and the lights mounted on the corners of the building lit up the scene as if it were daylight. Meg couldn't believe who walked out of the lab.

Whispering into her microphone, she spoke firmly, "Stand at the ready. Over."

"Roger." Voices echoed in unison.

Meg wanted to put herself in Jake's shoes and take one shot at the man who she had her doubts about since Washington, DC : the man who had her jumping through hoops with the Director since she'd arrived at Hampton Beach. Reggie's instinct had been on the mark, just as hers had been. Derek had played her for a sucker. Judas, what would the Director say, if she wasn't already listening.

Four men, one carrying a large rectangular, silver suitcase in front of him, similar to the kind one carries to hold poker chips, exited the building, their hands and arms shielding their faces from the pounding rain. Kranepool did not. He carried the case, cradling the precious cargo in his arms. Inside the well padded case was no doubt the virus and the vaccine. The Arab was getting what he wanted and pockets of the participants were going to be lined with millions of dollars. Or so they thought.

Eyes of those who'd exited the building darted in all directions: Fleming, Steeler, Kranepool, and Taylor. The four men looked in her direction, but Meg had hidden herself far enough into the copse of pines, but close enough to hear their ensuing conversations.

"Go!" Kranepool yelled to Taylor. "Baker's waiting at the dock. We've got to get out of here. Move it!"

Kranepool nodded to Steeler. "Wait five minutes. Then make your way down. Make sure there's no trap as we go down that path."

Steeler took his place next to Jim Fleming and simply nodded.

Odd, Meg thought.

Jake's voice broke in. "Be aware suspects separating. Over."

Meg chimed in, "Affirmative. Team will follow Steeler and Fleming."

The thought that a breach of security might exist crept into Meg's mind. Kranepool could be exhibiting extra caution due to insider information, but no matter what, the team would follow and attack from behind. Reggie, on the Navy cruiser with Sarah and his crew, had been circumventing the harbor undetected, now ready to jam the frequencies of the communication radios held in the hands of the four men and the Coast Guard vessel.

"Night Owl. Do you read me? Over." Meg was relieved to hear the Scottish voice.

"Copy, Sparrow, all is ready. ETA to intercept—fifteen minutes."

"Roger. Agents take position. I repeat, suspects taken alive per orders of the Director. Over."

Kranepool and Taylor, leaning into the wind, walked passed Meg. But she could hear every word of their conversation.

"Get your gun out, Taylor," Kranepool commanded gruffly. "I'm concerned there may be somebody on the trail. You've got to defend that case."

As the two entered the trees on their way to the cutter, Derek drew out his Sig Sauer and vanished from sight.

Meg knew their original plans had changed dramatically which could affect the mission's outcome. Originally, the Navy cruiser was to invade on one front. Reggie's team would infiltrate the lab, with a Special Ops team dropped in by air. But now the latter choice was an unavailable option due to the weather. The use of a SAR chopper at least was an impossibility as well, but how deep into the organization Draper's tentacles stretch?. The Navy's Seahawk SH-60 had been grounded when the wind speed picked up, the safety of its crew taking precedence. Given the hurricane making its way to Montauk Point, her confidence still ran high that her team could take down the men who had made Matt's life implode.

"Shadow, do you copy?" Jake's voice boomed in her earpiece.

Meg's attention diverted back to the two remaining men standing by the exit.

"What the f....?" Meg saw the flash of another silver box, just like the first, come from behind Steeler's back. Knowing Reggie had jammed Draper's radios, she had to think fast.

Jake's vantage point was far better than hers. "Identify object. Ready your weapon. Over."

"Identical suitcase, Shadow."

They'd been played. Under the impression the first suitcase was the one and only one to contain the virus, Draper may have turned the tables on them. Both cases would soon be on the Coast Guard cutter— one with and one without the virus.

"Stand down, Robin. Will apprehend both at the cove. Do you copy?"

"Roger."

Steeler began a slower paced trek to the trail. He suddenly stopped and turned to look for his partner. Fleming hadn't moved.

"Fleming!" he yelled,, the rain now coming down in torrents. "Get a move on. The clock is ticking! We have five minutes to be aboard with Mike."

Fleming stood motionless, his hands in his lab coat pocket. "You're not going anywhere. *Not with that case.*"

Seeing Fleming take a stand had Megan shaking her head in denial and disbelief. Could it be? No! It wasn't possible.

"Stand down! Do *not* fire!" Meg screamed into her microphone.

Steeler, who had walked half-way to the trees, pivoted in the direction of her voice, his attention drawn away from Fleming. Meg reached for her weapon, but was too late.

"No! No!" She cried out, her voice echoing even in the blowing wind. She prayed Mike and Derek had not heard her cry as they made their way down the path. Meg froze and watched in horror as Fleming drew a small caliber pistol from his pocket and fired off three rounds into Steeler.

Pop! Pop! Pop!

Steeler dropped to the ground, grabbing his right knee, the case hitting the pavement. Blood poured out the side of his leg, mixing with the rainwater on the pavement.

Meg and Jake ran toward Fleming, guns drawn. Meg covered Fleming while Jake searched Steeler for any more weapons that might still be on him. Steeler lay writhing in pain.

"Put your gun down!" Meg's pointed her Glock at Fleming's chest. Puzzled at his laid-back reaction to her coming at him fast and furious and as if rehearsed, he raised his hands in the air before she even shouted out the standard command.

"Don't shoot, Agent Spears." Fleming's eyes locked onto the muzzle of her gun aimed at his heart. "My ID. It's in the inside pocket."

Meg rummaged in the interior of his lab coat. It was hard to get it open due to the material being matted to his frame from the pelting rain.

Pulling out what seemed to be a wallet of some sort, she expected to open it and find a laminated ID card that would read, "Jim Fleming, BS Level 4". Instead, she found Agency-issued credentials, "Darius Sarkov, CIA".

"I don't understand. Jake! Take a look at this!" Jake, his gun still pointed at Steeler, came to stand beside her, taking Darius's ID in his hand. He looked at Meg quizzically, his face showing disbelief in their discovery.

"You're CIA." Jake and Meg stated in unison.

Fleming silently nodded.

Meg motioned to Steeler lying on the ground. "How bad is he hurt?"

Jake responded, "The bullets went clear through. Let's get him inside and doctor him up. But, we've got a problem. We're not going to be able to get off this island in one trip with him injured. You know what that means. Plan B.

"Yup. I know we have no choice. His getting shot has thrown a monkey wrench in getting out of here."

Meg was going to have to ride out the storm with the man whose primary role was putting Matt's business in the toilet. And worse, the hurricane was now literally on her doorstep. Matt had warned her of the dire consequences of riding one out on an island. If only she hadn't started an argument with him over doing her job versus saving the Sunfish. Her biggest regret of all was she'd neglected to say she loved him. How she couldn't live without him. That everything would work out. Now she might never have the chance.

Focusing on the present, Meg finally understood Jim Fleming's purpose in Operation Hurricane. Sarah had brought an item to her attention four weeks ago, but she'd dismissed it, shoved it out of her mind. Jim had spent his undergraduate studies at George Washington University. Then he'd gone on to MIT. He'd been a plant by Elizabeth Hallock far longer than the operation was in existence. The Russian's last name was known far and wide in intelligence circles around the world. Sarkov was the youngest son of Demetrie Sarkov, one of the best agents in the Russian-European Theatre. Demetrie had saved Katherine Hallock's life two years ago, and she had saved his.

Just as Meg was about to explain to Jake what they were dealing with and that she was going to make contact with Reggie to redefine a few elements to close up their operation, another round of gun shots came from the area of the cliffs.

"Shots fired!" she yelled, hoping Reggie and the others could hear her and the transmission had not been broken down with the communication system.

Jake looked to Meg, "What should we do? We've got to get out of here and back to the dock."

Meg knew what had to be done. "You go. Take Samantha. But go through the pines to get her. Don't let anyone know her position."

"Meg. I can't leave you here." Meg turned and stood next to Sarkov.

"That's a direct order from your lead agent. Get the hell out of here and find out what is going down in the harbor. Listen on your earpieces. I'll contact Reggie, shut down the place and pray he can get the boat back here in time."

"Meg…"

"Go."

Jake embraced her in a bear hug. "You take care of her, Sarkov. Otherwise, the Director will have us shoveling camel dung in Egypt."

Darius Sarkov put up his arm to stop Jake. "You need to know that case… the one that Mike and Derek took with them?"

Darius had Meg and Jake's undivided attention. "It's fake. I did my job. But we've got to get that one," he pointed to the case sitting in the puddle on the pavement, "the hell out of here. If that becomes airborne from the winds of the hurricane, the whole Northeast will be dead."

CHAPTER TWENTY-FIVE

Nearing Plum Island Harbor

The sailor raced up the staircase to the bridge where Captain Morton, Reggie, and Matt stood looking out the window. Waves crashed over the front bow of the large frigate as it moved closer into the waters leading to the harbor.

"Sir! Sir! Report's of shots fired!" The sailor saluted and stood at attention, trying to keep his balance as the boat rocked and rolled.

Even Matt, who'd spent many a day on rough waters, kept having trouble maintaining level footing and keeping his stomach on an even keel. Reggie had not let him have his own headset when he came onboard at the marina, so he'd not been able to follow what was happening. But one quick look in the Scot's direction told him the situation had turned dire. Matt swallowed, his fear for Meg making his heart thump wildly. Inner panic set in. She'll be all right, he said to himself over and over.

"We heard, Hartford. What else do you have for me? You wouldn't be up here if there wasn't something I needed to know."

"Ahead in the water, sir. Something's on the radar. Ensign Reed says we need to check it out."

Matt was amazed at the precision of the commands that took place among the officers. Reggie walked back to stand next to him, reaching for the pole that Matt had been holding onto and sat on the edge of the small bench close by.

"How bad?" Matt asked.

"We'll know when they come about. I hope this doesn't slow us down. We need to intercept that cutter."

The boat slowed. The lights on its bow flashed on, illuminating the activity on the deck below. Men were tethered to the side rails of the cruiser to keep from going overboard should a wave crash onto the decks.

Captain Morton motioned for Matt and Reggie to come to look out the window. Below, four sailors leaned over with grappling hooks and pulled something from the water—a body.

"Sweet Jesus." Reggie was the first to speak.

The Captain relayed to his crew to carry the body below deck. He turned to Reggie. "Full speed, ahead?" he asked.

"Aye, Aye. Let's go get those SOBs. Come, Matt. Let's hope he's not one of ours."

Grabbing the radio from its clip in the ceiling, Captain Morton called, "All hands on deck." To the man on his right, he said, "Set the course to intercept at Plum Island." He nodded to Reggie who took his leave.

Matt followed Reggie down a set of steep metal stairs. As they turned the corner, a bevy of sailors had gathered near the doctor's quarters. They broke apart, allowing for Matt to follow Reggie into the room. The door closed behind them. A sailor stood at attention, standing guard outside.

The body lay on a gurney, water dripping in puddles on the floor. Again, Matt felt his heart pound as if it were outside his chest and not in it.

"Couldn't have happened to a nicer person." Reggie took one glance at the body, and then stepped aside for Matt to take a look.

Matt stared down, sucking in a deep breath. No! Staring up at him, eyes wide open was Derek Taylor, Meg's "boyfriend", aka CIA agent.

"Don't feel bad, Matthew. He got what was coming to him. He went over to the dark side. Went rogue on us."

Matt had to ask, but the words failed him at first. "If he's dead, where's Meg?"

"I don't know."

"She's alive, isn't she?" Matt wanted to choke the answers he wanted out of the man next to him, but knew Reggie would keep him in the dark.

"Meg's on the island." Reggie put his hand up. "That's all I know. With the storm, we're now getting very limited communications. We don't know what's fully gone down. Meggie knows her job, Matt, and she's good, the best at what she does. She suspected this scumbag a long time ago." He pointed back at Derek's lifeless body. "Let's get back to the bridge. We should be nearing the harbor. You brought your gun. Sarah's going to need a partner for backup."

Matt didn't need to be asked twice.

* * *

The cruiser had successfully intercepted Draper's crew before their boat had a chance to head for the open waters of the Sound or the Atlantic. Reggie passed off an extra set of binoculars to Matt as he, Sarah, and several other members of the officers' crew watched the operation from the bridge.

Matt heard the conversation between his aunt and Reggie regarding the safety of her agents. It was then the captain informed the trio it was unwise for those not trained in high-level water rescues to take part in the mop up operation due to the increasing intensity of the wind and wave action. It was a dangerous task for even the finest trained team. It was evident the Coast Guard boat was taking on water, the waves rolling in from the sea, sending massive quantities of salt water across its bow and into the cabins below.

"Too much bobbing up and down." Matt peered through the eyepiece, trying to adjust the focus onto the people involved below his viewpoint. He was looking for one and only one person. And he hadn't found her… yet.

"Where the hell are Meg and her team?" Matt wiped at the window of the bridge knowing full well it would do no good.

The Navy Seals had secured a safety net between the ships and had begun the process of bringing Draper and his men over to the cruiser one by one. What Matt would give right now for any of them not to be wearing a life jacket. One good push overboard…

"Steady, lad." Reggie interrupted Matt's thoughts as if he'd read them. "I know this is hard for you. But the commander says all is going according to plan. They're doing the final search of the vessel now from top to bottom. We'll go below in a few minutes. I want to stay and see that everyone gets on board."

Sarah, who had been waiting silently at Matt's side, placed a hand on his arm. A simple gesture of reassurance. He knew she was as concerned as he was for Meg's safety and for the others in the dangerous storm. Derek's death had left them all shaken and wary of what had happened when communications became sporadic.

Suddenly, Sarah jumped up and down, her binoculars knocking into the window. "Look! At the back of the boat! Jake and Samantha managed to get on board! Reggie, can you see them?"

"I do, lass. Good eyesight. Captain Morton, radio the Director, if you will. I'm taking my team down to the conference area. See that your men keep each captive well guarded."

Nodding, the captain reached for his radio and began his transmission.

Matt stopped on the top of the stairway. "Is this where Aunt Elizabeth stops the money transfer?"

"She did it hours ago. Sent it to the account where Interpol immediately sent a false transaction to Kalil and his men. They have to show up in person at the Swiss bank with ID to take the cash out of the safe deposit box. We've found out Kalil's not a very intelligent man. Overlooks the finer details. His boss, the one he double-crossed, will be arriving at the same time to pick up the money as well." Reggie glanced up the staircase at Matt. "Are you two coming? Let's find out who's been on that boat."

Matt took the stairs two at a time, eager to see Meg. Then all would go as he planned. But first, he would tell her he loved her more than life itself. If today had taught him anything, it was the simple fact he couldn't live life without her.

Coming around the corner, Matt heard voices shouting and swearing from inside the door on the left hand side of the hallway. Mike Kranepool's voice could be heard cussing out the guards.

Following Reggie into the conference room, his eyes scanned the room not once, not twice but three times. No Meg. Where the hell was she? Jeff Draper sat handcuffed to a metal chair at the head of the table. Jake and Samantha stood in the corner, whispering, trying to dry off as much as possible. Baker sat mute in the corner, his eyes practically bugging out of his face. Like he'd seen a ghost...or worse.

"Well now, what have we here?" Reggie pounded the table with his fist. "Traitors. Treasonist terrorists! And you thought we wouldn't find out."

Kranepool was the only captive still struggling with two guards who held him in his seat.

"Shackle his hands and his feet!" Reggie commanded. "I'll start with him first."

Matt came farther into the room for a better view of the interview.

Kranepool's eyes landed on Matt. "You!" Mike snarled. "If you and your *girlfriend* hadn't gone shoving your noses in places they didn't belong, we'd be long gone. But she's not your girlfriend, is she?"

Matt stood mute.

"Don't let him get to you, Matthew." Reggie raised his voice so that he made it clear he was in command. "I've got a dead body in the room across the hall. Anybody want to lay claim to it?"

Mike and Draper looked at one another, but it was Mike who was the spokesman. "Derek got what was coming to him. He was playing both sides. I took him down on the path. He wanted the suitcase before we got to the boat. I said, 'Over your dead body.' Then, I shot him."

Matt couldn't believe what he was hearing. "Where's Fleming and Steeler, Mike? You take them out, too?"

Baker spoke up. "I had nothing to do with dead bodies. I signed on to get the virus...for the money, Matt. Only for the money." He turned on Mike. "Three weeks ago, you wanted nothing more to do with any of this. Remember? At the Liar's Club?"

"I changed my mind when Jeff offered me a higher stake in the action."

All eyes turned on Draper, who sat smugly staring at Matt. "Sorry. But you were the perfect cover, my friend. When you asked me to invest, I knew the club was what we'd been looking for. But I'm with Baker. I didn't sign on to kill anybody. So who's dead up on the mountain top?"

The room became eerily quiet.

Draper's eyes locked onto Matt's. "We heard another round of gun shots when Mike got to the boat. It came from the lab."

Matt clenched and unclenched his fists. He'd been waiting for just the right moment. He lunged at Draper, taking the guard by surprise, knocking him to the side. He pummeled Draper's face. One blow missed its target completely and slammed into the table, but the other squarely connected with Jeff's nose, blood spraying in all directions.

"Somebody get him off me!" Draper screamed in pain.

"Matt, stop! Enough!" It was Jake who took hold of his arms and spun him around away from Draper.

Matt panted heavily, looking down at his bloodied hands. He didn't move, but looked back over his shoulder, "Where is she? Where's Meg?"

Reggie bellowed, "Out! Jake, Samantha, Sarah! Get Matthew out of this room. This investigation is on hold until I get some answers from the two of you."

A roar came from the belly of the ship. The engines were revving up and coming to life.

"What's that?" Matt asked, panic in his voice. In the hallway, Reggie took Matt by the shoulders and gently pinned him against the wall.

"Matthew, lad, look at me. The captain had orders to get out of the way of this storm as soon as all the people on the Coast Guard boat were aboard the cruiser." There was a hitch in Reggie's voice as he continued. "Meg, Steeler and Fleming are still at the lab. If we can, we'll go back."

Matt looked at Jake, who simply nodded in the affirmative.

Matt gulped, his heart in his throat, "And what if you can't?"

Sarah started to cry. Samantha comforted her. Jake's hand came to rest on Matt's shoulder as he gently moved an emotional Reggie to the side.

Reggie, his eyes downcast, shook his head, "I just don't know, lad, I just don't know."

CHAPTER TWENTY-SIX

Hallock Farm

Meg didn't want to imagine what her beloved Beetle Bug was going to look like after the hurricane passed. She abandoned the car two miles down the road when a tree as wide as she was tall came crashing down in front of her. Turning into the drive that led to Hallock Farm, Meg marveled at the devastation and destruction of Mrs. Hallock's prized trees and shrubs. The wind buffeted her from all sides, one gust almost lifting her off her feet, as she made her way around the house to the back door by the kitchen.

Meg couldn't believe after all she had been through she was home.

Taking a seat on the back step, Meg took a few minutes to catch her breath from her long walk before she went inside. She knew those awaiting her safe return were frantic knowing that the SAR team and the Navy cruiser weren't able to come to her aid. But the back porch and stoop provided little shelter. Meg sorely needed to get warm and dry. A smile formed at the corner of her mouth. Matt could definitely help in that department.

Opening the door, she was surprised that all was eerily quiet. No Hannah cooking at the kitchen stove, although pots and pans lay strewn about. She hated the thought she was leaving a trail of muddy dirt and rain water on Mrs. Hallock's Oriental carpet runner as she made her way to the foyer, but it was the fastest way to get to her room at the top of the stairs.

Approaching the living room, Meg saw through the crack in the door that the room was filled to capacity.

"Matt, I'm telling you, no one...no one is venturing out on the water or roads right now. The supervisor declared a state of emergency. We stay put. People who didn't evacuate stay in their houses until the storm passes. We warned them. You've led mandatory evacuations before. We go in and clean up after. I don't risk the lives of my volunteers in a storm of this magnitude." It was Sam, from the rescue squad.

"But we're talking about Meg! My Meg!" There was a sense of urgency and desperation in Matt's voice. The happiness Meg felt by hearing him talk in such a way made her heart start beating rapidly, but she stood by the door and listened. "I can't simply wait and do nothing. It's been twelve hours."

"Yes. I know. Be rational. We've lived through this before. Don't you trust that she can handle herself in any emergency?" Sarah spoke in a more soothing tone.

"Megan has good common sense, Matthew. She and Fleming will be able to figure something out. There's a vault if need be. She's resourceful. Have faith."

"Aunt Elizabeth!" Matt sighed in frustration. Meg found herself standing at attention. What was the Director doing at Hallock Farm? When had she arrived? And how had she managed to arrive at the farm through the storm? Was she at Fox Hollow when Reggie returned with Draper and his men?

"Matthew Hallock, you stop right now. Sarah's right. We all need to be rational and let it pass. Oh my dear boy, I know you don't want the love of your life…" Mrs. Hallock, always the mother, was showing her maternal side.

Shivering in the foyer, Meg looked down at the massive puddle on the floor. She had to make herself known or she'd have hypothermia…again. Come to think of it, the last time had had its benefits. She smiled and walked in the door.

"Well, look what the cat dragged in," Jake smiled from across the room, his arm draped lovingly over Samantha's shoulder. Shouts of surprise and gleeful claps came from the room's occupants.

"Funny, Jake." Meg smirked at him. Then she turned to Helen and the housekeeper. "Mrs. H, Hannah. I always seem to be showing up on your doorstep making a mess of things. I'm afraid I've made a royal mess in your foyer." But as she talked Meg searched the room for one person and one person only.

And he was nudging his father's chair and jumping over the coffee table to get to her.

"Whoa! Don't kill your…" Meg never got an opportunity to finish her sentence. Matt engulfed her in a huge bear hug, lifted her off her feet, and twirled her around the center of the room. Meg didn't care who saw them. She hugged him back and firmly planted a kiss on his lips. He lowered her to the ground and kissed her back, far more deeply than Meg felt comfortable with in public.

"Matt, not here. Your parents are watching.."

"Oh, you go right ahead, dear. Don't mind us." Meg peeked behind Matt to see both Helen and Robert Hallock grinning broadly, the patriarch giving her a thumb's up. Meg laughed out loud.

"Master Matthew, you need to let that girl go and get changed into some dry clothes. I'm sure she knows we all are dying to hear how she got off the island." Hannah was carrying a tray of empty glasses as she passed by.

Meg nodded, "She's right. I have to get dry. I'll be right back and tell you everything." Glancing at Elizabeth Hallock, she got the nod of approval. The nod that said "within reason."

"I'll go with you." Matt went to follow her out of the room. Meg knew what would happen should he do that. And she didn't need to announce that fact to the world. Her hand went up. "Talk to the hand, Matt. What does it say?"

Sam laughed, knowing Matt's experience at the yacht club. "You better get the lady a good stiff drink, good buddy. I know your father has something hidden around here somewhere. She'll be back down in a minute." He whipped his hand up as Meg had done. Matt slapped it away.

Meg kissed Matt on the cheek and walked out of the room. Seeing him again made her think of her bucket list. Then reality hit. She'd be in back in DC within two days.

* * *

"It's truly amazing! I can't how you managed to vacate the island in the storm!" Elizabeth's soft, southern drawl was in awe as she spoke and then, took a sip of sherry. Gone was the Earl Grey tea. Today was a day for celebration. "Megan, I don't even to tell you to the depths my mind traveled."

Meg carefully chose her words relaying the facts of her mission to her captive audience. Even she marveled how things had taken a turn for the better. Hell, in her career she had sped down the Thames, skied ahead of an impending avalanche, and jet-skied through the canals of Venice. None compared to getting off of Plum Island.

"Jim Fleming was a pure genius with the electronics. He hooked up an old transistor radio to the batteries of our flashlights to beam a flashing beam of light skyward. We then set up five flares trying to get attention, thinking no one could possibly be left out in the storm. However, the fishing trawler saw the signal.

Its crew set out in a rescue boat to come for us. It took some work considering the delicate package we were carrying, and Steeler's bleeding leg, to board the craft. I had to laugh, though."

"Why is that, Meggie?" Reggie had cleaned his plate of pecan pie.

"The boat that picked us up was called 'Megan's Folly.' I believe you know it."

"Aye, I do, lass. Captain Henry. I suppose I'll be owing him a pint when I see him next?"

Meg slapped her thigh as she chuckled. "Oh, I think you're going to have to do better than that. The man was talking about installing a keg-i-rator in his kitchen." Meg rolled her "r" as she spoke making slight fun of her mentor's accent.

Everyone sitting around the dining room table erupted in laughter and everyone had smiles on their faces.

Matt cleared his throat. "I'd like to make a toast, if I may? Father?"

"The table's yours, Matthew. Make it a good one."

"Oh!" Matt's mother let out a squeal.

"Hush, Helen. Let the boy have his say."

Meg suddenly realized that Matt hadn't risen to say his piece but was kneeling next to her, on one knee, reaching for her hand. OMG! Her breath caught as she watched him reach into his pocket to take out an aqua colored box.

"Megan Spears. You know I love you. I can't imagine my life without you. I want to grow old with you, see your smile when I wake up every morning and at night when I go to sleep. I know getting married to me was on your bucket list under 'only in my dreams' but—"

Meg stopped him. "You read my diary?"

Matt shrugged his shoulders and nodded. "You're not the only one in this family who can do surveillance undetected."

Meg heard the snickers around the table.

"Well?" Matt asked.

"Well, what? I don't think you're quite done." Meg wasn't going to let him off the hook that easily. She wanted it all.

"Will you do me the honor of being my wife?"

Matt didn't wait for her answer. He slipped a ruby ring surrounded by diamonds on the ring finger of her left hand.

Meg looked down at the ring which sparkled back up at her and then flung herself into Matt's arms. "Yes!"

"Mother?" Matt lifted his head after thoroughly kissing Meg.

Why was the man questioning his mother at this most perfect, romantic moment of her life?

"I'm right on top of everything. Don't worry about a thing." Helen practically bounced in her seat. Meg had never seen the woman so excited.

Meg looked to Matt who smiled down at her, his eyes smoldering with banked desire.

"Mother has the wedding planner on speed dial." Meg pulled Matt to her. She pulled his head down and kissed him deeply while those gathered at the table whistled, hooted, and applauded their approval. The white flag resurfaced. All was well with her world. The hurricane of a life she had lived was gone forever.

EPILOGUE

"You're not going to tell him, are you?" Meg needed one last reassurance as she whispered her question to her two companions. The doors of the vestibule in St. Mark's Church were closed, the strains of a concerto played as the organist awaited the cue for her entrance. The church was filled to capacity with friends and family. *Her new family.* Today she was joining the Hallock family and crossing off another item off her bucket list.

"Love a duck, dearie!" Elizabeth Hallock bent over, adjusting Meg's white mantilla, cathedral length veil. "Stand still, Megan. Tell her, Sam. It's all going to be perfect."

Meg eyed Sam Tanner at her right hand side, struggling with his black bow tie. He winked at her. "Lizzie's got it all planned it out, Meg. Why are we talking about your new Agency position five minutes before we walk down the aisle? And no, to answer your question, Matt won't know unless you choose to tell him."

When Meg and Matt announced their plans to get married, Mrs. Hallock immediately dialed her event planner to set up the wedding of Megan's dreams. However, Matt threw a curve ball into the works when the plans got out of hand, announcing he wanted a destination wedding: just the two of them, a minister, and a beach, waves lapping onto the shore at sunset in a warm tropical climate. Meg should have hidden her feelings better, but a wedding was another item on that infamous list and she broke down in tears.

Wanting to give her anything, Matt changed his mind. It was then Meg broke down, sobbing uncontrollably. Finally, after cleaning out an entire tissue box, he found out why she'd become so upset. She told him he had no father to walk her down the aisle to give her away. No mother to sit on the left side of the church in the front pew and dab at her eyes with a hanky.

Hence the two people who now stood on each side of her waiting to escort her down the aisle. It was Matt who suggested Elizabeth and Sam, pointing out to her that they had been her family for almost ten years. When she'd asked Elizabeth to come shopping with her to choose her wedding gown, the woman promptly picked up the phone and canceled her lunch with the President of the United States. They were at one of the most exclusive bridal shops in DC within the hour.

Sam, on the other hand, had stood silent, stunned. But he quickly walked up to her, kissed her cheek, and whispered in her ear. "You've been like a daughter to me, Megan. I'd be honored." When he walked back to his desk at the Agency, she watched him wipe away a tear that had escaped and slid down his weathered cheek.

And here the three of them stood together today. Her family.

The "Wedding March" started and the doors to the church opened. As her maid of honor, Sarah took her place in front of Meg, a broad smile on her face. "You are a beautiful bride, Meg."

Taking Lizzie Clinton, Matt's niece and flower girl, by the hand, Sarah began the long walk down the red carpet to the front of the church.

"Megan, I can't believe you wanted me to walk with you and Sam." Elizabeth dabbed at her eyes with an embroidered handkerchief. "I could have just walked in with Helen."

"I know, but I wanted you both beside me," Meg replied. It was her turn to smile lovingly at both of them. Her head held high, she looked through her veil down the long aisle and locked eyes with the man of her dreams, the love of her life.

"That's our cue, ladies," Sam quietly whispered, taking a hold of Meg's arm, placing it through his own. He squeezed her hand as any father would at that moment. "It's time for Operation Happily Ever After."

THE END

Want to know what's next in store for another member of the Hallock clan? Continue reading an excerpt from THE ROMANCE EQUATION, the next book in the series, HAMPTON THOROUGHBREDS.

THE ROMANCE EQUATION

Chapter One

St. Regis Hotel
New York City

Thomas Hallock glanced down at the dial on his gold Rolex watch. The CFO of Hallock Farm Equine and Rehabilitation Facility noted only five minutes had passed since the last time he checked. Frustrated Rick Stockton hadn't arrived on yet, he drummed his fingers on the bar. He hated to be kept waiting. Tardiness ranked right up on the top of his list. It was one of his biggest pet peeves. Where the hell was Rick? Rick was never late. *Never.* And if he was, he had a damn good reason why. Since it was Thomas who'd invited Rick to meet him at the bar, the thought that his best friend and confidante was a no show sent a chill down his spine. Especially with knowing the state of affairs back at Hallock Farm in Hampton Beach.

Sitting on the tan velvet barstool, Thomas drained his order of scotch on the rocks, caught the eye of the bartender and signaled for another. Normally, he made it a rule never to drink before five o'clock in the afternoon, but today was different. Desperate times called for desperate measures.

Waitresses circulated among the intimate tables for two as well as those manned by the business crowd steeped in networking for the next power meeting during the busy lunch hour.

Uncomfortable with the roar of the chatter and the scrutiny of several women perched on nearby stools, Thomas looked down into the empty crystal tumbler, his mind drifting off. By nature, Thomas tended to be a bit of a loner. He detested crowds. Unfortunately his duties at one of the most prestigious horse training facilities on eastern Long Island, and for that matter the entire East Coast, didn't give him the option to live the life he wanted to live.

Thomas lost control over his life when it was decided by his parents to send him to the Wharton School of Business after graduating from Harvard. Why? In order that he take his "proper" place in the running of the family business. Thomas had had other plans: go to medical school, specialize in pediatrics, and volunteer with Doctors Without Borders in order to aid those less fortunate than himself. The Hallock Family Trust gave him enough money to live on for the rest of his life. Thomas had a burning desire to give back. But without warning, the tables turned on him. He'd been devastated, but duty to family, which had been drilled into all Hallock siblings from birth, had won out in the end.

Thomas clearly understood why now. But it had taken a few years to get the chip off his shoulder that it had to be him, the eldest son of Robert and Helen, to carry the torch forward, not his younger brothers, Ethan, Adam and Matthew, or his sister, Katherine. With his dreams in the way distant past, it was business as usual to be a part of the infamous Hampton social scene, hobnobbing with the rich and famous who lived and/or vacationed in Hampton Beach, Sag Harbor, East Hampton and Southampton. His social calendar was filled with invitations to wine and dine with hedge fund managers, power brokers, foreigner investors and celebrities. These people were the farm's bread and butter. And whether Thomas liked it or not, he had obligations to see that Hallock Farm's finances flourished. Thomas thought he'd done just that. Until now.

Slowly sipping the rich liquid, Thomas thought back to when his parents had promised he could live his life on his own terms if he would aide them in turning around the farm's financial mess. Once prosperous, they had told him he could move on. But promises were made to be broken, and it had been one mess after another that kept cropping up. Bloody hell, twenty years had now passed. Those dreams, so often thought about, were long gone. Kaput. He would be forty-two in a few weeks. As far as he was concerned, he deserved the right to live his life as he saw fit. Practicing medicine and Doctors without Borders were dreams in his rearview mirror, but life as a philanthropist was not. He could make life better for others less fortunate than himself. And he planned to do exactly that whether his parents liked it or not.

Thomas should have learned his lesson not to think about having a life of his own. He had bigger issues on his plate at that moment. What had brought him to the St. Regis was a simple five-letter word.

Fraud.

Someone, somewhere was swindling Hallock Farm. His gut instinct told him it was coming from deep within *his* inner circle. Rick Stockton was the only person Thomas could trust to get to the bottom of whatever the hell was taking place.

"So how long am I going to stand here before you offer to buy me a drink?" A deep familiar voice spoke in his ear, snapping Thomas from his musings.

"Rick!" Thomas stood up, relieved to see his friend at his side. He reached out to shake Rick's outstretched hand.

Rick gave an appreciative nod to the ladies at the bar as he sat down and indicated Thomas to do the same. He leaned in, his tone serious and ominous, "Get ready to get the hell out of here, cowboy."

Taken aback, Thomas sputtered, "Come again?"

"Do as I tell you to." Rick whispered out of the corner of his mouth. "You're being watched."

Thomas's immediate reaction was to swirl his stool around to scan the crowd behind him. Rick yanked hard on the sleeve of Thomas's sport coat and stopped him. "Trust me. I'm not late, if that's what you've been thinking. I got here long before you did. I had a suspicion you might be followed. I was right."

"But…" Dumbfounded, Thomas voice trailed off as Rick signaled the bartender.

Rick pointed to Thomas's glass. "Give my friend another…I'll do a tonic water with lime." Rick pulled a fifty-dollar bill out of his money clip as the bartender walked off to fill the order. Thomas saw wariness in Rick's eyes. "Keep the conversation flowing until I figure out how to get us the hell out of here."

Thomas knew to follow Rick's instructions to the letter. Rick was the best there was. He and Rick had been friends for thirty years, having met in grade school, but went their separate ways after college. Rick had taken his forensic accounting degree to Washington, DC, putting it to good use working for the FBI. Not happy with DC's bureaucracy, he left his lucrative job taking some key talented personnel with him. Rick now was CEO of one of the largest forensic investigative agencies east of the Mississippi: Stockton Investigative Enterprises.

Thomas watched as Rick made use of the mirror behind the bar to scan the crowd behind them.

Keeping up the ruse of casual conversation, Thomas remarked, "It's good you could make it. How long's it been?"

Glancing at Thomas, a sly grin crossed Rick's face. "Too long. Right after you broke up with Tamara."

Rick had a knack of pushing the right button. Tamara Thompson. Ouch. Thomas was still raw whenever her name was mentioned. It had been over a year since they'd parted company. He thought he'd found the love of his life. Boy, had he been taken for a fool! A doctor at Peconic Hospital, Tamara professed to want to follow his dreams when the time came, whatever they might be. They'd spent hours discussing ways his money could be put to good use by helping others. Fortunately, his sister, Kate, had been home at a country club event and eavesdropped on a conversation between Tamara and two of her girlfriends. It was then Thomas discovered Tamara had only been in their relationship for the Hallock name and the connections that could catapult *her* career into being one of the premier concierge doctors in the Hamptons. Ever since that night his luck with love and life hadn't changed. His was convinced his life was cursed. And to prove it, he was sitting with Rick with a hell of a mess on his hands.

"She's history." Thomas itched to turn and watch as well, but he did as he was told. He swirled his scotch around in his glass. "Enough about me. You're a hard man to get a hold of. Every time I tried to call your office over the last month your secretary said you'd get back to me. And every call I made to your personal cell phone went to voice mail. Where the hell have *you* been?"

Rick tipped back his stool and took a sip of tonic water, his gaze clearly fixed on the mirror. "Been working a case. I finally closed it up last week. Your Aunt Elizabeth had me globe trotting all over the damn place." Suddenly, Rick righted his stool, but this time he actually turned to look to the back of the restaurant area. Curious, Thomas followed the direction of Rick's gaze. His eyes landed on two men in dark blue suits supposedly deep in thought over lunch menus. Thomas couldn't help but notice how the taller of the two kept peering up and over his menu to casually glance in their direction. Trying his best to keep his face void of any expression, Thomas could practically see the wheels churning inside Rick's brain. Suddenly, Rick swiveled his chair back around and continued as if nothing were amiss, "Paris, Rome, Athens. You name it, I think my passport says I went there."

Curious, Thomas asked, "Aunt Elizabeth, huh? Was she trying to recruit you to work for the Agency again?"

Thomas's aunt, his father's sister, had, over the course of many decades, developed a reputation as one of the nation's top global operatives in the European theatre. Having retired from life on the road, she'd spent the last four years working for the current presidential administration as the Director of the CIA.

Rick laughed and smiled in response, but, at the same time, nodded toward the exit leading into the main foyer of the lobby. That was Thomas's clue they would be on the move. He was ready. He knew the drill. Rick chuckled, "She sure as hell tried. But my involvement with her is a story for another time."

Unable to stop himself, Thomas glanced over his shoulder once more to view the two men who'd piqued Rick's interest. One was engrossed in texting, the other talking on his phone. Neither man had his sights on Rick or Thomas. Bad mistake.

Rick nudged him in the side, "Time to move. Follow my lead. Come on. I'm assuming you let your driver go to lunch?" Thomas nodded in the affirmative. "Great. Now we've got to flag a cab and hope we lose those two bozos in the process."

Thomas didn't even remember walking through the hotel lobby and out the front door. Rick hailed the first cab that came down East Fifty-fifth Street, leaving the hotel doorman to stare at the both of them in surprise. As the cab pulled up, Thomas felt a hand push him hard from behind through the open door. He landed askew on the back seat. Rick leaped in, practically landing in his lap. Rick glanced over his shoulder out the rear window giving the driver an address Thomas knew quite well. Thrown back into the seat from the cabbie putting the pedal to metal, Thomas grabbed the edge of his seat to maintain his balance while the car weaved its way into the heavy New York City traffic.

* * *

"You bring the thumb drive from your safe?" Finally, having buckled himself in for the long ride to their destination, Thomas pulled the requested item out of his jacket pocket and passed it to Rick. "Did you get the documents yesterday?"

"Yes." Rick answered. "I've looked over everything you sent. You've got more than a simple case of fraud on your hands, my friend." Looking over his shoulder once more, Rick turned and rapped on the partition separating the cabbie from his passengers. "Step on it! I think we've got company. There a couple of hundred extra in your tip if you can lose that black Town Car."

The cabbie looked in his rearview mirror, muttered something unintelligible and stepped on the gas. The cab lurched forward.

Thomas's eyebrows shot up. "What do you mean there's more?"

"I don't know the exact specifics. My team's hard at work examining everything. That's why I need that thumb drive with the PDF spreadsheets."

"I can read your face, old friend. It's worse than you thought. Isn't it?" Thomas's heart began to rapidly pound in his chest. The fast car ride wasn't the cause of his anxiety and panic. The unknown was. He clenched his fists in his lap.

"It's a good thing you're sitting down," Rick stared directly at him and quit scanning the surrounding scenery that flashed by the cab's windows. "You're not just missing thousands, Tom. My best IT guy started going through your papers."

Thomas had his own suspicions, but even with numbers being his thing, he knew something was exponentially askew with the farm's records. Warily eyeing Rick, he braced himself. "How bad?"

Rick waved the coveted thumb drive. "If this has what we want…"

"Yes?" Thomas grew impatient. Why didn't Rick just spit it out? Seeing recognizable landmarks, Thomas realized they were nearing their destination.

Rick tucked the red drive inside the breast pocket of his navy blue blazer. He placed a reassuring hand on Thomas's knee. "I'm just going to say it. Three million is missing…and that's just from *one* account."

Feeling like a football player who'd just had the wind knocked out of him, Thomas felt ill It wasn't the drinks he had had at the bar that made his head and stomach reel. He shook his head trying to clear away the nightmare of "what if's" brewing in his brain.

Three million! How could he explain to Aunt Elizabeth and his sister, Kate? They'd trusted him to do the hiring of the new CEO to replace Kate when she decided to leave the post and follow her true love, former Special Agent John Clinton, to live in Virginia two years ago. And he'd have to confront the Board of Directors as well as telling his family. Everyone, himself included, depended on the income from the farm's stock dividends to contribute to their affluent lifestyle and business ventures. His sixth sense told him things were going to go from bad to worse.

In an attempt to calm himself, Thomas tried drawing in deep breaths and exhaling while counting to ten. The one good thing he had going for him was the man sitting next to him. Rick Stockton was a specialist in weeding out corporate fraud. His friend had spent a great deal of time building his business on investigating embezzlement cases. Thomas knew he'd made the right decision to call Rick. The fact that his best friend happened to be one of the best forensic investigators in the business was an added bonus. Rick would have Thomas's back. He always did.

A VERY SPECIAL THANK YOU:

One of the fondest memories this author has, as a child and teenager, is sitting at the counter of Eckart's Luncheonette on Mill Road in Westhampton Beach. Eckart's was known for its root beer floats. The author can attest to spending much of her hard earned allowance there on many occasions. Mr. "Red" Eckart, dressed in his white shirt, apron wrapped around his waist, would smile and ask, "A root beer float?" If the author closes her eyes, the memory of the taste is in her mouth and she can lick the imaginary foam off her lips.

As many of the "townies" will attest to, the Hamptons have changed drastically over time, but not Eckart's. When the author gets a chance to visit the old homestead, one of the first places she heads for is the lunchonette. When she opens the door, it feels as she has traveled back in time to her childhood. Not much has changed. The old newspapers of world events still hang on the walls or sit in the glass case. Old bottles surround the tops of the wooden cupboards and the wooden booths are still there, as well as the stool the author used to sit on.

And if the author is lucky enough, the loving arms of Shirley, Red's wife, embrace her. It is then "Diane" knows she is really and truly home.

Here's hoping Dee and the family can keep this Hampton institution going for many more years to come.

ACKNOWLEDGMENTS:

The author would like to thank the following people who answered her countless questions regarding the Hampton area and waterways as well as those who provided research for topics related to the book's plot development:

Dr. Elaine Brooks Bohorquez – Dr. Bohoroquez is a professor at William Peace University with an expertise in microbiology, immunology and genetics. She holds a Masters in Science from NC State and researched avian influenza before studying for her Ph.D. at the University of NC – Chapel Hill.

Aram Terchunian of First Coastal, Westhampton Beach, New York – Aram has been a champion of the waterways and the preservation of the coastal environment for as long as the author can remember. She would like to thank him for the countless times he answered her questions in regards to which way the winds were blowing, hurricane information and for providing her with maps of the eastern end of Long Island. She is forever grateful and knows she owes him another breakfast at Eckart's on her next visit home. For more information regarding First Coastal visit www.firstcoastal.com.

Sandy Oliveto, known to many as "The Balloon Lady" – Sandy was invaluable in helping the author understand the changes that have been made to Gabreski Airport since the author's youth, as well as the working of the National Guard. She provided research on SAR: how the operation of Search and Rescue takes place and is carried out. The author hopes that all who live in the Hamptons realize the dedicated work that these brave men and women provide to save those trapped in storms on the bays and ocean. Thank you, Sandy, for your many years of service to our country.

ABOUT THE AUTHOR

Diane Culver was born and raised in Westhampton Beach. She spent her first twenty-one years soaking up life in the Hamptons. After a career as an award winning mathematics teacher which spanned thirty-one plus years, Diane has retired, residing in a small community in Central New York on the outskirts of Syracuse.

Diane is probably the only person (except for the crazy ski people) who looks forward to the snow piling up outside her window so she can put on a pot of Earl Grey tea, cozy up on the sofa by the fireplace, and work on her next book. Contact her at dianeculverbooks@gmail.com or visit her website: www.dianeculverbooks.com to find out what's up and coming in the series: **Hampton Thoroughbreds**.

Diane would like to extend a very special thank you to the following people: Jessica Lewis, who helped format the book for publishing and helped create publicity posters for book signings and Meet the Author dates. Contact Jessica at (www.authorslifesaver.com). Also she would like to thank her friends in the Central New York Romance Writers Chapter of the RWA and, finally, those who belong to the Long Island Romance Writers Chapter of the RWA(www.lirw.org) who keep her in touch with what goes on in the Hamptons when she can't be there to enjoy the sand, surf and long walks on the beach by Jetty 4.